THE
GREEN JOB

Detective Inspector John "Winner" Nguyen returns to investigate the murder of a research scientist working on how to improve wheat.

Rob Gerrand is a novelist, editor and publisher living in Melbourne, Australia. The Green Job is his second mystery, following on from the well-received The Millennium Job.

Also by Rob Gerrand

Transmutations (editor)
Fortress
The Best Australian Science Fiction Writing: A Fifty Year Collection (editor)
Rewrite Your Life! (with Eve Ash)
Rewrite Your Relationships! (with Eve Ash)

Inspector John Nguyen mystery
The Millennium Job

THE
GREEN JOB

ROB GERRAND

NORSTRILIA PRESS

NORSTRILIA PRESS
norstriliapress.com

Norstrilia Press
11 Robe Street, St Kilda, Victoria 3182, Australia

Cover and book design by David Grigg
Typeset in Adobe Garamond Pro and Crimson Pro

ISBN 978-1-7638516-4-1 (paperback)
ISBN 978-1-7638516-5-8 (eBook)

Prologue

Dr Chen Du placed a tray of test tubes on the laboratory bench, and sat back to check the levels. Another wave of nausea flowed up from his stomach, worse than before, and his headache became a blinding, stabbing pain at his temples. The pain subsided but his brain was fogged. He sat back, rubbing his temples. A sudden urge in his bowels had him stumbling to his feet.

He glanced at the lab equipment. Everything was okay. Reaching out a hand to steady himself, he slipped and knocked into the tray of test tubes, sending them crashing to the floor.

He grasped the edge of the bench and, despite the beads of sweat on his forehead, he shivered. He raised one hand to his brow. Then his knees gave way.

He tried to grab the bench again but missed and tumbled backwards. He gasped a muffled shout and collapsed completely, the back of his head hitting the floor. Sluggish and exhausted, he half rolled over, bending his knees in an effort to stand up, at the same time reaching for his phone in the pocket of his white lab coat. He had to call——

All went dark.

Some hours later, around five in the morning, the cleaner moved her trolley into the lab, took out her mop, looked around—and screamed. A man lay on the floor. She approached cautiously and stared down at the motionless figure. She saw it was Dr Chen. There was a pool of vomit at his mouth, and a tray of smashed test tubes spilling their contents above his head. Heart racing, she dialled 000.

1

THE DEAD SCIENTIST WAS at the Badeker Institute, next to the Alfred Hospital. A cleaner had phoned it in, and an ambulance and uniformed police had attended.

Detective Inspector John "Winner" Nguyen looked at the building in front of him, six floors of coloured glass and concrete. The doors automatically parted and he entered a foyer of polished aluminium and white tiles. Detective Constable Carol McTeish followed him. McTeish, 23 years old, was new to detection, and this was her second time working with Nguyen.

The foyer was cool, impersonal. There was a reception desk, and a stout woman in her thirties, dressed in a blue security uniform, looked up. She had glasses, a tight mouth and the appearance of a smile. "Can I help you?"

Nguyen held out his identity card. The woman made a sound, a sort of muffled sob, and picked up her phone, spoke, listened, and looked up at him.

"The Director is on level five." She handed them electronic visitor passes. "These will let you through."

They passed through the gates and entered the lift. At level five the doors opened on to a small area, with a young man at a desk facing sideways to the lift, who stood up—he was tall and lean with a slight stoop. "Inspector Nguyen? Come this way, please. Dr Penrith is expecting you." He knocked and opened the door.

As they entered the Director immediately stood and came around her desk towards them. "Thanks, Derek," she said, and he closed the door Dr Penrith was slim, skinny even, and almost the same height as

Nguyen. She wore a dark suit and her hair hung straight to just above her shoulders. Her elegant face was strained. Nguyen saw her desk, light wood with a dark glass top, had one sheet of paper in the middle of it, a laptop to one side next to a cell phone. Nothing else on the desk, not even a pen.

Nguyen introduced himself and McTeish.

"Olga Penrith." Her voice was low, quiet. She gazed at him. The stare was not friendly. "Please sit down." She indicated four leather chairs around a coffee table.

"I'm sorry. There's no easy way to do this, but I have to ask some questions. Who was the dead man?" Nguyen always thought the blunt approach best. Interesting to see the reactions.

Olga Penrith tightened her lips. "Dr Chen Du. One of our research scientists. The cleaners found him." She spoke as if she were talking about a stocktake. "Some police have already been. Haven't they spoken to you?"

"That's why I'm here."

"What, you suspect foul play?"

"A death like this has to be investigated. Please tell me about him."

"Doug was one of our leading scientists."

"Doug?"

"He used that as his first name. He was very smart, a leading scientist. And healthy. Never took a day off. One of our stars. He headed one of our research teams." She cleared her throat. "What do you need to do?"

He considered her for a short time, but kept silent, waiting for her to say something more.

"We need to keep this quiet. You understand?" She shook her head, looked back at her desk as if to pick up the piece of paper, then looked up. "If it gets out, the Greens will try to shut us down."

"If what gets out?"

"Dr Chen's death. The media will have a field day."

"You can't keep a death confidential, Dr Penrith. What do you mean, the Greens?"

"The environmentalists are running a campaign against us. Frankenfurters …" her voice trailed off.

Frankenfurters? Sausages? Nguyen waited, glanced at McTeish, who sat with her face expressionless.

"Frankenfood?" McTeish said.

"Yes, that's what I said. GM."

"Genetically Modified?" McTeish said.

"That's what they call it. But what we do here is not exactly GM." Penrith gave an irritated sigh.

"What was he working on?"

"Plants—working on how to improve things."

"I see," Nguyen said. "Could you have someone show us Dr Chen?"

"He's—the body's in the lab."

"Do you know if anyone touched the body?" He watched her discomfit.

"How would I know? An ambulance came, and some police. Shouldn't you be able to find out?"

Nguyen stared at her, wondering at her abrasiveness. "Of course we can find out, Doctor. Could you take us to the lab?"

The Director walked to her desk, picked up the phone. "Get Shildduck here," she said.

After a few minutes a stocky, grey-haired woman entered the room.

"Dr Shildduck--this is Detective Nguyen. And Constable—" she rolled her eyes up— "McTeish. Could you please take them to your lab."

"Of course." Dr Shildduck extended her hand, and Nguyen shook it.

"Detective Inspector John Nguyen," he said.

She had a firm grasp, and met his eyes directly. She gestured for them to follow her, and left the room. They walked to the lifts, Shildduck remaining silent. She pushed the button for the third floor, and they entered a clean, white, bright open plan room, with lots of computers. There were large devices the size of washing machines, and groups of small test tubes in trays with an automated pipette dipping into them. Not what he expected.

A body in a white coat lay on the floor, face up. And as he'd been briefed, there was a small pool of liquid near the mouth, and smashed test tubes near the body.

"This is Dr Chen?" Nguyen asked.

"Yes. It's Doug—Dr Chen Du."

Nguyen inspected the body, walking around it, careful not to disturb it. It lay on the tiled floor, head facing one of the banks of machines, at roughly a 45-degree angle, the right arm above the head, the left by its side. His eyes were bulging, and there was spittle, or was it a slight froth, on his lips. McTeish used her phone to photograph the body from both sides, above, from the head and from the feet.

Nguyen took a pair of gloves from his jacket pocket, put them on and rolled the body half over, looking carefully at the clothing. Nothing appeared disarrayed. He stood and took out his phone to call Forensics.

"We have a body." He gave a brief description. "Uniform attended and called us in. How soon can someone get here? And can you get on to the coroner's office, alert them?" He shut off his phone and crouched down again to look at Dr Chen's face.

"What was he working on?" McTeish asked Shildduck

"Plants."

Nguyen looked up at her. "Plants? That's pretty general."

Shildduck looked away, as if arguing with herself. "Researching their genome." She seemed evasive. As they faced each other a tall young man walked in, saw them, paused, and started to turn to leave.

"Hello," Nguyen said. The young man hesitated, and came towards them.

"This is Dr Tamas Kosic." Shildduck said. "He's part of our research team. A post doc."

Nguyen introduced himself. Kosic seemed distracted, said nothing, looked away from the body.

"Can we get away from here?" Nguyen asked. "Is there an office we can use, Dr Shildduck? And can you make sure no one comes in here?"

Shildduck led them out and shut the laboratory door behind them. She turned and said, "If anyone wants to come in they'll have to buzz me." She took them to an office in the far corner. There was a dark wood-topped desk with a laptop and a phone on it, no paper, and behind it a bookshelf with magazines and several books, and next to it a credenza with a vase with pink roses on it. There was a faint antiseptic smell. Three visitor chairs in front of the desk, a leather chair on wheels behind it. Fairly stark, Nguyen thought. It reminded him of his boss's office, except all the furniture here was new, went together, and was not battered.

"Carol," Nguyen said, "can you please wait with Tamas outside?"

McTeish nodded.

Shildduck picked some magazines off one of the visitor's chairs and put them on the credenza. She sat behind the desk, indicating the chairs, and Nguyen sat facing her.

"Tell me about your … former colleague." Nguyen said.

"Doug, er Dr Chen—" Shildduck broke off. "He was gifted. He was harmless. Wouldn't hurt a fly. How could this happen to him? He's too young." She clasped her hands, rubbing them together.

"We'll find out soon enough. Did he have any history of heart problems, any ill health?"

"Not at all. Not as far as I know. He never took a sick day all the time he was here."

"How long was that?"

"Three, four years."

"The cleaners found him. Who was that?"

"The cleaner who does this floor, I presume. I don't know who that is. I was rung by Dr Penrith."

"I'll need to speak to the cleaner. Can you find out who he or she was, and let us know?"

She nodded. "I can call now … "

"Maybe best after we finish. When did Dr Penrith call you?"

"About seven this morning." Nguyen wrote down the time.

"Could you tell me a little more about what Dr Chen and you and your team were doing?"

Shildduck glanced at the door, looked up at the ceiling, and said, as if reciting, "We are investigating the genome of plants—of a particular plant, Triticum aestivum."

"What's that when it's at home?" Nguyen asked.

She looked at him as if he were a sample of Triticum. "Wheat."

He stared back, then wrote it down. "And?" he said.

"Look, this is very confidential." She must have seen his exasperated look before he masked it, because she smiled briefly. "All research is to some extent confidential, of course, until we publish. But we have added difficulties. Politics. So we don't talk about it much."

Seeing Nguyen's blank look, she continued, "All I can say is that we're on to something of great importance, and Dr Chen is a key player. Was a key player." She shook her head. "His loss won't stop us, but it will slow us down for a bit."

Nguyen decided to let this pass for the moment. "Can you tell me what he was like?"

"Look, he was very focussed on his research. He wasn't much of a socialiser," she said.

"Was he cheerful? Sad? Tell me about his personality."

"I wouldn't say he was sad. Not at all. But he did tend to keep to himself."

"Who were his friends?"

"Well, no-one in particular—at least not here, as far as I know."

"Was he any different recently?"

"How do you mean?" She stared at Nguyen, puzzled.

"Well, any change in his usual behaviour?"

"No, not at all. Not that I noticed."

"Why was he here last night?"

"We often work late. He would have been seeing a process through."

"What process?"

"When you start a run, you have to wait until it all finishes. You can't just leave unless someone can take over from you. We do it all the time."

"Would anyone else have been with him last night? Where were you, for example?"

"I was here," Shildduck said. "Until about 8 o'clock."

"And Dr Chen didn't want you to stay?"

"No. Why would he want me to stay? He was fine. He knew what he was doing. I think Tamas was with him for a while."

"What did he last say to you?"

"Tamas, or Dr Chen?"

"Dr Chen."

"He just said, 'See you tomorrow'."

2

"I WAS HERE UNTIL ABOUT 8 OR, 8:30," Kosic told McTeish. He was tall, with dark wavy hair, and he seemed nervous. They were in an office adjoining Shildduck's.

"How did Dr Chen seem?"

"Seem?" He paused. "The same as ever. The usual."

"And what was that, the usual?"

"I don't know. Focused. Not very communicative."

Like you, McTeish thought.

"Were you friends?"

"Friends? Not really. It wasn't that he was unfriendly, but I wouldn't say we were friends. He was bit of a loner."

Also like you? she thought.

"So he was just a colleague?"

"Colleague. Yes, that's it. He was my colleague." He seemed relieved to use the word. "But also my boss."

"And did you like him? Or dislike him?"

"Like him?"

McTeish was getting irritated at the way he kept repeating her questions.

"He was okay."

"Did he have any enemies?"

"Enemies? No. No. Not that I was aware of."

"Then why do you think he was killed?"

"Was he killed?"

Maybe I've jumped the gun, she thought. Oh well.

"Dr Shildduck said he didn't have any health issues. We have to investigate that possibility. We can't rule it out."

Kosic looked thoughtful. He also looked very pale.

"Dr Penrith mentioned something about GM, Frankenfoods," McTeish said, trying to trigger some useful information.

Kosic flinched. "Frankenfoods! That's what some of my friends say. The environmentalists don't like what we're doing," he said. "But we're not doing what they think we are."

"And what's that?"

"They think we're into GM foods, and that we'll poison the planet. The last thing we'd do. I'm a member of the Greens, myself."

"So what are you doing, if it's not GM?"

"Do you know what GM is?" He looked directly at her for the first time, concentrating.

"Genetically modifying food?"

"Well, yes. Gene splicing, like putting in something that kills insects, so farmers won't need insecticides."

"Isn't that a good thing? Stop putting all the chemicals on our food?"

"Chemicals? Everything is made of chemicals. Water is a chemical. H 2 O." He noticed her reaction and stopped.

"You know what I mean," she said. "Fewer pesticides. Isn't that a good thing?"

"Yes and no."

He seemed incapable of giving a straight answer. She waited.

After a time he said, "The idea's good. I mean reducing pesticides, or getting rid of them. The problem is when the big agribusinesses patent them, and then charge farmers for the seed. In the third world farmers can't afford that. And of course, there's also the risk the genes will jump across to other species, and cause all sorts of unexpected problems."

"So, you're not doing that?"

"Not really. I should say, no. Not at all. And before you ask, I can't tell you what we are doing. We've all signed confidentiality agreements."

McTeish nodded. "So it's not GM, not frankenfood, and you can't talk about it."

Kosic nodded. He managed a half smile. Sheepish.

"Look, what we do here, if we succeed, will be worth a fortune. Some people want to stop us. Others want to buy us."

She'd talk to Sergeant Brothers and Nguyen about that.

"How important was Dr Chen to all this?"

"Doug was crucial. It's basically his IP. He's the pioneer. Was the pioneer. It's his theory we're working on."

"So, would anyone benefit from his death?"

"What? Benefit how? What an awful thing to say." He shuddered.

"Well? Would anyone? You said some people want to stop this work."

"Yes, but that's just some of the environmentalists. Not the sensible ones. There are radicals, you know." He paused. "They might picket the lab, or throw paint on our cars. But that's completely different from murder." He stood up. "Please, excuse me. I need—the toilet …" he gasped. He rushed out of the room.

A few minutes later he returned, sat down again. He looked pale; greenish. "Sorry," he said.

"Are you okay?"

He looked embarrassed. "I threw up."

McTeish studied him. "A natural reaction," she said.

"I never throw up," he said.

"It's normal—shock." She waited. There was a carafe of water on the desk, and three glasses. She poured him one. He drank it down in one long gulp.

"Feel better?"

He nodded.

"Is there anything else you want to tell me?"

He shook his head, wiped his mouth with the back of his hand.

"You okay?"

"Yes. Sorry. Don't know what came over me."

"As I say. It's natural. Shock." She waited another moment, stood up. "Thank you, Tamas," she said. "That's all I need for the moment. I'm sure my colleagues will want to talk to you and everyone again, later."

"Okay, uh, Detective."

"Carol," she said.

He smiled. Was that a look of relief?

THERE WAS A KNOCK on Shildduck's door and a short, stocky man put his head in.

"Er, Inspector?"

Nguyen looked at him. "Yes?"

Shildduck beckoned. "Come in, Les."

"I'm Leslie Smithson." A man in his thirties came into the room, a large chest and belly leading the way. He had small eyes in a reddish face. A faint whiff of aftershave came in with him.

"I'm Corporate Counsel for the Institute. Dr Penrith asked me to help." He reached out a hand.

Nguyen stood and shook it. He could almost hear the capitalisations: Corporate Counsel. The hand squeezed his hard. "And how can you help?"

"Well, rather than wasting everyone's time, maybe you could let me know any questions you have, and I'll make sure you get the answers you want. My job is not just to protect the Institute, but of course to assist the authorities. This, er, unpleasantness, is something I'm sure you can clear up pretty quickly."

"That's very thoughtful of you. And of Dr Penrith."

"We aim to please." There was an edge in the tone of his voice, though he held a smile. Interesting.

"Did you know Dr Chen?" Nguyen asked.

"Of course. He led one of our teams. Of course I knew him." Smithson paused, frowned. "But not well, of course. I wouldn't say I knew him well. I didn't see him outside of work meetings."

Nguyen stared at the man. "It would assist us if you could get me a list of all staff of the Institute, and let me know all those who worked with Dr Chen. All who did know him well. Including the cleaners.

We'll need to speak to all of them. Also, we'll need Dr Chen's home address."

"All of them? Okay. Inspector, I can help speed things up for you. Just let me know what you want to know, and I'll get the answers for you."

"You say you're Corporate Counsel?"

"Yes." Smithson stuck out his jaw. "There's a heap of work to protect our IP. Negotiations with the pharma companies. We're a growing concern. It keeps me pretty busy."

"Pharma companies are interested? And you look after the intellectual property."

"That's right. Patents, negotiations with investors. We have a lot of interest in our work. Could be in the hundreds of millions if all goes as we expect it to." He smiled with his mouth. His eyes remained cold. "As soon as this—blip—is taken care of, we can get back to our work."

Nguyen stared at him, trying to keep his face bland. "You regard Dr Chen's death as a 'blip'?"

"Sorry. An unfortunate word. I meant, of course, it's tragic that Dr Chen died. But life, and work, must go on."

"So intellectual property. But not criminal law?"

"Criminal law?" He sniffed. "Of course not."

"Then perhaps that's why you might not understand we'll need to ask our questions directly. When can you get me the list of people? With contact details?"

Smithson frowned again. He blinked. "I'll get my assistant on to it straight away. Of course, Inspector." His lips tightened. "Of course."

"How soon? I'll need it before we leave."

"I'll see what we can do," Smithson said. He stuck out his jaw.

"Do you have a card?"

Smithson took one from the lapel pocket of his jacket and handed it over.

"Thanks." Nguyen glanced at it. "How long will it take to get the list?"

"Um, not long. Can I have it emailed to you?"

"Make sure you do," Nguyen said. He handed Smithson one of his own cards.

"I'll get on to it. And Inspector, any other questions, please call me." He left the room.

Dr Shildduck stood up. "Is there anything more you need from me, Inspector?"

"Not for the moment, but I'll need to speak to you again, of course."

3

THAT AFTERNOON SUE GOSSITER brought in the forensic report. Gossiter was head of the forensic team, and despite her quirks, Nguyen liked her. Maybe because of her quirks.

After greeting him, she said, "Clear as mud."

Nguyen waited, then said, "And?"

"Well, we think he was poisoned. The question is, how? We haven't worked that out, yet. What we do know—" she paused, scratched her chin— "his body has gone through a massive internal meltdown. Catastrophic organ failure."

Nguyen was startled. "Well, certainly not a heart attack."

She shook her head.

"Not an accident?"

"Don't be too quick, Winner. We don't know what he was working on. Maybe a bit of his GM chemistry got into his system. And, voila!" She grinned.

Nguyen had thought he had got used to her macabre sense of humour, but she still managed to unnerve him from time to time. "You for real?" he said. "He wasn't working on germ warfare, was he?"

"I don't know. Was he?" Gossiter raised her eyebrows.

That gave him pause. He realised he had no clear idea at all what Chen or his team were working on.

"I thought it was to do with food," he said.

Gossiter nodded, grinned again.

"You don't know, do you. But, with all that security downstairs— maybe it is chemical warfare, what, I don't know, for the Defence department?" She paused. "Just kidding." She paused again, thoughtful. "Or am I?"

"We'll have to talk to the Director, find out what he was actually up to. The last thing you'd want is poisonous food."

"Yeah, well—I just like to cover all bases. You know me."

Nguyen frowned. Gossiter laughed.

"But he was poisoned?"

"You got it."

"What about the details? Any fingerprints on the body, or clothes?"

"None we could find. I reckon time of death was around midnight, no later than 1 am. Could have been 11."

"Anything in his stomach?"

"It looks like he might have had a burger and fries some hours earlier."

"When would he have eaten?"

"At least six hours earlier. Possibly 6 o'clock."

Nguyen said, "We checked his wallet. A couple of credit cards, Medicare, driver's licence, movie club, health card. Nothing odd." He thought of the body as it had lain on the laboratory floor. Had someone sneaked up on him? Or had he been poisoned before he got to the lab? "You say his body had catastrophic organ failure. Do you know what caused it?"

"Not yet. But it wasn't polonium—no radioactivity."

Nguyen raised an eyebrow.

"We'll do checks. These can be a real bastard to find out. The agent, poison, whatever it is, can break down, as the organs collapse."

"So, no clues?"

"It could be ricin, but it's a bugger."

"Ricin?"

"It can cause what happened. It takes some time, but it can cause multiple organ failure." She smiled again. "By the way, ricin is a waste product from making castor oil. You said the deceased was doing something with food?"

"Wheat. Not as far as I know castor beans. Anyhow, let us know as soon as you can."

"Of course. See ya."

She left, waving her hand.

4

Nguyen knocked on the open door of Superintendent Robin Forell's office.

"Detective. Come in," she said. "Sit down."

Nguyen glanced at her. She didn't seem pre-occupied. He wasn't sure whether he preferred her irritated at being interrupted, or focused on him as she was now.

He filled her in about the dead scientist, Dr Chen; told her he was probably poisoned.

"Badeker Institute. That rings a bell. What do they do again?"

"Research into food, it seems—but they're pretty cagey about what sort of research. They seem to be trying to do a big deal with a pharma company."

"I remember now. There've been protests outside the Badeker Institute, haven't there?" she said.

"Greenies protesting, apparently about GM foods."

"That's right. There were some arrests, weren't there—are they researching GM foods?"

"Not too sure."

"You don't know?" Forell sounded incredulous.

"They say it's not GM, but maybe it could be GM related in some way."

"Have you checked who's involved." Forell had rested her chin on her clasped hands, and peered at him over them.

"In the protests? We think some local Greenies." Nguyen rubbed his cheek. He made a mental note to check whether any arrests had been made at the protests.

"Yes, but who? There could be some real nuts among them. Someone who would try to infiltrate the labs." She put her hands back on her desk and looked down at some papers in front of her.

"What, and kill Dr Chen?"

"I presume someone did." She looked up from the papers and glanced at him.

"We'll check, of course." Of course, he said again to himself.

"And let me know what the pharmaceutical company side of it is."

What the hell, Nguyen thought. "Sure," he said.

As he stood up to leave, Forell said, "By the way, what do you think the media interest will be?"

"There's bound to be interest. The Greenies will love it."

"Why is that?" Forell gazed at him, her face bland.

"Shit. Of course. More evidence of bad GM. Even if it's nothing to do with GM. Especially if it's nothing to do with GM, knowing the media." He paused. "We'll try to keep a lid on it."

"Is that realistic?"

"The Badeker people don't want a fuss made of it."

"Naturally."

He pondered some more. "I suppose Dr Chen's friends will let people know."

"Prepare a statement with the pr team—play it down."

After leaving Forell, Nguyen called a team meeting with Detective Constable Carol McTeish and Detective Sergeant Graham Brothers. Brothers had worked with Nguyen for several years, and McTeish had joined the team for their previous case. He recapped the news from Sue Gossiter. "He was poisoned."

"What with?" Brothers asked.

"She didn't say—hasn't found out yet. But he apparently had massive organ failure. Could be ricin."

"Did she say how long he'd been dead?" McTeish asked.

"He definitely died in the lab, if that's what you're meaning. Around midnight."

"Um." She frowned.

"Yes?" Nguyen looked up at her.

"I meant, could he have died while someone else was there? Such as Tamas Kosic? He said he left around 8:30, but he was pretty evasive when I talked to him."

"Yes?" Nguyen said again.

"I got the impression he wasn't saying everything he knows. In fact, I'm sure of it."

"Good, good," Nguyen said. "We'll have another little talk with him."

"Anything else?"

"What about the boss?" Brothers said.

"The Director is Dr Olga Penrith. Not the most accommodating of individuals. Someone we'll need to talk to again. Speaking of which, they've got a lawyer. A pompous know-all. Smithson. He's meant to have emailed me the staff list, and all those who worked with Chen. We've got to find out more about them all. Who they live with, who their friends are, who they see, who they do business with. And of course who Chen knew."

"So. How do we do this? Do we need help?" Brothers said.

"I'll get support in, if we need it."

Brothers seemed about to say something, but then nodded. "O-kay," he said, drawing out the second syllable.

"Right. I'll take Dr Penrith. Carol, you can follow up with Kosic. Talk to his friends. Once you have more info, if necessary I'll talk to him myself. Graham, you go round to Chen's place. Find out who his family and friends are. It could be personal—does he have any enemies? We'll probably need the forensics team to go to his place, so be careful. I'll talk to Shildduck again."

"Have we got his address?" Brothers said.

"His wife is Lucy Bottega. Or maybe partner. It's in Carlton North, 70 Fenwick Street," Nguyen said.

"Kosic said that Dr Chen was the key behind some new IP the lab's developing," McTeish said. "Apparently it could be worth a fortune. And he said that some of the Greens didn't like what they're doing. Maybe one of them could have targeted Chen?"

"Smithson said something similar," Nguyen said. "The Green angle is helpful. When you talk to Kosic again, try to find out who his Greenie friends are."

"I'm not sure if they are friends," McTeish said.

"To summarise: we're looking at Dr Chen's family and friends, at his work colleagues, and at any Greenies who have been linked to the Badeker Institute. And when I talk to the Badeker Director, I'll try to find out exactly what research Chen was doing. Any more questions?"

"I'll get on to it," Brothers said.

5

Brothers drove through the city to North Carlton, up Rathdowne Street and turned right into Fenwick Street. No. 70 was a small Victorian era single story brick house.

He knocked on the door, and after about twenty seconds the door opened and a face with striking dark eyes peered out.

"Yes?" The face belonged to a woman in her thirties, short and petite, dressed in black pants and a tan jumper. Her face was quite round, framed in reddish hair.

Brothers introduced himself. "Ms Bottega? May I come in?"

"What's this about?"

"It's about Dr Chen. I have some bad news."

She stared at him for a while, as if trying to find a reason to bar him from entry, then shrugged, opened the door and let him follow her in along a short hall to a front living room. The floor was polished boards, with a rug. He could smell coffee.

"Please sit." She gestured at a chair; she sat on one facing him.

"Sorry to disturb you, Mrs Bottega."

She nodded. "It's not Mrs, though. We're not married."

He glanced up. "Oh. Right." Brothers took out his notebook.

Before he could speak she said, "What's the bad news?"

"I'm afraid Dr Chen is dead. He was discovered in his lab early this morning." He breathed out heavily.

"Dead?" Her face paled. "Doug dead? What happened?" There were tears in her eyes. "He was too young. Was it his heart? Should I go down to the Badeker?"

"We don't know all the details yet, but it seems he was poisoned."

"Poisoned?" She shook her head. "How can that be?" He lips trembled and she gasped.

"We're investigating it. There's nothing more I can say at the moment. I'm terribly sorry." He broke off.

She stared back, her face drooping. "Doug dead?" She started crying quietly.

Brothers was still awkward talking to the relatives of the deceased, even after all these years. He did not know what to do to comfort her.

Bottega groaned, cradling her face with her hands. "Who would do such a thing?"

"That's what we'll find out."

"But why? Why would anyone want to kill Doug?"

"Did he have any—" Brothers broke off. "Did he have any enemies?"

"Never." She answered without a pause. "He was a bit of a loner, but he got on with everyone. He didn't even have arguments."

"Arguments?"

"About his work."

"Ah. And what was his work?"

She looked up, surprised. "He was researching a better way to grow food."

"How do you mean?"

"It was secret, of course. But then I suppose all research is secret. But he was trying to make food more productive. Wheat, in fact. Some people didn't like that. But it wasn't what they called it. It wasn't GM— genetic modification." She smiled bleakly at him. "So if someone tried to argue with him about it, he changed the subject. You know, saying, that's not right, but I can't talk about what it really is until we have the patents in place."

"Were many people trying that on him, arguing?"

"Not many. Just occasionally at a party or drinks somewhere. Not often."

"And do you know what he was really doing?"

Bottega looked up at him, a little more energy in her body. "Not really. But even if I did, I wouldn't tell you—if it was secret."

"We'll need to speak to close friends. And, if you can remember who tried to argue with him, could you let me have their names?"

"When do you need the names?"

Brothers had noticed that just doing something could take people's minds off their worries, so he said, "Could you let me know now?"

She thought for a moment then reached for her phone. "Just a sec." She scrolled through her contacts list, and Brothers opened his notebook. "Thanks. You don't need to worry about the details of the work colleagues. We're talking to them already."

"Look, I can't think who might have argued with him, but here are some friends." She read out some names, and Brothers wrote them down. Sally and Kane Churchill, Yvonne Wisher and Ronnie Manser, and Yasmin and Simon Lee. "Three couples we see a bit of. Apart from his work colleagues."

"Thanks. When did you last see him?"

"This morn—" she broke off. "Yesterday morning. He said he was working overnight."

"Did he do that often? Work overnight?"

She paused, rubbed her forehead. "From time to time. It depended on what the work was. Sometimes he had to follow it through. He, he—" She sobbed.

"Take your time." Brothers went to hold her shoulders, then stopped himself. You never knew how that might be interpreted these days.

"He'd work through the night sometimes. I think that's normal in his sort of work."

"And what time did you last see him yesterday?"

"After breakfast. He was still home when I left for work, at about 9 o'clock."

"What do you do?"

"I work at the uni. Melbourne University. I'm a tutor, so my hours aren't regular."

He could see she was trying to pull herself together. "Did you speak to him during the day?"

"He rang in the afternoon."

"Anything out of the ordinary? Did he sound different in any way?"

"No, not at all. He just confirmed he'd be working late. Said he might not be home till today. She clenched her hands together and closed her eyes, then blinked. "I'm sorry. I just can't believe it. Can I see him? I mean his body?"

"The forensics people are examining—finding out how he died. Of course, after that you'll be able to see him." Bloody hell, Brothers thought. It never gets easy.

"I'm sorry," Bottega said again. "I haven't even offered you a cup of tea or coffee."

"No, no," Brothers said. "No, thank you." She said nothing further.

"As soon as we know anything we'll get in touch."

6

"Carol," Nguyen called across the office. "Can you please set up another meeting with, whatshername, the Director of the Badeker Institute."

McTeish walked to his office door. "Olga Penrith? What time?" she said.

"ASAP. Thanks." He looked down at the notes on his desk.

"Do you have her card?" McTeish asked. "It'll take forever going through the switchboard."

He rummaged around his desk, handed her a card. McTeish used her mobile phone and dialled. The call went through to voicemail. "Detective Inspector John Nguyen would like to come in to see you," she said. "What time this morning is best?" She closed the phone and grinned at Nguyen. "If she doesn't get back, you should just go in when it suits you."

He nodded, suppressing a smile.

A moment later McTeish's phone rang, with no caller ID.

"Hello. Can I speak to Inspector Nguyen?" It was a man's voice.

"Who's calling?" McTeish said.

"Les Smithson. I'm corporate counsel at the Badeker. I understand that the Inspector wants to speak to our Director. Unfortunately she's tied up today. Can I help?"

McTeish muted the phone. "It's Smithson, the lawyer at the Badeker."

"Two can play at that game. You handle it," Nguyen said.

McTeish unmuted the phone. "Detective Constable McTeish here."

"Ah, Constable. The Director is tied up—can I help you?" Smithson's voice was cheerful and bombastic.

"I hope so," McTeish said, "but you'll need to make sure Dr Penrith is available too, if you can't answer all my questions."

"What do you need to know? I'm sure I can help you. Did the Inspector get the list of names from my assistant?"

"Yes, thanks. We need to know exactly what research Dr Du was working on."

"Dr Du? You mean Dr Chen, don't you?"

McTeish cursed silently to herself; how could she get that wrong? And with that turd Smithson, to boot. "Yes, Dr Chen. Chen Du."

"I'm afraid that's bound up with confidentiality agreements." Smithson's voice contained a self-satisfied element not too far removed from gloating.

"Just a second. Here's Detective Inspector Nguyen." McTeish said, handing the phone over.

"Hello?" Nguyen said.

"Hello, Inspector. I was just saying that I'm afraid we're tied up with confidentiality agreements. Concerning the nature of our research."

"I'm *afraid*," Nguyen said, grimacing, "that we have to know what it is. We need your co-operation."

"Just a moment." There was silence, then he heard a muffled conversation in the background, and Olga Penrith came on the phone.

"Inspector," she said. "As I mentioned to you yesterday, Dr Chen's work is highly confidential."

"Dr Penrith. Hello." Nguyen put on a cheerful voice. "I understand the work was secret, but the fact is we need this information. We will treat it confidentially, of course. We don't need to know the detail, just the import of what he was doing."

"Why is that?" There was a patronising tone to her voice.

"We've established that Dr Chen's death is suspicious. We still don't know the exact poison." He heard an intake of breath. "We need to establish whether it had something to do with his research. It would be great to rule that out. Then we could focus on other possibilities."

"I see." She paused.

"I'll come in. In half an hour's time. Would that suit you?"

Again he heard a muffled conversation including, he thought, "…get him off my back …" then she said, "Okay. I'll expect you at 10:00 am." She hung up.

"Come with me," he said to McTeish. "They can't keep farting us around."

7

They drove to South Yarra, twelve minutes from the police station, and parked in a staff space labelled "Visiting Doctor" and walked up to the reception desk, and after signing in went straight up to Level five.

Smithson was standing at the lift when its doors slid open, and he smiled his fake smile and took them into the Director's office.

Penrith met them at her door. "We're very busy, Inspector," she said. "Please take a seat. I have to prepare for a meeting with some US visitors in an hour."

"Thanks for seeing us at short notice," Nguyen said. "This shouldn't take too long."

McTeish took out her notebook.

"Are your visitors related to Dr Chen's work?" Nguyen asked.

"They're from Howarth-Acfield. They fund a lot of our research, but not Dr Chen's."

"Howarth-Acfield. Who are they?" Nguyen asked.

With tightened lips Penrith said, "A US pharmaceutical company." She seemed on edge.

"What was Dr Chen's field of research?" McTeish asked.

"I thought we'd covered that. Can't we do this another time? Or get Dr Shildduck to answer your questions?"

"Would she give us any answers?"

Penrith breathed out heavily. "Okay."

She nodded at Smithson, who said, "He was working on wheat."

"So we've been told. What sort of work?"

"How to make it more productive."

"Then why are the Greenies so concerned? Surely that's a good thing?"

"Of course it's a good thing," Penrith said. "The Greenies somehow think we're into making GM foods. It's not that at all. Or rather, not what they think of as GM."

"What's their beef with it?" McTeish asked.

"Genetically modified foods have their genetic material, their DNA, modified," Penrith said, as if to a primary school child. "New genes are inserted so, for example, a plant becomes toxic to an insect pest. That could remove the need for pesticides. You understand?"

McTeish nodded. Nguyen stared at Penrith, rubbed his chin.

"The Greenies think we're tweaking the DNA like that, such as introducing a gene from a different organism."

"That sounds like GM to me. Was that what he was doing?" Nguyen said.

She looked at both of them, breathing out heavily again. "That's what we're *not* doing. Doug was *not* doing that."

"Then what *was* he doing?" Nguyen said again. It was infuriating how she kept going round in circles. "This is a murder investigation," he repeated. "You can rest assured we'll keep your science completely confidential."

"We're trying to make wheat, any grain, more productive. Increase the protein content. We've got a couple of teams. Doug headed one. If it works, it will revolutionise agriculture. That's why the secrecy. It could be huge."

"Careful," Smithson said to Penrith.

"How do you mean, Dr Penrith? Just how would Dr Chen revolutionise agriculture?" McTeish said.

"You don't need to know that. Just take it from me that it would. It will. I think we are done here," Smithson said.

"Oh, for God's sake, we'll have to let them know." Penrith stood up and paced behind her desk.

"I'll get a couple of confidentiality agreements," Smithson said, his face flushed in annoyance. "You'll have to sign them first."

"We don't sign confidentiality agreements," Nguyen said. He sat up straighter, and addressed Penrith. "So, what is it?"

"Dr Chen was working on improving plant photosynthesis."

"So?" Nguyen said. He glanced at McTeish. "That mean anything to you?"

She nodded. "I think I know what photosynthesis is. But why would anyone want to kill a scientist over photosynthesis?" she said.

"We're trying to change how plants get nitrogen. One team is working on cyanobacteria. If the bacteria can get their nitrogen directly from the atmosphere, farmers won't need to use fertilisers. How good would that be for the environment?"

"How?" Nguyen asked, again, not trying to hide his growing impatience.

"As I said, certain bacteria do it. We know the genes that allow them to do it. We're trying to get wheat to do it, too. Actually," Penrith smiled, "Dr Chen wasn't doing that. That's the other team."

Nguyen's jaw dropped. "Then what the f—" he broke off, bit his tongue. "What *was* Dr Chen doing?"

"He too was working on a new form of photosynthesis. He was hoping to make the wheat three times more productive."

"Then why would anyone want to stop that?" Nguyen said again. He tried to restrain his growing anger.

"Some Greenies have been protesting. They apparently fear it will damage humans, and must be stopped," she said.

"Who knows the paranoia the extremists think up," Smithson put in.

Penrith made a shushing motion with her right hand. "Actually, if the Greenies knew, they might endorse what we're doing."

"Then why for …" Nguyen mastered himself. "If it's so beneficial, why don't you tell them, get them onside?" He glanced at McTeish, who didn't look up, but kept taking notes.

"Don't you understand?" Penrith said. "We can't let people know before we get our results, and not before we have it all patented."

Smithson broke in. "If we let people know what we're doing, others will get on to it. There are millions, if not billions at stake here. That's why the secrecy."

"And the other team?" Nguyen asked.

"They're working on the cyanobacteria approach, as I said," Penrith relaxed her steely look. "I don't think you understand the enormous potential of what we're doing. Whoever gets there first could win the Nobel Prize."

Nguyen stared at her for a moment, then asked, "Who leads the other team?"

Again Penrith glanced at Smithson, who nodded. "Dr Felix Robertson. I suppose you'll want to talk to him as well."

"That would be helpful." Nguyen thought about stones and getting water from them. "So you have two teams, one run by the late Dr Chen, and one by Dr Felix Robertson."

Penrith nodded. "Two teams working on wheat. Are we done? I do have my visitors arriving."

"Carol, you'll need to talk to Dr Robertson."

Penrith said, "Les—could you take the Constable here to see him?"

Smithson frowned, but when Penrith made a quick gesture with her right hand he stood up and led McTeish out the door.

As they left, Nguyen asked Penrith, "And you said that the US pharma, what's their name?"

"HA—Howarth-Acfield."

"You said they fund this research?"

"They fund Dr Robertson's, but not Dr Chen's."

"Why is that? I may be a simple copper, but wouldn't a huge pharma want to cover both bases?"

"Dr Chen gets his funding, er, got his funding from the National Health and Medical Research Council. I'm sure HA will want to bid to develop it if it works. They already have rights to Robertson's work. My meeting—" she glanced at her watch "is in 40 minutes. It's about just that very thing."

Nguyen nodded, and thought for a while, digesting the implications. "Then I'll get out of your hair." He stood up. "While I'm here, I'll need to speak again to Dr Shildduck."

Penrith nodded. "Okay. I'll get Derek to call her for you. If you don't mind, could you wait outside?" She pointed towards the door.

"Thanks," he said, and left. The tall young man who was Penrith's assistant beckoned him. "Dr Shildduck will be down shortly. Please take a seat."

8

Dr Felix Robertson looked up as Les Smithson ushered McTeish into his office. He stood to shake hands as Smithson introduced her. Robertson was tall and thin, with a bright yellow T-shirt under his lab coat. McTeish guessed he was in his late thirties. There were files and paper piled up on his desk, and books and papers haphazardly spread on two bookshelves against the wall. The small coffee table was also overflowing with papers.

Robertson picked up two books from a chair and added them to a stack on his desk.

"Sit down," he said. He sat opposite McTeish. Smithson looked around as if to find another chair.

"That's okay, Les," Robertson said. "We'll be fine."

Smithson looked annoyed, and seemed to be about to say something.

"We'll be fine," Robertson repeated. Smithson shrugged, nodded at McTeish and left. Robertson's voice was a baritone, and McTeish looked at him more closely. He smiled at her.

"What can I do for you?" he asked. Did his eyes twinkle?

"We're investigating—"

"Yes. Poor Doug," Robertson interrupted. "We may have had our … disagreements, but …" he broke off.

"You had disagreements?"

"Well …" Robertson's voice seemed, bizarrely, like chocolate. "We were competitors. Rivals, I suppose you could say."

McTeish shook her head, and took out her notebook.

"Rivals?" she repeated. "You mean in your research?"

"Yes, scientific rivals, I mean. We're determined, or rather, we were, that is each of us, determined to get there first. You know?"

"With wheat?"

"With wheat." He smiled, folded his hands across his chest. "Looks like my team will get there first, now." He looked at her. "No disrespect to Dr Chen and his team. But with him gone, I can't see how Shildduck and Kosic can continue. At least not for a while. And a while can be a long time, a very long time, in the lab. You understand?"

He looked at her again, smiling. His smile, she noticed, was open, not fixed like that creep Smithson's.

"So, his death puts you ahead?"

"Yes, indeed." He frowned. "I mean it takes him out of the picture."

She studied his face. "Who else would gain from his death?"

"You mean me?" He laughed, a sort of quick snort. "Of course I gain. But I'm sure we'd have got there first anyway. I certainly don't go round killing off my colleagues. No matter how arrogant they might be."

McTeish jotted down some more notes while he talked.

"He was arrogant?"

"He—well we all are at times, I suppose, in this line of work. You have to believe in yourself to get anywhere. Don't you find that in your work too?"

McTeish refused to be distracted. "So, no more arrogant than anyone else. Or you?"

"That's right." He grinned. He seemed to think for a while. "Do you understand what we're doing?" he asked.

"Improving wheat—somehow," she muttered.

"Exactly. I'm researching how we might get nitrogen absorbed into wheat, directly. Bypassing the traditional mechanisms. We're trying to insert genes from cyanobacteria." He broke off. "You've signed a confidentiality agreement, I take it?"

"No."

"What?" His eyes opened wide.

She liked the way his face looked shocked. "We're police. We don't do confidentiality agreements. At least not while we're investigating murders."

"Murders? Plural? Someone else as well?"

"Bound to be. But not here, as far as I know." McTeish mentally kicked herself for being flippant. Yet it seemed the way to relate to this odd bod.

"Well then, if you haven't signed anything—"

"This is a murder investigation," she repeated, more firmly. "We don't put stuff out there, not even on social media. Unless we want to, of course. I can assure you that this won't go further than our team."

Robertson shook his head, then grinned. "If Smithson brought you here, things must be okay, I suppose."

"Cyanobacteria," she reminded him. "Is that the term?"

"Yes. By inserting the right genes, we hope to get the wheat to convert nitrogen directly into protein, bypassing photosynthesis. You know what that is?"

McTeish vaguely recalled high school biology. "Yes. I mean I know it's something to do with the sun and plants…they convert the sun's energy. Is that right?" she couldn't recall anything else.

"Well, yes." Robertson smiled at her, which annoyed her. "Photosynthesis is how plants turn light into chemical energy. It's pretty inefficient. If *we* succeed, we'll make wheat three times more productive than by photosynthesis. When you think of the billions of people all needing food, it'll make a huge difference."

"And is that why Howarth-Acfield is funding your research?"

"Of course. They'll own a big chunk of the patents. It's what they do."

"And Dr Chen? I understand they weren't funding him."

"Not for lack of trying. They wanted to. Really wanted to. Cover all bases, you see."

"So why didn't they fund him?" McTeish looked around the messy office. Was this how real brains worked? Funny how everywhere else she'd seen in the building was neat, tidy, antiseptically clean.

"They would've, but Doug didn't want them to. He wanted his stuff to be public domain."

She looked at him, raising an eyebrow in question.

He smiled. "He would have given the rights away, so no one had to pay to use his IP."

She digested this. "Who would want to kill him? Do you have any ideas?"

"I've no idea." He stood up, took a couple of paces, then sat down again.

She watched him. "There've been protests. Any Greenies?"

"Greenies? They don't like this gene insertion stuff. And they assume we're doing stuff that can affect other plants. Which we're not. But killing someone? Come off it." He smiled again. "Why would anyone do that?"

"Someone did."

He shut his mouth.

"You're right." He pulled on an earlobe. "It doesn't add up. There's security here at the labs. How could anyone have got in?"

"He was poisoned. That could have been done before he arrived here."

"Oh." He looked more serious. "Yes, I suppose. Yes, they could certainly have done that. Do you know what he was poisoned with?"

"No. Not yet. But forensics will get there. By the way, have you thought, if they killed Dr Chen, could you be next?" McTeish asked.

"What? Me?"

"You haven't thought of that?"

Robertson sat quietly for a time. His face went a little grey. "I suppose that makes a weird sort of sense. Fuck!" He glanced up at her. "Sorry. I mean, should I take precautions?"

"Better safe than sorry."

"What. Are you serious? I should get protection? My team?" He thought for a moment. "Look. I said earlier that with Doug … gone, his work will stop. But that's not completely true. Shildduck and Kosic might not have Doug's smarts, but they'll work on the main theoretical basis that Doug worked out. So killing Doug won't stop the work. Slow it down, yes, but not stop it. Same goes for me. If I get taken out of the equation, the work will still go ahead. Anyone really wanting to stop our research, if that is the motive, would have to do more than that. But was that the motive? Could it have been personal? Hmm." He scratched his chin, then looked at her more closely. "I don't envy you your job."

She looked up at him from her notebook.

"It has its moments." She thought of her boss: Nguyen was scrupulous in acknowledging each person's work. He seemed to be gender blind as well, evidenced by the fact she was given the responsibility to do this interview. "You've just got to focus on the detail."

"Yes, I get that. But you have to deal with death, and all that goes with that."

"You get used to it." Though she wouldn't let him know this was only her second murder investigation. "Anyone else who might have had it in for Dr Chen? You mentioned it might be personal. Do you mean it might have nothing to do with his work?"

"Just a suggestion."

"Well, you said he was arrogant. Did he have any enemies?" She watched his face as he thought.

He shook his head. "He was a scientist. He could be prickly, but— enemies? No. None that I know of."

"Did you see him socially?" she asked.

"We didn't mix outside work. My scene is different to his."

"And what is your scene?"

"My partner and I don't get out much. I'm afraid I'm a workaholic. We travel when we can. We do subscribe to the MSO."

At her puzzled look, he said, "The Melbourne Symphony Orchestra. We go to their concerts."

"And Dr Chen?"

"You'd have to ask Lucy."

She raised an eyebrow.

"His partner," Robertson said.

"Oh. Right. One of my colleagues is doing that." She smiled, hoping to encourage him. "Anything else you can think of, that might help?"

"Well, no. Not really." He shook his head.

"Thank you for your time, Dr Robertson." She put her notebook away, and he stood up. "If you think of anything else, no matter what, please give me a call." She handed him her card.

He studied it for a moment, put it down on his desk among the papers. He looked up at her. "Hang on. You do know the reason for all the secrecy, don't you? There could be millions at stake here. So maybe consider the money angle. Eh?" He shook her hand. "Nice meeting you."

She glanced back as she left for the lifts. Dr Robertson was staring out with his hands on his hips. He seemed to notice her glance and waved with his fingers, then turned around and went back into his office.

9

WHILE DETECTIVE INSPECTOR NGUYEN waited on the ground floor foyer for Carol McTeish, he thought about aspects of the case. The early dope from forensics was that Dr Chen Du had been poisoned with something like ricin. The poison, Gossiter had said, was likely slow acting, so it might have been administered outside this building. Equally, given the nature of the biological research at the Badeker Institute, it could have been given to him here. But that was maybe unlikely, he thought. He'd get Brothers to check for any video footage, even though it was pretty clear when he'd gone to his lab, and when he was found.

Who else did their first sweep of interviews need to cover? The cleaners, of course. He knew he'd assumed they'd had nothing to do with it beyond discovering the body. But why assume that? What about the Greens? They had to check who had been demonstrating outside the labs. McTeish was talking to, what was his name, Robertson. He doubted professional jealousy was a factor, but again, he had to keep all options open. They all knew there were too many cases where detectives had decided early that the evidence had pointed to a likely culprit, who turned out not to be likely at all, with huge efforts wasted, or worse the wrong person getting convicted, or the right person getting away.

Who benefited from Chen's death? Was it to do with his research, or was it personal and completely unrelated to his work? If it was to do with the research, did that point to some Green nutter? Though from what Olga Penrith had said, surely the Greenies should have embraced what he was trying to do, rather than try to stop it. But, of course, they didn't know what he was trying to do. The nutters probably just saw GM. That was enough for some people to go off the deep end.

What sort of rewards would the successful research team get? Was there a race between Robertson and Chen? Was Penrith bullshitting when she mentioned Nobel Prizes? That would be some reward, if that was true. That would be a motive. He shook his head, as if that would clear it.

And how was it done? Chen's wife, or partner, whatever she was, would have had the opportunity to lace his food. Who else could have? He made a mental note to check with Sue Gossiter about timelines, assuming her forensics team had got more information. The actual time of death, and how many hours before that he would have ingested the poison. Where was Chen when he was poisoned? At home? In the lab? At a fast food joint?

He heard a ping, and Carol McTeish walked out of the centre lift.

"Hi, Boss," she said.

He looked at her questioningly.

She filled him in. "I don't think Robertson was involved. Though of course you never know. But he did say something strange as I was leaving."

Nguyen waited. McTeish was proving effective. Full of energy, no doubts, eager as all get out. And smart, too. He remembered himself at her age. He'd been driven, and anxious not to put a foot wrong. It had taken him nine years before he'd been accepted into an investigative role. He didn't want to wish that on anyone like McTeish. He realised he'd missed what she'd said. Something about money.

"Sorry, Carol. Just been thinking over the ins and outs of the case. What was that again?"

"He said, follow the money."

"Hmm. Good point." Penrith and Smithson had both emphasised that hundreds of millions were at stake. "Did Robertson say what he meant by that?"

"No." She flushed. She should have asked that question. "He just said it as I was leaving. Should I go back?"

"No. No. We can follow that up later. We don't want him to know what our thinking is."

"What is our thinking?"
He smiled at her. "Too soon to know, eh?"

10

IN THE CAR BACK to the station McTeish drove. Although the car was only two years old, it had already gained the faint smell of cop cars—stale hamburgers and coffee.

"Carol," Nguyen said, "I think you're the best person to check out the Greenies."

McTeish glanced across at Nguyen, her eyes widening.

"Get in touch with Chen's research assistant, Kosic is it?

An idea occurred to her. "I could do it in a social way. Have a drink with him. He knows the Greenie scene, I think. I might be able to get more from him than you or Brothers. At least more quickly. You okay with that?"

"A drink?" Nguyen raised his eyebrows. "If you're comfortable with that."

"Yes, Boss," she said. She grinned, then stifled it. "Yes," she said again. "When should I try to see him?"

"ASAP."

She nodded. "I'll see if he'll meet me for a drink tonight."

"Be careful. But I think this guy can give you the state of play—you know, who's obsessed with GM and doing stuff about it. He'll be able to point them out to you." He saw her tense a little. "That is what you said, isn't it? That he has Greenie friends?"

"Yes. That's what he said." She let herself smile.

"TAMAS?" HE'D ANSWERED HIS PHONE on the second ring.

"Yes—who's this?"

"Detective Constable McTeish. Carol. We spoke earlier. At the Badeker."

"Right. Yes. Hello, Carol." He sounded in better spirits than just after Dr Chen's body had been discovered. Natural, she supposed. "How can I help you?"

"I was wondering if I could pick your brain. Maybe over a drink. Are you free this evening?"

"What do you mean, pick my brain?" She could imagine him starting to panic.

"It does seem that someone poisoned your boss. We're trying to find out who might have been aware of what he was researching. We're talking to a wide range of possible contacts. You mentioned you're a member of the Greens."

"The Greens had nothing to do with it." He was emphatic. "That's a ridiculous suggestion."

"I'm not saying they did. But I need to talk to some of your Greenie friends. Maybe one of them will know someone who knows someone. You know what I mean? After all, someone must have had it in for Dr Chen."

There was a pause. "Yeeess, I suppose so." Another pause. "Yes, that might make a sort of sense."

"So are you free this evening? Can we meet for a drink? Informal. Not a proper interview. Just a chat."

She waited.

"Okay. Yeah, I suppose that'll be okay." Another pause. "Where do you want to meet?"

"How about a bar or pub near you?"

"I'm in Port Melbourne."

She thought for a bit.

"Do you know the Vincent, in Albert Park?"

"Where's that?"

"In Victoria Street."

"The Vincent. Okay, I'll find it. Would about six be okay?"

"Six it is. I'll see you there." McTeish hung up. Speaking to Kosic was like dragging … she couldn't remember what. But it was difficult.

11

McTeish arrived at the Vincent a few minutes after six. The bar was crowded, noisy with laughter and the hubbub of chatter. Maybe this wasn't a good choice after all. She looked around. There, in a corner, Kovac sat at a table. He happened to look up at that moment and saw her, and waved. She walked over to him through a huddle of drinkers.

"Hi." He stood up, shook her hand, gestured towards a chair.

"Hi, Tamas. Thanks for meeting me here." She sat down and smiled at him.

He nodded. "What can I get you?"

"A glass of white." She noticed he had yet to get himself a drink.

"Just a sec." He walked to the bar, and presently returned with two glasses of wine, one white and one red. "It's a sav blanc—is that okay?"

"Perfect." She took the glass and raised it to clink against his. "Good health." She took a mouthful. "Delicious."

He sipped his red, then asked, "How can I help?"

He seemed anxious, and she tried to reassure him.

"As I said, we're talking to anyone who might have been in touch with Dr Chen. Recently, I mean. And I thought you'd know people I could get in touch with. You know, professionals, and also some of your environmental friends might know others."

He nodded. "I see." He sat stiffly.

"But before we get into that, tell me a bit about yourself." She looked directly into his eyes, willing him to relax.

"What do you want to know?" He sat there, his face reddening a little.

"I don't know. How did you get into this? I mean research." She had to raise her voice to be heard over sudden shrieks of laughter coming from a nearby table of young women.

"How do you mean?"

"Have you worked at the Badeker long?"

"About a year." He considered. "No, year and a half."

"And how did you get the job?"

"It's a post doc."

She must have looked blank.

"I did my PhD at Melbourne uni, and this job came up. I was pretty lucky to get it. There was a bit of competition." He seemed to be relaxing a bit.

"So what's it like at the Badeker?"

"It's not all that exciting. Long days and nights, lots of computer programming, then testing reagents. Seeing if something works. Trying to find out why it works. I think we are close to a breakthrough."

"What sort of breakthrough?"

"I can't talk about the detail." He spoke not to her but down at his drink.

"Well, what's a breakthrough mean?"

"The breakthrough is the wheat grows extra protein, and the mice we feed it to don't get sick." He looked up and grinned.

"So, mice are the test?"

"Most research ends in failure. Less than one in a hundred projects get through to proper human trials."

"So if the mice don't get sick, then it's safe for humans?"

"It's not that simple. But it does have to pass the mice test." He looked at her, waiting for the next question.

"You mentioned you're a member of the Greens."

"Yes—that's one reason I'm doing this work." He smiled. "There's a real chance that what we're doing could help save the planet."

"Save the planet! That's pretty amazing. Can I ask you how?"

"If we make food more productive, it'll feed more people. Simple arithmetic." He smiled complacently.

"Your friends must be happy."

"They don't really know what I'm doing." He scratched his head. "Some of them assume the worst. And I can't really tell them what we're doing—except to try to reassure them. That it's all for the good. They're fixated on the evils of GM seed. You know, that poor third world farmers will be held to ransom by the big companies that sell the seed. We're not doing anything like that."

"But if you make wheat more productive, won't that make the improved wheat seed more expensive?"

"It will—to a degree, I suppose. But the benefit will be huge, and far outweigh the small extra cost. A win-win for everyone.""

"But some don't believe that, do they?"

"As soon as you say Big Pharma, some people jump straight into the conspiracy theories. Of course, there are good reasons for some of them. But not all. And not what we're doing." He sat back and drank more wine.

She decided to be direct. "Well, someone poisoned Dr Chen. We can't rule out someone who was disgruntled with his research."

"I see, so it's whack a Greenie, is it?"

She took another sip, regarded him. "Tamas. We have to do our job. I'm not suggesting your Green mates poisoned Dr Chen. But they might know who were protesting outside the lab. What do you think of the protesters?"

"They've got the wrong end of the stick. I've tried to tell them. I mean, hint, I suppose. I can't really talk about what we're doing, as I said. But some people can't get beyond 'GM is evil'. That's not to say they'd do anything about it."

"Well, isn't protesting doing something about it? Do you know any of the protestors?"

"A few, I suppose. But protesting isn't poisoning."

"That's why I want to meet them. If I can talk to them, that should clear them from our inquiries."

"I suppose." He drank some more of his wine.

"Who should I talk to? Who organises the demos?"

"I don't know that, but I could introduce you to a couple of my friends. They might know."

"When's a good time for that? Or could you just give me their names, and I'll get in touch. I don't want to slow things down."

He sipped his wine, put the glass down and rubbed his chin.

"Okay. You could talk to Rhys Meadows, and Sonia Yee."

"Who are they?"

"They're both pretty het up about Green issues. They've both demonstrated outside the lab."

And they're friends of yours?"

"Well." He seemed to shrink back into himself, then shrugged. "Yes, they are friends, I suppose. Not the closest, but I do see them from time to time."

"Will they talk to me?"

Kosic sipped his wine. "I don't see why not. They'll be appalled that Doug was killed. I'm sure they'll try to help you. But—" he shook his head. "I don't see how they can help you much."

She took out her phone. "Can you share their contact details?"

He nodded, and after a few seconds did so.

"Thanks."

"Like another drink?" he blurted out.

McTeish had thought she'd go and start getting in touch with his friends, but she decided, having got him here, that would be too rude. "Okay. But let me get them this time. The same again?"

"Yes, please." He straightened up in his chair, a smile on his face.

"What was your red?"

"A pinot noir."

"Right. A pinot noir it is."

She returned shortly with the two drinks.

He raised his glass. "Cheers." They clinked them. "Are you hungry? We could get something to eat."

She shook her head. "No, I'm right. Got another commitment later on."

"Okay," he said. His face fell.

"What else do you do? I mean apart from your work," McTeish asked.

He brightened. "I listen to music. Read sf. See a few films."

"What sort of music?"

He reddened. "Don't laugh, but I like ABBA, and the Beach Boys."

"Old time music, hey?"

"Have you heard any of their stuff?"

She was sure she'd heard an ABBA song. What was it? "Didn't they have a song about money? I think I've heard that."

"Yeah. *Money, Money, Money.*"

"In a rich man's world." She remembered it now. "And the Beach Boys?"

"My dad used to play *Good Vibrations* all the time. It's a great song. Brian Wilson was a genius."

She looked blankly at him.

"Brian Wilson. He wrote their songs. You're bound to have heard them, even if you don't know they're the Beach Boys."

He was happy to talk about music, but he hadn't asked her one question about herself. She held a smile, then finished her wine. "Thanks for seeing me, Tamas. I've got to make a move."

"Oh, no worries." He drained his glass. "You sure you have to go?"

She nodded. "I'll call your friends. Thanks again."

12

MᴄTᴇɪsʜ ʟᴇꜰᴛ ᴛʜᴇ ᴘᴜʙ. It was cool and there was a sprinkle of rain, and she walked quickly to her car. She sat for a moment, thinking about the conversation. Again, Kosic had been pretty unforthcoming. Though at least she did have two names and contact details. And had he tried, in his awkward way, to come on to her? Men. She shook her head, then started the car and drove to her apartment in St Kilda. Once home she decided to ring Kosic's friends, Rhys Meadows and Sonia Yee. She'd try Sonia Yee first.

The phone rang, and went to voicemail, and she left a message. "Hello. Sonia Yee? This is Detective Constable Carol McTeish from Victoria Police. Could you please call me back?" She left her number. Then tried Meadows. This, too, went to voicemail.

Oh well, she thought. I'll try again tomorrow if they don't call back. She went to the fridge, looked at a bowl with cling wrap. Yesterday's pasta. She grabbed it and stuck it in the microwave.

Her phone rang. She glanced at the screen. It was her mother. "Hi, mum."

"Hi, darling. How are you?"

"Fine." She waited. Always there was some ulterior motive in her mother's calls.

"How was your day?" As if she cared.

"Fine. The usual. What's up?"

"Just wondering when you could pop over. I hardly ever see you."

"I'm still working, mum."

"At this time of night?"

"I keep telling you, I'm always on duty." She waited for the next comment.

"Why did you want to be a policewoman, anyhow? You could be anything you want."

"Mum. You know why. Do we have to go over that again?"

"Sorry."

Had she heard right? Her mum saying 'sorry'? "Look, I can't come over now. I'm expecting two important calls. I can call in tomorrow evening. Will that be okay?"

"It's just …" Her mother hesitated.

"What?"

"I'm being bothered. By some young hooligans. If they saw you, they'd clear off."

"How are they bothering you?"

As she spoke another call started ringing.

"Mum, I've got to go. I'll call you back shortly."

Before her mother could say anything, she ended the call and answered the new one. "Carol McTeish."

"Hello. This is Sonia Yee. You rang?"

"Hi, Sonia. Thanks for calling back."

"What sort of car are you looking for?"

"A car? I'm not looking for a car. No. I was wondering if I could talk to you."

"We are talking, aren't we?" The friendliness had left her voice. "Why do you want to talk? How did you get my number?"

"We're investigating the death of Dr Chen Du. Do you know him?"

"Dr Chen Du? He's dead?"

"You know him, then?"

"Isn't he the one who works on GM at the Badeker? You say he's dead? Well, bad luck for him. Why ring me?"

"How do you know him?"

"I don't. I know *of* him. I know who he is, but I never met him. You say he's dead? How did it happen?"

McTeish thought for a moment, then said, "He was poisoned."

"Poisoned. Ugh."

"That's why I want to talk to you."

"Me? But I've just told you I never met him." A new note of suspicion entered her voice, "How did you get my name?"

"Tamas Kosic gave it to me."

"Tamas? Why would he give you my name?"

"I'm talking to people who were protesting outside the Badeker. You've done that, haven't you?"

"Why? What's that got to do with him being dead? Are you trying to say I had something to do with it?" Yee's voice rose in pitch and volume.

"No. No. Listen, when can we talk?" She kept her voice calm.

There was a pause. "Uh, I'm working tomorrow."

"Whereabouts? I could meet you at your work."

"I'm at Preston Motors. I'm a saleswoman. You could come there. But how can I possibly help?"

"It's just routine. We're talking to a wide range of people. I'll explain when we meet. Would ten am suit?" She took down the address.

"You sure this is necessary?"

"Yes. It's important. Thanks for your cooperation, Ms Yee. I'll see you at ten tomorrow."

"Okay—maybe I could change your mind about a car."

13

Would Meadows return her call? She checked the time: 8:45pm. She'd call him again in the morning. But now she had to do it—return the call to her mum.

"Hi, darling. You cut me off." Her mother's voice had that long-suffering tone she had perfected.

"What were you ringing about?" McTeish tried to keep her voice even, friendly, but knew it had an edge to it.

"As I was saying before you so rudely terminated the call, I want you to come home to help me with these young hooligans."

That word again—where had she got 'hooligans' from? "Mum. I told you. I had an important call coming though."

"You have a boyfriend?"

"It was a work call." It was exasperating. "And no, I don't have a boyfriend." Unlike you, she thought, with her long stream of losers. "I'm investigating a murder, Mum. That has to come first. Surely you understand that."

"I understand that I will always come last. That's okay. I don't care if you find me bashed up or dead. What do you care?"

"Mum." She gripped her phone tightly. Willed herself to relax. "Are the 'hooligans' there now?"

"I'm not sure. Hang on a sec. I'll check." She heard the sound of a door opening and shutting. "Not at this minute. But who knows when they'll come back?"

"Okay. Look. You know I have to focus on my work. But I will come round tomorrow. Okay?"

"Promise?"

"Yes, promise. See you around sixish."

"Will you bring some takeaway?"

Shit, as usual her mother was driving her mad. She took a deep breath. "Okay. Fish and chips, all right?"

"Thanks, darling."

Before her mother could launch into anything else, McTeish hung up.

She went to the fridge, poured herself a glass of sav blanc, took a gulp. Get a grip, she told herself. Focus. Breathe. She took a slow deep breath, held it for the count of three, then slowly exhaled, also to the count of three. She did it again, then took another gulp of wine.

She sat down on the couch. Anything worth watching? She scrolled through Netflix, shook her head, stood up and found her bag, took out her notebook, and reviewed her notes. That calmed her. She finished her drink, and stopped herself from refilling her glass. She put in her earbuds and listened to Billie Eilish's *Lovely*.

14

Nguyen held his regular team meeting at eight am. Brothers and McTeish sat on chairs in his office, and he listened while McTeish recounted her meeting with Kosic, and her intended meetings with the two names Kosic had supplied her, Rhys Meadows and Sonia Yee.

"Good, good," he said, nodding. "Graham, have you got anything for us?"

"Not since seeing the widow," he said.

"Well, I want you to follow up with her and Dr Chen's friends. If he was poisoned before he got to work, then it must have been by a friend or an acquaintance. Maybe even by his wife."

"Partner," Brothers said.

"What's that?"

"Dr Chen wasn't married. Lucy is his partner." He shut up.

"Thank you, Graham." Nguyen was feeling annoyed. "If Lucy wasn't his wife, why did you call her his widow?"

Brothers reddened.

"Where was I? Yes. His *partner* could have done it."

"What? Lucy Bottega? You think? She was pretty upset," Brothers said.

"People have been known to act, fake their responses." Nguyen regarded Brothers and smiled.

Brothers shrugged. "Just saying. When I told her, she started crying. I didn't get the impression she was faking it."

Nguyen stared at him.

"I know. I know. So, she may have bumped him off. But why would she do that?"

"Maybe she really was upset. More than likely. All I'm saying is, let's not rule anyone out just yet. Okay?"

"No worries, no one is ruled out. And I'm speaking to their friends to see what they have to say."

"Good." Nguyen paused. "I'm going to have to speak to some of the backers of the research."

"Why's that, Boss?" McTeish said.

"No one's ruled out," he said with a grin.

"What, a pharma exec knocked off the guy they're funding?" Brothers said.

"Apparently they weren't funding Dr Chen." Nguyen rubbed his jaw. "It's not likely they were involved, but we need to get a better picture of what's been going on. They may have some answers."

But when Nguyen rang Olga Penrith, she was again uncooperative.

"These are busy people, Detective Inspector. What on earth can they tell you? They are business people. Investors. We can't afford to lose their interest. Particularly after this … tragedy. Especially after this tragedy." He could hear the annoyance in her voice.

"Dr Penrith. I seem to keep needing to remind you that this is a murder investigation." He thought for a moment. "Just as I am sure you are very effective in running your research institute, let me assure you that I too am very effective in my job. That includes talking to those who need to be talked to."

"Detective—" he heard the disdain in her voice—"that is precisely my point. If there were something they could tell you, then there would be no problem. It's very simple." He thought he heard a sigh. "But I cannot afford for you to put these people off. I've already told you that millions of dollars are at stake. Again I ask, what possible help could they give you, that my people can't provide?" She paused. "Be reasonable."

He had to give her marks for persistence. It just didn't wash. "It's my judgement who we talk to. And the way we work is sometimes to talk far and wide. And this is one of those times." He decided to play a card, which he knew would get back to the Super. "Let me put it this way. Which would you prefer? The slim possibility your pharmaceutical colleagues might get upset with me—and you might not believe me, but most people get some perverse pleasure in being involved in a murder inquiry, if they're on the periphery, as you assure me they are. Rather than being put off, they'll probably get a bit of a kick out of it."

"Or? You implied a choice." Her voice was icy, aggressive.

"Or I may have to charge you with obstructing this inquiry, this murder inquiry." He waited, let it hang there.

"I see." The tone was still icy. "Very well."

"You'll help me talk to them?"

"Why, no, Detective. You'd better charge me."

Fuck, he thought. Would Superintendent Forell go along with this? Who knew what people Penrith knew, what connections she might have? "Very well," he said. I'll get back to you later today." He hung up.

15

As HE WAS CURSING HIMSELF for forcing the issue and being out-manoeuvred, a thought occurred to him. Why the resistance to him talking to her investors? Ah, he relaxed. Maybe I haven't been out-manoeuvred after all.

He buzzed Superintendent Forell.

"Can I see you for a moment, Supe?"

"No time like the present." She hung up.

Shit. It was so hard to predict what reaction she'd have. He took the lift to the floor above and knocked on her door, even though it was ajar, and put his head in.

She looked up. "Detective. Come in. I was going to call you anyhow. How's the Badeker situation going?"

"That's what I want to talk to you about. A difficulty has come up."

"Difficulty?" Forell spoke the word as if as a caress. Her eyes narrowed as she regarded him, a faint smile on her lips. "Difficulties can be interesting, can't they, John?"

Damn. She'd reverted to his first name.

"Except when they're not. Which is it? Interesting, or … ." She let it hang there.

He explained the choice he'd given Olga Penrith, and how she was trying to block him talking to the pharma company investors about Dr Chen. How she'd challenged him to charge her with obstructing the inquiry.

"The first kind of difficulty, then. The interesting kind." She looked at him again, the smile still on her lips.

"I reckon you might be getting a call from the Commissioner to suggest I be more … diplomatic," Nguyen said.

"As I said, the interesting kind." She broke off for a moment, as if weighing possibilities. "Let's hope I do get such a call. Haven't spoken to Jim for a little while."

What could that mean? He felt himself growing anxious.

"Sorry, Boss, if I—"

She cut him off.

"Bullshit!" She spoke in her quiet voice, but the emphasis was there, perhaps intensified. "John, John. If Jim calls me, what does that tell us? Eh?"

He couldn't help himself and let out a sigh of relief. "They're afraid of something."

"Quite. You did well to keep me in the loop. I'll let you know if I get pressured. Meantime, I suggest you carry out your threat."

"Arrest Dr Penrith?"

"It may not come to that. But certainly offer to do so. See how she reacts." Forell sat back, picked up a file and opened it. She looked up. "You still here?"

"Just going, Boss."

"Remember. Where there's a bluff there can always be a counter bluff."

16

NGUYEN LEFT FORELL'S OFFICE, took the lift back to his level, and grinned to himself. That hadn't been so bad. Now Forell had his back, he'd see what happened next. In fact, rather than call Penrith again, he'd go in and see her. Put her on the spot.

He looked around the office. McTeish was out—that's right, she'd be chasing up Sonia Yee and what was his name, Meadows. Brothers was on the phone. He caught his eye and signalled for him to join him in his office.

He sat at his desk, made a couple of notes about the conversation with Forell, and Brothers came in.

"Something up?"

"You free at the moment? I need to go in to the Badeker Institute to see Dr Penrith.

"Yes, I'm okay. I'm going around to see Lucy Bottega, but that can wait. Will it take long?"

"I hope not." He explained to Brothers how he was going to threaten to arrest Penrith.

Brothers' eyes sparkled. "I like it! Maybe that'll help you get a straight answer or two."

"Never know your luck in a big city." He glanced at Brothers, put down his pen. "You can drive."

THEY ARRIVED AT THE Badeker Institute a little after ten thirty. They parked underground, finding a visitors parking spot on basement level one. The lift lobby was quiet as they approached the reception desk, behind which sat the same woman as earlier. Nguyen gestured to Brothers, who said, "Two passes, please."

"Who do you wish to see?"

Brothers flashed his badge. "This is official police business. Just the two passes, please."

The woman dithered, then seemed to make a decision and passed over two key cards. "These will get you through the barriers."

"Thank you," Brothers said, and handed one to Nguyen. He gave the woman a wave as they walked over to the lifts.

"What floor is Dr Penrith on?" Brothers asked. "It's five, isn't it?"

Nguyen nodded, and pressed the 5 button.

The lift rose uninterrupted and pinged gently as they arrived at level five. They got out and walked across towards Penrith's office.

Outside at his desk, Penrith's assistant looked up. "Yes?" he said. "Can I help you?"

"Is Dr Penrith in?" Nguyen said.

The young man glanced at the door before saying. "She's tied up at present."

He ignored him and knocked at the door, opening it. Olga Penrith was on the phone, and looked up, glaring.

"Excuse me. Can I call you back?" She put the handset down and stood up. "What's the meaning of this?" She frowned, and her voice was angry.

"I'm following up on your request." Nguyen said.

"Request? What request?"

"You asked me earlier today to charge you, didn't you?" Nguyen said. "So here we are."

Penrith stared at them, her jaw rigid. She breathed out slowly and seemed to relax. She sat down. "You want to arrest me?" Her tone was one of wonder. "Really, Detective. Are you serious?"

"Perfectly serious. If you don't want to help me speak to your investors, then I'm afraid we have no choice."

Penrith regarded him steadily for a few moments. "What precisely is the help you want?" she said.

"Simply the names of the executives from Howarth-Acfield you've been dealing with. You might like to let them know that I'll be talking to them. You can smooth the way, if you like. Let them know this is purely a necessary procedure. Nothing to be concerned about. Right?"

She considered this, then reached for her phone. "Derek. Can you get me the HA file?" She put the phone down and said to Nguyen. "Very well, Detective. I'll give you their contact details. But let me tell you, a lot is riding on our research. Not just here at the Institute, but at senior levels of government. If your provocative actions jeopardise anything, I doubt it will be me who will be paying the price."

"Thank you, Dr Penrith. That's all we need. I'm sure your anxieties will be allayed."

The young man came into the room with a manila file.

"Derek. Please give these gentlemen copies of the business cards of Frank Robarts and Sheila Ostarkie."

He took a page from the file. "Here's a photocopy of their cards." He handed the piece of paper to Nguyen. "Anything else?" He looked at Penrith.

"Thanks, Derek. That's all for now," she said.

He left the office.

"So, Frank Robarts and Sheila Ostarkie," Nguyen said, reading the names on the paper. "Is that all?"

"They're the two who've come out here. I also deal with people in their head office, in Baltimore. Surely you don't want to talk to them as well?"

"Are these two in Melbourne?" he asked, waving the sheet of paper.

"Until next week, I believe."

Now that she'd decided to co-operate it was if she'd never been anything else but helpful.

"Then we'll call them later today. Give you time, if you wish, to let them know we'll be in touch. We'll see ourselves out."

Penrith nodded.

Brothers jumped up and followed Nguyen out to the lifts.

"When are you seeing the *widow*?" Nguyen asked as they descended to the carpark basement.

"I'll call in after I've dropped you back at the station."

"Good. Check who Chen saw in the last day or so, if she knows. Particularly anyone unusual. I can't imagine any friend would suddenly want to knock him off, unless there was some long-standing rivalry or jealousy." He glanced at Brothers. "Maybe an affair?"

"Gotcha, Boss. Don't rule anyone out."

They exited the lift and got into the car.

Brothers said, "Her nibs seemed to give in pretty easily, didn't she?"

"Penrith? Yes. Maybe she talked to her counsel, Smithson. He would know there's no point in being difficult."

Brothers started the engine.

"On the other hand," Nguyen said, "maybe she just came to her senses. Or more likely she's already spoken to them and discovered they are okay with talking to us."

They drove for a while, then Nguyen said, "By the way—have you had a chance to talk to the cleaners?"

"Yes—nothing there. The poor woman—" he reached into his jacket pocket with the other hand on the wheel, found his notebook, and somehow flipped it open—"Zenya Dubcek." He put it back in his pocket. "All she did was call the ambulance when she saw Dr Chen's body. She said she didn't touch anything. And that the ambos called in the police."

"Hmm. Thanks. Glad that's tied off."

17

At his desk Nguyen looked at the two names on the sheet he'd been given. Frank Robarts was Director, Research, for Howarth-Acfield, and Dr Sheila Ostarkie was Vice-President Commercial. Derek had underlined their cell phone numbers. He decided to call Ostarkie first.

"Who's calling?" a melodious voice asked.

"Dr Ostarkie? This is Detective Inspector John Nguyen, from Victoria Police."

"Detective Nguyen. I've been expecting your call. Olga said you wanted to talk to me. How can I help?"

"Would it be convenient if we met? Do you have any time today?"

They agreed to meet at her hotel, the Park Hyatt, at two pm.

"Will Mr Robarts be available, then as well?"

"Yes, I'll make sure he can see you too."

"Thank you." He hung up.

So he'd been right—Penrith had already eased the way.

At two pm Nguyen entered the lobby of the Park Hyatt: marbled floor with circular designs, walls panelled in dark timber, and leather chairs and sofas. He approached reception where a young woman with short blond hair in a dark suit looked up Sheila Ostarkie's room number. She rang the number, then passed the phone over.

Ostarkie's voice was calm, and she suggested they meet on the Mezzanine floor; he climbed the curved staircase and sat on a chair where he could watch the bank of lifts. After several minutes a woman in her forties emerged, dressed in a light grey suit with a white blouse.

She was followed by a stout older man also in a grey suit, with a bright blue open-necked shirt under his jacket. The two looked around.

Nguyen stood up walked over and introduced himself.

"How can we help you?" Ostarkie asked, after they had sat down. Before he could answer a waiter approached and they ordered coffees and a ginger and lemon tea.

Ostarkie was elegant, severe, and her calm voice had a no nonsense quality to it. Robarts lounged in his chair, clearly impatient. Nguyen decided to get straight to the point. "As you know, I'm investigating the murder of Dr Chen Du." Neither said anything, just looked at him. "And my job is to talk to as many people as possible who had dealings with him. So I'd like to ask you both a few questions."

The two still made no comment but looked at him expectantly. Then Robarts said, "Will this take long? We didn't exactly have dealings with Dr Chen." He smiled in what Nguyen thought of as a self-satisfied way.

"We would have liked to have had dealings, you understand," Ostarkie interjected, her tone a quiet drawl. "He just wasn't interested."

"We mainly dealt with Dr Robertson. You know him?" Robarts said.

"We've talked with him." Nguyen watched them both. They seemed relaxed. "Could you fill in a few things for me? Food research is not something I know much about. What's your relationship with the Badeker?"

"We're investing in their work," Ostarkie said. "We've put a bunch into Felix Robertson and his lab. We were hoping to do the same with Dr Chen. Until the unfortunate events …" she left her sentence unfinished.

"So you'd met him?"

"Oh, yes. A fine man. But not commercial, not at all." Her eyes remained trained on Nguyen as she spoke.

"What was he working on?"

Robarts looked around, as if he were afraid of being overheard, and muttered, "He was working on wheat, and a novel method to increase the protein levels."

"As is Dr Robertson," Ostarkie said. "But he has a different approach."

"And why are you investing in the work?"

"If it pays off, it will transform agriculture. It would be crazy for us not to be part of that." She smiled, but there seemed little warmth in the smile.

"Which team was making better progress?" Nguyen asked.

"Both of them seemed to be going okay. But I have to say Dr Chen seemed to be more promising."

"You said he wasn't commercial. What do you mean?"

Ostarkie looked up at the ceiling, then back at Nguyen. "He didn't want his work to be commercialised."

"Load of crap," Robarts said. "Of course it would have been commercialised—just not necessarily by him. The Badeker would have made sure of that."

"So the fact he didn't want your money made no difference?"

"Detective," Ostarkie said. "Scientists have deals when they do their research. They might own a small percentage of any IP they develop, but the Institute would have the rest. Maybe a university, too—sometimes scientists get their ideas when they were academics, researching at their university. Then they take them to research institutes so they can earn some money."

"So where does Howarth-Acfield come in?"

Robarts chuckled. "Excuse me, Sheila. We've bought into the Badeker in a big way. We're providing the funding. We'll make sure the work gets developed."

"You mean commercialised?"

"Exactly." Robarts lent back in his chair. "What's the point of good work if the world can't benefit from it?"

The waiter arrived with their drinks, and set them down on the small table in front of them. He put the tea in front of Ostarkie without having to ask.

"Do you have any idea why someone would want to kill Dr Chen?" Nguyen asked.

"Any professional jealousy, you mean?" Ostarkie said.

"Any reason."

"Look, we're from Baltimore. How would we know?" Robarts said.

"Are other pharmas interested as well?" Nguyen asked.

"Of course they are," Ostarkie said. "We just happened to get there first. We're building a strong relationship. But tell me, Detective. Why do *you* think he was killed?"

"Far too soon to even speculate," Nguyen said.

"Come on," Robarts said, sitting up straighter. "You must have some idea. Or why talk to us?"

Nguyen smiled. "People always want us to make guesses. We don't do that—make guesses or share them. Look, we're still gathering information. That's why we're talking now."

"Frank," Ostarkie said, putting a hand on his arm. "Relax. We'll find out, all in good time." She took her hand off the arm and sipped her tea, looking across at Nguyen. "Anything else we can help you with?"

"If anything else occurs to you, please let me know." They stood up, shook hands and Nguyen left.

18

CAROL MCTEISH DROVE NORTH to Preston Motors, in High Street. It was a large dealership, and she noticed several hybrids were placed out the front, to catch the eyes of passers-by.

She drove in and pulled up near the showroom between a row of cars. Soon an overweight middle-aged man in a suit appeared; he lent towards her window.

"How can I help you?" He had a slight wheeze.

"I'm seeing Sonia Yee. Is it okay to park here, or should I move?"

The man gestured. "You can park at the end of this row. Okay?"

She nodded.

"Sonia is in the showroom."

"Thanks." She pressed the button to raise the window and re-parked the car.

She entered the showroom through sliding doors, and walked around three new cars to reception, noting several cubicles along the window. There was a scent of eucalyptus cleaner in the air. The receptionist, with caked on makeup over a tan, real or fake she couldn't determine, eyelash extenders and shiny blond hair cut shoulder length, was on the phone, repeating "Yes, yes" every so often. She looked up, saw McTeish, and looked back at her desk. "Yes. Yes. I understand. Look. I've got to go. I'll call you back." She put the phone down and smiled. "Can I help you?"

"I'm here to see Sonia Yee."

"Is she expecting you?"

"Yes. Carol McTeish." She checked her phone. "At ten."

The receptionist pushed a button and spoke. "Sonia? A Carol McTeish to see you." She looked up at McTeish. "Would you like a coffee or water?"

"Water would be good."

She reached under her desk and handed her a bottle of spring water branded Preston Motors.

"Hi there. Carol?"

A young woman in a white blouse and dark red skirt, with black straight hair, smiled at her, arm outstretched. She led McTeish to a cubicle facing the cars parked outside, towards High Street.

"Thanks for meeting me," McTeish said. She noted that Yee used a minimum of makeup, and her hair seemed to move freely without the use of hairspray.

"No worries. You said you're not looking for a car?"

"Not at the moment."

Yee nodded. "Oh, yes."

"It's about what I said last night. Dr Chen and the Badeker Institute."

"Yes? So Dr Chen was poisoned. Nothing to do with me."

"Well, that's good, if it had nothing to do with you. I'm talking to everyone who had some sort of connection with Dr Chen."

"But I already told you I never met him."

"We have to talk to everyone, just to rule people out."

"So, am I a person of interest, is that what you call it?"

"If you never met him, then no. That's one of the things I'm establishing."

"Well. That's pretty straight forward." She smiled defiantly. "Never met him."

"But you may still be able to help. Look. One line of our inquiry is whether any unusual people were taking an interest in Dr Chen. You said you demonstrated outside the lab."

"Against GM food. Do you know the harm it can do?"

McTeish ignored the question. "Who were the others there?"

"What do you mean, others? We're a small group, GOCH."

"Gotch? As in 'gotcha'?"

Yee smiled bleakly. "No. GOCH." She spelt it out. "G O C H—Greens for Community Health."

McTeish couldn't resist. "What's the O for?"

Yee looked at her a moment, sighed. "How would you pronounce GFCH?" Clearly she'd had to answer this before.

"Okay." McTeish grinned. "Right. Got you. You were saying? About who else was there?"

"A few of us. Maybe a dozen. We'd take it in turns to be there."

"How are you organised? Is there a roster?"

"Rhys Meadows does the co-ordination."

McTeish noted down the name. "Were there any strangers who joined in, people you hadn't seen before? Who weren't members of GOCH? Take your time." She undid the cap of her water bottle and took a sip.

Yee thought about it. "Now you mention it, there was a man in his thirties, maybe a bit older, not one of us, who came along a couple of times. I don't know his name."

"What did he look like?"

"Let me think. He was quiet. Didn't say much."

"Australian?"

"What do you mean Australian? Am I Australian?"

"Of course." McTeish held her hands up. "I meant was he from overseas, a visitor? Not a local."

"Well, okay. I suppose, yes. About average height, maybe six foot. He had a sort of beard. More like designer stubble. Darkish hair, I think."

"He didn't befriend anyone?"

"Not me. He kept to himself, apart." She hesitated. "But he did ask about Dr Chen, now I come to think about it. Wanted to know if any of us knew him."

"You don't remember his name?"

Yee shook her head. Then sat up. "Hang on. I think it was Terry." She tugged an ear lobe. "Maybe not. Not sure. But, yes, Terry."

"No surname?"

"Not that I recall. Rhys might know. Do you want his number?"

"I've got it, thanks."

"Tamas?"

"Yes." McTeish smiled at Yee. "No one else joined in, that you didn't know?"

After a moment Yee shook her head. "Sorry. No one else that I can recall."

"Thanks for your help."

"Is that all?"

"Unless you can think of anything else."

Yee reached across the desk and took McTeish's hand. "What about having a quick look at a car while you're here? We've some very good deals on hybrids at the moment." She stood up, and McTeish found herself standing as well. "Look," Yee pointed at a Corolla Hybrid near them on the showroom floor.

"Thanks, but another time, perhaps."

"Come on. Just a quick look."

The car was a bright glossy blue. Yee opened the driver's door. "Hop in."

McTeish was tempted. It had that new car smell, and the seats were leather. She wrenched herself away. "Another time, okay?"

Yee smiled. "Okay."

They shook hands and she left.

19

Frederick Lovell, President of Howarth-Acfield, rang Dr Sheila Ostarkie from Baltimore. "What's happening?" he asked.

Typical Lovell question, Ostarkie thought. What did he mean? "About the police investigation?" she asked.

"What else? I mean to say, with Chen out of the picture it sure makes our work a little easier. You signed the new deal with Robertson?" As usual, Lovell sounded a mixture of satisfied and impatient.

"We're close. They're having their lawyers look over the agreement."

"Got to get that signed before anything else happens."

"It'll be signed." He was such a worry wart. Of course it would be signed.

"Water tight. It's got to be water tight. Right?"

"Fred, stop worrying. If they didn't have their lawyers look at it I'd be worried. It's just the normal process. You know that. We'll own the IP completely."

"I know. I know. It's just with Chen gone …" he paused.

"Yes?" What now?

"Can his team keep going?"

"No doubt. But it'll put them behind, slow them down. No doubt about that." She imagined that the Badeker would promote Helen Shildduck to lead the team, at least in the short term. But they'd probably have to recruit someone else. That would be difficult. Where do you find distinguished scientists?

"They can't be shut down?" Lovell's voice was again impatient. "Disband the team?"

Ostarkie considered. Could the team be disbanded? "Without Dr Chen they'll have difficulty with their next round of funding. If they still try for the government grant. Maybe we could offer them something."

"Yes?" Lovell interjected. "What do you mean?"

"Now Chen's gone, the others will be wondering about their future. They may be willing to sign up with us. They may not share Chen's concerns about IP ownership. If we offer the right amount, who knows? Then that line will be locked away, too."

"Atta girl," Lovell said.

Ostarkie winced. "You can't say that, Fred. Jesus!"

"What do you mean, Sheila?" He had that satisfied purr again.

"You know what I mean. In any case, Frank and I will work on it."

"Good. We can't have any loose ends. Okay?"

"Okay." She waited. "Anything else?"

"The police have spoken to you?"

"Yes, the detective, Nguyen. The one leading the case. He spoke to Frank and me."

"And?"

"Fine. It went fine. They haven't got a clue. Apart from knowing he was poisoned. No idea who did it, or why. We just told him about our involvement."

"Our involvement?" Lovell sounded annoyed. "Our involvement?"

"Yes, our involvement. Our investment. Calm down." She breathed deeply. "It's all okay." She moved her phone to her other ear. "As I said, all they seem to know is Chen was poisoned. How could that have happened? They don't know."

"Well, okay."

She heard him mutter something to someone else at his end. "Let me know as soon as the agreement is signed," he said. "And work on Chen's team. Okay?"

"Okay." What did he think she was going to do? He treated her like a school kid. She decided to change the subject. "How is Josephine?" This was a sore point; Lovell couldn't keep his zip closed. Before she'd flown to Melbourne they'd had dinner, Fred and Josephine, her and Barry, and Frank and Alain. During the meal, it became clear that Josephine suspected something of Lovell's proclivities. She'd made several pointed barbs, like, why wasn't HA working on drugs for men with mid-life crises? "We're fine."

Lovell again spoke to someone else. "Listen. I got to go. Speak soon." He hung up.

Ostarkie smiled. Then she called Robarts. "I've been speaking with Lovell. Can you get us to talk to Chen's team?"

"What about?"

"See if we can sign them up, now Chen's gone."

"Sign them up?" Frank sounded both shocked and puzzled. "Is that a good idea? With the police all over the place?"

"Why not? How does that affect anything?" She waited while Frank thought it through.

"Okay. I get it."

"Exploratory stuff. Clear it with Olga. She'll love it. Save her from having to think up ways to keep them on. Imagine her putting another grant application in—it would take the best part of a year. Or she has to sack them. So, she can set up a meeting for us with Chen's deputy, Shildduck."

"You're sure it's not too soon after the death? That it won't upset them?"

"Frank. So what? They're upset anyway, I presume. Getting funding is their bread and butter. They'll be shitting themselves that their project will be shut down. We will reassure them, not the reverse, will we not?"

Frank said nothing.

"Okay?" she asked.

After a short time, he said, "Okay. You're probably right." He thought some more. "We would be offering a lifeline, and they'd be able to continue their work. Yeah, the more I think about it, you're dead right."

20

Carol McTeish was at her desk when her phone rang.

"Hi. Rhys Meadows, returning your call. Is this Carol?"

"Hi, Rhys. Thanks for calling back. This is Detective Constable Carol McTeish."

"Detective Constable?" His voice tailed off. "What's this about?"

"It's to do with Dr Chen Du. I think it's too difficult to discuss over the phone. We need to speak face to face. When can we meet?" She waited a moment then said, "Have you any time this afternoon? Whereabouts are you?" Too many questions at once, she scolded herself.

There was a pause. Then Meadows said, "I'm in the city. We could meet a bit after five, if that suits you."

"Great. Five fifteen okay?"

They agreed to meet at the Alexander Bar at the Savoy Hotel in Little Collins Street.

The bar was art deco, with leather chairs and couches in groups of two and three, with small marble-topped tables between them. McTeish seated herself on a chair with a view of the door so she could watch for Meadows. Shortly after 5:20 she saw a tall gangling man enter. He was in his mid-twenties, with ginger hair and a trimmed beard. She guessed and stood up.

"Hi, Rhys?" She held out her hand.

"Constable." He shook it. "Sorry I'm a bit late."

"Thanks for coming. As I said, I'm working on the case of Dr Chen Du." She looked up at him. "You knew him?"

"Not really. Of course I knew who he was, I mean his job. I did meet him once."

"Well, I'm interested in the GOCH demos you helped organise outside the Badeker. They were about Dr Chen's work, weren't they?"

Meadows looked uncomfortable. "Well yes. We were protesting GM food research." He sat up straight. "But that has nothing to do with this death. How could it possibly?"

"I'm not saying it did." She sighed. "Look. We're trying to understand the different views people have of Dr Chen."

"How do you mean?" Meadows sat back, not slumping but losing his stiffness.

"Look, was there anyone there who seemed odd to you? At the protests. Maybe someone who was there for possibly another purpose. You know what I mean?"

Meadows smiled.

Nervously, she thought.

After a while he said. "There was one guy."

"Not called Terry, was he?" she asked.

"How did you know?" he said.

"Sonia Yee."

"Ah. Sonia. Of course." He breathed out heavily and smiled. "Sonia."

"But, tell me, Rhys. Do you know him? This Terry?"

"Is Terry involved somehow with Dr Chen?" His eyes lit up. "He did ask about his work, as if he had no idea, which was odd. Why would he be there with us if he had no idea about it all? That's a good question, now I come to think about it. A good question." He stopped for a moment, stroked his beard, then shook his head. "The only other thing. He said he was a photographer, and he did take some pictures. That's about all I remember of him."

"You don't have his details, do you?" McTeish tried to restrain her excitement. "Doesn't GOCH have a membership file?"

He blinked at her, and grinned. "Of course. It should have his address. Are you sure you need it? He's probably got nothing to do with the terrible ..." his voice petered out.

"We need to talk to everyone. Terry included. It would be great if you could get the membership details. When can you get them?"

He grinned again, waved his right hand. "Now," he said, and picked up his phone. After a second or two he opened a file, passed the phone over. "Here. The GOCH membership list."

McTeish looked at the phone. She quickly scrolled: there were only about 30 names. Excellent. She scrolled down again, looking for a Terry. Bingo. She looked up at Meadows. "Was it Terry McCauley?"

"McCauley," Meadows repeated the name. "Yes, that would be him. You know, I think it was McCauley."

McTeish noted down the address and phone number. "That's all you have on Mr McCauley?"

Meadows shook his head. "Sorry. That's all."

"Could you forward me the address file?" She saw his questioning look. "I'll need to talk to the others."

"Oh. Yes. Okay." He fiddled with the phone. What's your email address?"

21

McTeish dialled the number for Terry McCauley, and after a couple of rings a man answered.

"Mr McCauley?" she said.

"Yes. That is he. Or rather, me. Who is this?"

"I'm Detective Constable Carol McTeish from Victoria Police."

"Yes? Detective Constable McTeish. Hmm. To what do I owe this—is honour the right word?"

"I need to talk to you—"

"Well, that's a nice surprise," he cut her off. "Always happy to meet someone new and, without overstepping the line, youthful. You are on the youthful side, Constable, are you not?"

McTeish was flustered. How could he tell her age?

As if reading her mind he said, "If you're a constable, you're either young, and therefore not yet promoted—or not very competent, so not promoted. I'm guessing the former."

She opened her mouth, recalling for a moment a goldfish she once owned, before the cat got it. She came to. Best to ignore smart arses. "When's the best time to talk? I can come to your place. Or you can come to the station. What suits you?"

"Hang on, Constable, as the film director said to Harold Lloyd. What's this about?"

McTeish started to feel angry. And who the hell was Harold Lloyd? She calmed herself. "We're interviewing people with some connection with the Badeker Institute, following the death of Dr Chen Du."

There was a pause. "Chen Du is dead? Well, well, well. You're sure about that?"

"Yes." She felt pleased to be able to be definite. "He was poisoned."

"Very sad, for Dr Chen, and his family, no doubt. But what's that got to do with me?" His voice had dropped its playfulness. "I never met him, so how can I help?"

"You are part of GOCH, aren't you?" She liked again being able to be specific. "We're talking to people who were demonstrating outside the labs."

"Ah. I see." There was a pause.

"You were demonstrating?"

"Well, yes. Demonstrating my prowess with the camera, I suppose. But more, if you like, protesting—against GM foods."

"That's why I need to talk to you. As I said, I can come to you, or you can come to the station."

There was another pause. "Okay, Constable. Can you come around this afternoon?"

They agreed to meet at his house in Henry Street, Windsor, at half past two.

AFTER SHE'D HUNG UP she turned to Brothers, who was sitting at the next desk perusing the morning paper. "Sarge. Got a moment?"

Brothers looked up. "Sure."

"I've got this, this—" she floundered for the right word, then settled for the prosaic. "This photographer. He was at some of the demos outside the Badeker. I think taking photos there, or maybe that's just what he does for a living, when he's not demonstrating."

Brothers gave her his attention. "What's he like?"

"I'm seeing him this afternoon. He came across pretty showy on the phone, just now. A bit full of himself." She tailed off. She wasn't going to tell Brothers that he'd called her young.

"Why don't you check the files, see if we have any photos of the demos? You could take them with you, see if he can identify any of the faces. There was some media coverage, TV and so on. I'd reckon the Baedeker would have taken some shots themselves."

"Good point. Where can I find that?"

"It so happens I was looking for the stuff myself. I'll send you the link." He turned to his computer.

"So you know there are photos?"

Brothers laughed. "You could ask to see *his* photos."

"What?"

"If he took any at the demos."

She still felt annoyed with herself, and wasn't thinking straight. "Of course. Yes."

22

As she drove to Windsor, McTeish thought, what am I worrying about? So he took photos. So he demonstrated. So he sounded like a smart arse. So what? She felt better, and pulled into a parking spot a few doors from McCauley's house. It was a small Federation red brick bungalow, half of a duplex, with an overgrown garden and brick pavers leading from the wire gate to the front porch.

She knocked on the door. It was immediately opened by a man in his forties, solid, dark-haired. He had a mole on his left cheek.

"Ah. Detective Constable McTeish? Do come in!" His voice had a fruity overtone.

"Mr McCauley?"

"You got it." He shook her hand, a somewhat limp clasp, and turned and led the way into the house, along a hallway—polished timber floor with a faded narrow carpet runner—into a sitting room with another ageing Turkish carpet. The walls were white and bare of any decoration. There were three armchairs and a couch, all upholstered with what looked like had once been white linen, a fireplace with some sort of heater installed in it, a low credenza with large TV.

"Please." He indicated a chair. "Would you like a drink?" Seeing her face he said, "I mean tea, coffee, water?"

"No thanks. I'm right."

He sat down facing her. "Now, what can I do you for?"

She ignored the comment. "You were at the demos? Did you take any pictures?"

"I certainly did. That's my game."

"How do you mean?"

"I'm a freelance. I sell to the media." He smiled and made the motions of taking an imaginary photo.

"Can I see them?"

"Some have eyes but see not. You look like you use yours, so of course you can see them."

She stared at him. "Before we do that, could you tell me why you were at the Badeker? And how many times?"

"Let me see." He put his chin on his hand, in an exaggerated parody of Rodin's Thinker. "Three times. And as I said on the phone, I was concerned about GM foods."

"Oh? Why is that?"

"It's a free society, is it not? I can demonstrate if I wish. I don't have to tell you why."

"Of course not. I'm just curious." She reached into her bag. "Here. Take a look at these." She pulled out a folder of photos, held one up. "You can see there are about a dozen people here." She handed it to him. He took a quick look.

"Actually, eleven." He handed it back. "I just don't agree with people making artificial food. Surely you're aware of the horror stories?"

McTeish ignored the question. "Can you identify any of them?" She handed it back.

McCauley looked again, taking his time. "Yes, I can." He handed it back.

She grimaced and handed it back again. "Well, please do so, Mr McAuley."

He stood up. "Let's sit at a table," he said and walked into the adjoining room, a kitchen with a small round oak table, and sat down, putting the photo on the table top. She joined him.

"This," he said, pointing at a figure in a yellow jacket, "is Rhys Meadows. He's the organiser of our little group." He smiled.

"Anyone else?" She pointed at Sonia Yee. "Her, for example?"

"That's dear Sonia. Lovely lady." He pointed at two others, men in their twenties with dreadlocks. "These are Jim and Gary. Lovely boys.

I'm afraid I don't know their surnames." He looked up at her. "As I said, I only went to three of these events, so I don't know everyone."

He gave her first names of three others, Madge, a thin tall woman in her sixties with grey hair, wearing overalls and bangles, and two women in their twenties, one very large and the other short and petite, both dressed in black with metal in their eyebrows and nose. "Sammi and, I think, Yash."

"Yash?"

"That's her name." He pointed at the short woman. "Very committed."

"That's all you can recognise?"

"Oh, I recognise them, but not, unfortunately, their names."

"I notice you're at the back?"

"Just being polite. One doesn't want to get in anyone's way."

"And your photos? Would you mind if I take a look-see?

"Of course, Constable. Just a moment." He stood up and returned shortly with an iPad. "Here." He showed her a set of images.

The Badeker was clear in the background, and some of the photos showed a couple of security guards watching the crowd. There were a few shots of the protesters.

"Who would want to buy these?" she asked, pointing at the images.

"You never know, do you? Such is the life of the freelancer." He gave an exaggerated sigh.

"What I don't understand," McTeish muttered, as if to herself but looking at McCauley, "is why you were there."

"Eh? What do you mean? I told you."

"Yes, but look at you." She pointed at the figure of McCauley in her print out. "Notice anything?"

"That's me." He chuckled.

"Yes, at the rear of the group. And you're dressed differently."

"What, a guy can't wear dark jeans and a black jacket?"

"I mean, you don't look like your regular Greenie, do you?"

"These days, Constable, who does?"

"I was told you were asking about what Dr Chen did, what his work was."

McCauley blinked, then smiled. Or his mouth did. "Of course I asked about it. I didn't know precisely who was who in the zoo. They did. So of course I asked who he was and what his work was." He straightened himself in his chair and smiled again at her with his lips. "Wouldn't you have done the same?" He turned to the iPad and flicked through some images. "Here," he said. He pointed at two men in lab coats in front of the Badeker entrance.

McTeish looked at the photo. The two men were Dr Felix Robertson and Dr Chen Du.

"Do you know who they are?"

"Yes. They're researchers. They came out at the last protest I went to. That's when I asked about Dr Chen."

"What were they doing?"

McCauley smiled again. "They came out to speak to us. To explain what they were doing. To reassure us. They were very general."

"Did they reassure you?"

"Me? Perhaps. The rest, not so much."

She stared at him again. If the two scientists had explained their work, then why would McCauley have asked his friends what they were doing? He must have asked them earlier. He was lying, at least about that.

"Thanks for your time, Mr McCauley."

"Detective Constable. Great to meet you." He stood up, led her to the door. "I hope I've been of help." He shook her hand. This time he grasped it firmly. "Come again any time, or call me, if you need anything else."

23

As McTEISH DROVE BACK to the station her phone rang, through the car's sound system.

"Yes? Detective Constable McTeish."

"Darling. You haven't forgotten, have you?" Her mother had that whiny tone again.

"Forgotten what?" Steady, she told herself. Calm down.

"See. You have, haven't you." There was tinge of delight in her mother's voice. "Why is it so hard for you to make time for me?"

Time—Fuck, she had promised to see her this evening. She racked her brains. At six. "Mum. I'm coming round this evening. You know that."

"Are you? You haven't forgotten?"

"I said around six. So that's when I'll be there." She gritted her teeth.

"And you'll still stay for dinner?"

McTeish automatically began to say no, but caught herself. Better to get it over with. But she'd check first. "Will anyone else be there?"

"Anyone else?" Her mother sounded perplexed. "Who else could be there? You don't expect your father to return, do you?" Her voice took on an angry, bitter tone.

McTeish let it pass. "I'll bring fish and chips. I'll see you six." She cancelled the call before her mother said anything else. There was a sudden beeping from another vehicle and she realised she'd almost swerved into the left-hand lane. Get a grip, she told herself. Calm down. She breathed in deeply, held it in for a moment, then out, three times.

Feeling better, she returned to the office, took out her notebook and flipped through her notes. She keyed into her computer the key points from her interviews with Yee, Meadows and McCauley. Something didn't gel. Yee and Meadows seemed straightforward, but McCauley? Was he trying to impress her, or just being a patronising dickhead? He certainly seemed sure of himself. But regardless of his comment about how could you tell what a Greenie dressed like these days, he did seem different. And he'd clearly lied about asking about the research. So what was he really doing there, and why was he part of the GOCH group?

She stood up and stretched her shoulders, then peered into Nguyen's office. He was sitting behind his desk so she knocked.

Nguyen looked up, beckoned her in. "What's up?"

"Boss, can we do a search on a guy, on the database?"

He regarded her for a moment. "Tell me about it."

"It's this guy McCauley. Something's not right." She told him of her interview. "He may be just what he says, but he seems suspicious to me."

"Have you checked online where his photos appear?"

McTeish reddened. Why hadn't she done that already? "I'll do that. He was taking photos at the GOCH protests—"

"GOCH? What's that?"

"Greens for Community Health. That's the group who were protesting."

Nguyen smiled. "GOCH, eh?"

"Yeah." She grinned back. "He was taking photos at the demos. He reckons he sells them, says he's a freelance."

Nguyen nodded. "Okay. Let me know if you can find more on him, and his photos. Then we'll search the database." There had been recent cases where police had been hauled over the coals for illegally accessing the police database, sometimes when a police relationship had split up over domestic abuse, and the angered had wanted to visit some vindictiveness on the injured, and needed to know the new address. Or sometimes a driver had annoyed a traffic cop. So her boss's approval was needed to get access.

She went back to her desk and keyed in 'Terry McCauley, photographer' into Google. A list of photographic studios appeared, but no Terry McCauley. She deleted photographer. Several Terry McCauleys and Macauleys came up. She checked and none matched the man she had interviewed that afternoon. She took out her phone and photographed the group shot of the protest, then forwarded it to her email address. She then edited it down to just McCauley's face, and fed that into the search engine. Again she had no luck.

She knocked on Nguyen's door and told him of her fruitless research.

"Okay," he said. "Let's see if he's known to us, one way or another. Check with LEAP first."

McTeish grinned, went back to her desk, and logged in to the Law Enforcement Assistance Program database. It was notoriously slow, and after a time it opened in a new window. She keyed in Terry McCauley. Result: nothing. She tried Terrance McCauley, and variations with MacCauley. Still no result. "No luck, Boss." She called across the office.

"Try the national. See if he's had a police check, or working with children," Nguyen called back.

She tried these with the same result. She returned to Nguyen's office. "What about Sergeant Ladbroke?" she said. "Should I call him?" Gershon Ladbroke was the Federal policeman who'd helped Nguyen and his team by intercepting two mafiosi attempting to leave via Melbourne's Tullamarine international airport.

"Worth starting with him. He can either check it out himself, or put you on to someone who can. I'll text you his number."

24

MCTEISH CHECKED THE NUMBER and phoned Gershon Ladbroke, who answered after two rings.

"Ladbroke."

"Hey. This is Detective Constable Carol McTeish from Victoria Police—"

"Carol. Long time no see. How are you? And how's Inspector Nguyen these days?"

McTeish was thrown. He remembered me? "He's well," she said. "He asked me to pass on his thanks again for your help with the mafia guys."

"You know, sometimes people say it was a pleasure and it's just, you know, a form of words. But let me tell you, it *was* a pleasure. Glad we could be of help, in putting those miscreants away."

She hadn't heard that word used by anybody before. Read it, of course.

"So, what's up?" he said.

"We're working on a case and I've just interviewed a guy who isn't on our database."

"Ah. A cleanskin?"

"He could be, but I wonder if you could check him out for us, Federally. Or help me find someone who could."

"What's the bozo's name?"

"Terry McCauley." She spelled it out and described the case of the poisoned scientist, and how McCauley had been part of a protest group outside the Badeker Institute. "He's not on LEAP, and I can't even find him on Google."

"Has he done anything wrong that you know of?"

"No, not really. Except I'm pretty sure he lied to me. That's why I want to check him out."

"Hmm. I'll key it in myself. Do you have his address?"

She gave him the details. "And by the way, I'll text you a photo of him. Hope that helps."

"Good. Give me a little while. I'll call you back. On this number?"

"Yes. Thanks so much." She found the photo on her phone and sent it on its way to Ladbroke. Phew. She grinned to herself. That went well. Straightforward. He'd been friendly but completely businesslike. No innuendo—no "in your endo". Not her usual experience with older more senior cops. Nor with her mother's succession of boyfriends. She must remember to get the fish and chips. She checked her watch. Four past four. She'd have plenty of time.

LADBROKE RANG BACK FORTY MINUTES LATER. "I think your Mr McCauley is not quite what he seems."

"You found him?"

"Not under that name. The photo's what did it. I had to pull a few strings with Home Affairs They have the database linked to passports and I asked them to check. The mafia case seems to have honeyed the road. Anyhow, the photos identified him as Terry Euston. That's the name on his passport."

"Euston? Has he been travelling?"

"To and from the States a few times over the past couple of years."

"Do they know where he visited?"

"Come off it, Carol. Our Home Affairs guys fancy themselves, but they're not quite Homeland Security yet."

"Homeland Security? You mean the US?"

"Yes. Our ASIO guys can tell us which airport he flew to, but not where he went afterwards." He laughed. "But I suspect Homeland Security could, if they were pressed."

McTeish waited. She was sure Ladbroke had more to say.

"Hello? Are you still there?" Ladbroke said.

"Yes. Just waiting for what else you're going to tell me."

He laughed again, a guffaw. "Nothing much. We've got nothing on him. As I said earlier, maybe a cleanskin. But it is odd, don't you think, that he changed his surname?"

"Yes it is. Maybe he got married," McTeish said.

"What, you think he's gay?"

"Just a joke. I'm not sure what he is. But I'm going to find out."

"You do that. And let me know if there's anything we should know."

"Will do. I thought you were going to tell me where he flew to."

"And I am, I am. He made five trips in the last two years. To LA, New York and three times to Baltimore. Does that mean anything?"

"I'm not sure. I'll check with the boss. Thanks, Sergeant."

"Gershon," he said.

"Thanks, Gershon. So just those three cities? And just to the States?"

"Yes. Is that helpful?"

"I hope so. I'll follow it up. And thanks again. I owe you one."

"Tell you what, when next I'm in the city, let's all of us have a drink—you, me, Winner and Brothers. It'll be good to catch up."

25

McTeish knocked on Nguyen's open door. "I spoke to Gershon," she said.

"Gershon, eh?" Nguyen, sitting at his desk, beckoned her in. "What did *Gershon* have to say for himself?"

She grimaced. "This Terry McCauley is really Terry Euston." She grinned.

"Euston? How did they find that out?"

"Through passport photos." McTeish, deciding two could play at his game, said, "*Gershon* got his mates in ASIO to check a photo I sent him."

"Good work, Carol. That's great."

"He also said that Euston, or McCauley, flew to the US five times in the last two years, to LA, New York and three times to Baltimore. And the Baltimore trips were in the last year."

"Baltimore." Nguyen sat up, his eyes thoughtful. "Now that's very interesting." He stood up and poked his head out of his door, a sweeping glance around the office. "Graham, got a sec?" To McTeish he said, "Take a seat." She sat and Brothers came in and did the same.

"Some interesting news, that Carol here has prised out of the Feds. This photographer, Terry McCauley, is really Euston, and he's traveled to Baltimore."

"Who's this McCauley again? asked Brothers.

"The photographer, you know?" McTeish said.

"Ah, right. And Baltimore? Is that important?"

"Baltimore, Graham, happens to be where Howarth-Acfield has its headquarters. HA, the funders of the Badeker." He gazed at both

McTeish and Brothers, a smile on his lips. "It may be pure coincidence, mightn't it? Or it might not, hey? I think we'd better have another chat with Mr McCauley or Euston. Let me think." He stood up again and walked over to the white board positioned against the blinds along the wall of his office. He wrote down McCauley/Euston in a box with a question mark, and near them Ostarkie and Robarts in a box marked HA. Then he wrote another box, labeled it Badeker, and in it wrote Penrith, Robertson and Chen. Under Chen he wrote Shildduck and Kosic. "We might need to talk to Robertson's team, too," he said, indicating a space he'd left under Robertson. He then wrote Bottega in another box, with a line to Chen. "And Graham, when you find out his friends, we'll list them here." He pointed to the box with McCauley/Euston in it. "And Carol, please add in the names of the other protesters here."

"I've got the names of some of Chen's friends, from his partner," Brothers said. "Three couples. I'm talking to one of them early this evening, after their work, and should get to the others tomorrow."

"Good. When we speak to Euston, we'll get back to the HA guys, Ostarkie and Robarts. See what they have to say."

"What are they like?" McTeish asked. "Ostarkie and Robarts?"

Nguyen raised his eyebrows, then said, "Ostarkie's the boss, or the more senior of the two. They're both pretty smart. They appear to be trying to be helpful, but I wonder if they really are? I suppose they have their financial interests to protect, but even so," Nguyen paused and reflected for a moment. "It'll all come out in the wash once we speak to this Euston or whoever he is. Carol, can you set it up for first thing tomorrow. You did say he asked you to call him back. You needn't mention I'll be with you. Okay?" He glanced at them both, dismissing them, and sat back at his desk.

26

McTeish bought two pieces of whiting, grilled, with chips and calamari rings in two packets from Heads and Tails on the way to her mother's house in Foam Street, Elwood.

She found a park a few doors down from an establishment called Femmes on Foam, and walked up and rang the doorbell.

Her mother opened the door, dressed in a pink lycra top and grey yoga pants. She had kept her figure and despite a garish use of lipstick and face paint looked younger than her forty-three years.

"Darling," she said, air kissing McTeish's cheeks. "You came after all."

"Yes, mum," McTeish said, proffering the hot food.

Her mother took the packets, peeked inside the white paper, and McTeish followed her as she walked down the hall and placed it on the kitchen table. "Can you set the table, darling?" she said as she took a bottle of white wine from the fridge and poured two glasses.

"I bought just for the two us. Is that okay?"

"Of course. Why wouldn't it be?"

McTeish bit her tongue.

Her mother looked her up and down. "How come you're not in uniform? Did you go home first to change?"

"I'm a detective, now, Mum. We don't usually wear a uniform. You know that."

"How would I know that? You never tell me anything." She inspected McTeish's hair.

"What?" McTeish said.

"When's the last time you went to the hairdresser, dear? You can't always keep your hair in a pony tail."

McTeish rolled her eyes.

"No wonder you don't have a boyfriend."

"You're looking good, too, mum. What's new?"

"As if you care!"

They sat down to eat.

"What about the hooligans?"

"What hooligans?"

"You said yesterday you were being pestered."

"Oh, *those* hooligans. They're not so bad. Just a few young men with nothing better to do."

"How do you mean?"

"This is tasty. Where did you get it?"

"The local, Heads and Tails. You were saying, about the hooligans?"

"I went out and spoke to them. They were moving in a few doors down. Quite gentlemanly, actually."

"So, nothing to be afraid of?"

"Afraid? Who, me?"

"By the way, how's—" she racked her brain. "Alex?"

Her mother sniffed. "Don't mention that bastard. We broke up."

Good, she thought. He was another of her mother's long line of users and losers. "So, no boyfriend now?" At that point McTeish's phone rang. "Yes? Tamas. How are you?"

Her mother looked at her, a smirk forming on her face.

"Just a sec." She stood up and moved towards the laundry. "Hi, Tamas."

"Hi." There was a pause.

"Yes?" She waited.

"I was wondering if you'd, er, like to go to a movie?"

Well, that was unexpected. She thought for a moment. Would it be too unethical to go out with him, when her only interest was in the Chen case? "Which movie?"

"Have you seen *Dune*?"

She hadn't, and had no desire to see it. "Is it on again?"

"They're screening it again, along with the second part as a retrospective. I wouldn't mind seeing it again, if you haven't seen it, that is."

From what she recalled it was at least three hours long. "Maybe something else?"

"Um. Any suggestions?"

"When did you want to see it?"

"Whenever it suits you. How about tomorrow night?"

"Let me check what's on. Can I call you back?"

"You mean you're free tomorrow?"

"Yes. Thanks, Tamas. I'll call you."

She walked back to the kitchen table and sat down.

"I thought you said you didn't have a boyfriend." Her mum had perked up.

"*Mum.* I don't. It's just a guy, to do with the case."

"Right." She raised her eyebrows and patted her hand. "Just a guy to do with the case. Of course. I suppose I'll be the last to know, as per usual." Her mother withdrew her hand and took a gulp of wine.

McTeish sipped some wine too, and they resumed eating. After they finished, she took the dishes to the sink, scraped them and put them into the dishwasher. Then she checked her phone to see what movies were showing. There was a French Film Festival season on at the Palace Cinemas. She had no idea what any of the films were like, but anything would be more to her taste than *Dune*. Though, come to think of it, *Dune* had had good reviews, and the photographer had won an Oscar. Photography reminded her of McCauley. Shit. She hadn't rung him yet to make arrangements for tomorrow. She extracted his card from her bag, went to her old room, and dialled.

"Constable McTeish! How delightful," McCauley said, answering straight away. "How can I be of help?"

"I was wondering if I could call in tomorrow morning. A couple more questions."

"You can't ask me over the phone?"

"I'd prefer to see you."

"See me? Well, in that case …" he was almost purring.

"Are you free around nine am?"

"Nothing better to do, I suppose, than help the local constabulary. I'll look forward to seeing you then."

"Carol!" her mother called. "Who was that?"

She returned to the kitchen. "Just another man, to do with the case."

"So," her mother said. "Two boyfriends! You always were a dark horse. You do know you can confide in me, darling. That's what mothers are for."

"Not a boyfriend, mum." And, she thought, you'd be the last person I'd ever confide in. She texted Nguyen that they could meet McCauley at nine am. He texted back within moments, "Good. See you tomorrow in the office. You can drive me."

She texted Kosic about the French Film Festival, asking him to choose a movie, and saying she could go to any session after six pm.

27

THE NEXT MORNING MCTEISH arrived at her desk just before eight. Nguyen was in his office, so she knocked at his open door. "Ready when you are, Boss."

"Where does he live again?"

"Windsor, so only about fifteen minutes away. We can leave at quarter to if you like."

"Okay. When we get there, you start asking the questions. I'll sit back until I need to ask something."

McTeish beamed. "Thanks, Boss."

"Don't thank me. It makes sense."

She frowned at him in puzzlement.

"Look. He's already spoken to you. So you're the one he's misled. Or lied to. That'll put a little bit of extra pressure on him. We'll see how embarrassed he is. That assumes he is embarrassed. He certainly wouldn't be with me. With you? Perhaps. Then we'll see where it all goes."

"Got you." She went back to her desk as Brothers came in, bearing three cups of coffee.

"I assumed everyone wants one?" Then, as he handed one to McTeish, he said, "Your turn tomorrow."

"Thanks, Sarge." She remembered, and called across to Nguyen who had emerged to take his coffee from Brothers, "I'm seeing Kosic again tonight. He's asked me out to a film."

"Has he indeed," Nguyen said. He nodded to himself, looking at McTeish who stared back at him expectantly. Then, as if he'd confirmed something, he raised his coffee in a sort of salute. "I don't need to warn you about getting involved with witnesses, do I?" He grinned.

McTeish reddened. The fact that she'd blushed annoyed her. "Of course not," she said. "It'll give me another chance to find out more."

"Of course," Nguyen said, straight faced. He returned to his office.

THEY ARRIVED AT HENRY Street, Windsor just after nine. McTeish found a park with a one hour limit out the front, and they walked up the brick pavers. Nguyen looked around with interest.

"Not much of a gardener, I see," he said, pointing to the overgrown garden. "Very sad." He shook his head.

"Sad? What's that, Boss?"

"See over there. A couple of rose bushes trying to get out. Bonica and Grandiflora, if I'm not mistaken."

McTeish looked. She could see bushes, one with pink flowers, two with orange.

"You like to garden, Boss?"

"No. Don't have time for it."

She halted.

"As a kid I worked at the market. Didn't like it much at the time. But, of course, you always can learn a thing or two, if you keep your eyes and ears open. They sold flowers there."

McTeish glanced at him in surprise. She hadn't heard Nguyen talk much about himself, ever. She looked at the door, which was a deep reddish brown, almost black, with a tarnished brass knob in its centre. He nodded, and she rapped on the door.

After a short time, it opened and McCauley, dressed in dark grey pants and light blue shirt said, "Welcome, Constable!" Then he paused as he saw Nguyen. "Hello, hello, hello! What have we here?"

"Hello Mr McCauley—" McTeish said.

"Terry, please!" he said.

"— this is Detective Inspector John Nguyen."

"Terry McCauley. This is a turn up for the books. A Detective Inspector!"

McCauley held out his hand and Nguyen shook it. "So pleased to meet you, Inspector. Do come in." He led the way down the hall to the kitchen area and indicated the table. "Please, take a seat."

They sat down and before McTeish could ask her first question McCauley said, "Can I offer you a cup of tea or coffee?" He chuckled. "Of course, I *can* offer you a tea or coffee. I should have said, shouldn't I, Inspector, *may* I offer you a tea or coffee."

Nguyen said, "No thanks." McTeish shook her head.

"So, how can I be of assistance, as the actress said to the bishop," McCauley said looking at Nguyen.

McTeish began, "Mr McCauley."

"Yes?" he turned to her. "Speak, dear lady."

"Why do you call yourself McCauley? Isn't your name Euston?"

McCauley snapped his mouth shut for a moment and a quick glare escaped him, before a smile reappeared on his face. "Does it matter? I've simply changed my name. Is that a crime?"

"Not necessarily," Nguyen said. "Only if you are perpetrating a fraud or a deception. Are you, Mr Euston?"

"McCauley, please. And I am certainly not." He glanced from one to the other. "Is that all? Surely the Constable could have checked that with me over the phone."

"So, do you still prefer to be called McCauley?" McTeish asked.

"With you, Constable, I prefer to be called Terry."

"Why the name change?"

"I had my reasons."

"Care to explain?"

"Private reasons. There's no requirement, as far as I know, to have to explain myself. As long as, as the Inspector has said, I am neither defrauding nor deceiving. Which," he waved his hand in a flourish as if he were about to bow, "I have not done." He smiled, and she noticed his eyes were cold.

They sat staring at each other for some seconds.

"Mr McCauley. Terry. We haven't suggested you have done so. We were just curious."

He seemed to relax. "Curious, eh?" he said to himself.

"Could I ask whether you've travelled recently?" she asked.

"Yes you can. And you may!" he beamed at her.

"Well, where have you travelled, then?" she asked, a little flustered.

"Hmm. Let me see. I've travelled from here to South Yarra to the Badeker on, I think, three occasions. And back. Is that what you mean?"

"That is not what she meant," Nguyen said. "Have you travelled internationally in the last year or so."

"Why, Inspector! Constable McTeish is quite capable I'm sure of asking her questions herself." He grinned at McTeish, or was it more a grimace? "As it happens, I have travelled overseas. And as it also happens, it's none of your goddamn business." He stood up. "If that's all, I'll bid you both good day."

"Steady on, Mr McCauley," Nguyen said. "We're investigating a murder, as no doubt Constable McTeish has informed you. That means we ask questions. A wide range of questions. Please don't take these things personally. Please sit down."

"What, I'm being asked to 'please sit down' in my own house?"

"Yes. Please sit down. We do have a few more questions. Or you might prefer to answer them down at the station."

McCauley sat. "Very well." He breathed out a heavy sigh. "When needs must the devil drives." He looked up at them both, a smile back on his face. "Have at me, lady and gentleman."

McTeish was again momentarily flummoxed. She almost burst out laughing, but pinched her thigh hard and managed to keep a straight face. She decided to try to make it more personal. "Terry," she said, "Have you visited Baltimore?"

He snapped his mouth shut, then appeared to relax. "Ah, Baltimore. The great city of *The Wire* and *Pink Flamingos*. Of John Waters and Frank Zappa." He gave a short snort. "If you must know, it's quite the cultural and political icon. Home also to Edgar Allan Poe, H. L. Mencken and Anne Tyler, and politically, to Spiro Agnew and Nancy

Pelosi. If you're into sports—" he looked questioningly at them both—"No? It's also home to Babe Ruth and Michael Phelps. Of course I made my pilgrimage. Baltimore. City of dreams." He leant back, crossed his arms.

"You didn't happen to visit a pharmaceutical company, Howarth-Acfield, while you were making your pilgrimage?" Nguyen asked.

"No, I did not. Nor did I visit Johns Hopkins University. Also in Baltimore."

"The reason I mention Howarth-Acfield is that they are funding the Badeker Institute. Outside which you were protesting, and where the late Dr Chen was poisoned."

"I see," McCauley muttered, "as the blind man said though he couldn't see at all." He sat up straight. "Anything else?"

"Not for the moment, but I'm sure we'll be in touch. Maybe you can let Constable McTeish in on some of the wonders of Baltimore another time." Nguyen stood up, and McTeish followed suit.

At the door McCauley said, "As I said to the Constable yesterday, I'm always happy to help."

28

THERE WAS A FAINT DRIZZLE and they jogged to the car.

"Well, Carol," Nguyen said as she started to drive off. "Certainly food for thought there. And we know, through your friend Gershon, that McCauley visited Baltimore three times. Not just the once."

"He must know it well, the way he reeled off those names. I've heard of *Pink Flamingos* and John Waters, but not many of the others," she said.

"*Pink Flamingos*? What's that?"

"An early film of John Waters." McTeish looked carefully at Nguyen. "You don't want to know."

"I certainly do want to know what Ostarkie and Robarts make of Mr Terry Austen-McCauley. Do they know him? It seems too much of a coincidence that he didn't get in touch with someone at Howarth-Acfield, if he went to Baltimore three times, and turned up three times at the protests outside the Badeker."

"Maybe he was employed by them to photograph the protesters. That would explain why he had to ask what Dr Chen was up to. But why would he lie about that?" McTeish jammed on the brakes as the van in front suddenly stopped. The police car brakes worked and they juddered to a halt with room to spare.

"Possibly, possibly," Nguyen said, ignoring the traffic. "But it seems an odd thing for a pharma to fly someone to Baltimore and back just to hire him to take photos. Were they employing him? Surely they could have got Olga Penrith to arrange that, if that's what they wanted. But why would they want that, anyway?"

"Good point, Boss. But if it's not the photos, what was he doing there? Maybe he just likes Baltimore."

McTeish focused on her driving and soon pulled into the entry to the basement carpark at the South Melbourne station. As they got out, Nguyen said, "You come with me when we go to see the HA guys."

"Thanks," McTeish said.

"Call them to set it up. I hope they're still at the Hyatt. Oh, and you're seeing Kosic tonight, aren't you?"

"Yes. We're seeing a movie."

"*Pink Flamingos?*"

McTeish smiled. "No way. Something in the French Film Festival. I asked him to choose." She looked at him. "You sure you haven't seen *Pink Flamingos?*"

He shook his head. "Hadn't even heard of it before McCauley mentioned it."

"I saw it with my girlfriends as a teenager. It's funny, but pretty gross."

Nguyen looked at her in mock shock, then shook his head again. "See if you can find out if Kosic knows anything about this McCauley guy. From his Green friends."

She nodded. It was great being treated like a colleague. Not just a junior.

They entered the office, and McTeish checked the phone number for Ostarkie, and rang it. Ostarkie answered and agreed to meet them at eleven thirty, at the Badeker.

29

Brothers checked his notes for the contact details of Dr Chen's friends: Sally and Kane Churchill, Yvonne Wisher and Ronnie Manser, and Yasmin and Simon Lee. He rang and set up appointments. The Churchills could see him that day, Sally at her office and Kane at lunchtime.

Sally Churchill worked at the University of Melbourne, a lecturer in the biochemistry department, and she arranged for them to meet at the Faculty Club. She was waiting outside at the door when he arrived at 11 am, a short woman in her late thirties or early forties, with pink highlights in her hair, bright eyes behind rimless glasses, dressed in a black suit with a bright yellow scarf draped around her neck. She was solidly built and held herself erect as if she'd been a ballet dancer. After introductions she led him to a table, and as they seated themselves he took out his notebook. A waiter with bits of metal in his eyebrows and ears approached and they ordered, coffee for her, water for Brothers.

"So you want to talk about Doug," Churchill said, when the waiter had departed.

Brothers nodded.

"Do you have any idea who did it? Oh, I don't suppose you can tell me, can you?" She gave a brief laugh, a sort of titter. "Sorry. But who would want to kill him? He wasn't the easiest man, but murder?"

"Well," Brothers said, thinking, yes, you're right, even if I had a suspect, I wouldn't tell you. "That's what we're trying to find out. You say he wasn't the easiest man. How long did you know him?"

"Lucy and I were at Uni together, doing science. When she hitched up with Doug, Kane and he got along."

"Not the easiest man?" Brothers repeated.

"Oh, he was pretty single minded. Didn't suffer fools. Didn't understand at all why people could think what he was doing was wrong."

"How so? Was what he was doing wrong?" Did she mean the Greens?

"Of course not. But some thought he was. He'd get into arguments—he was trying to help the world with his research, and yet some people had this fixed idea that GM was evil."

The waiter brought their drinks, placed the coffee and glass of water in front of them and left.

"What sort of arguments? Were they heated?" Brothers watched her as she sipped her cup. She seemed calm, dignified, and in turn regarded him cooly over the rim, a slight smile appearing on her lips as she thought.

"Sometimes. But they wouldn't get into a shouting match or anything."

"Do you remember who he argued with?"

"Well, Ronnie, for one."

"Ronnie Manser?"

"Yes. You've talked to him? He's a dear man, but he's Green through and through. A real idealist and worrier. Always on about climate change, toxic chemicals in cosmetics, plastics affecting our hormones, that sort of thing. I don't mean climate change isn't a serious problem. Of course it is. Nor that we need to get rid of parabens. He's just obsessed with them. And frankly, though Kane and I get on with Yvonne and Ronnie, Doug and Ronnie would go at each other." She took another sip. "A clash of personalities."

"How big a clash?"

"What? No. No. Nothing serious. You don't think Ronnie could have had anything to do with—" she broke off. "That's ridiculous."

Brothers watched her. "Any others?" he asked.

"Any others what?" Churchill looked annoyed.

"Any others get into arguments with Dr Chen?"

"Oh. Of course." She put her cup down and stretched her shoulders.

"A few, I suppose. Me for one." She smiled seeing his expression. "I'd tease him a bit." Her face fell and she shook her head. "And now he's dead. It's awful."

"Did you and Kane see much of Dr Chen and Ms Bottega?"

"Yes—the eight of us used to hang out. That's Yas and Simon—the Lees—and Ronnie and Evie Wisher. We'd do stuff together. Go to a movie or a play. Or a concert. Or out for a meal. Have people over, you know."

Brothers made some notes. "And there's no one you know who had a grudge against Dr Chen?"

She shook her head, without hesitation. "No. No one I can think of. There were those protesters outside his work, I suppose. But did they actually know him? I mean to hold a grudge? And even if they did, why would they want to kill a scientist? There are protests about all sorts of things, all the time. Scientists don't get killed."

Brothers cleared his throat. "And Dr Chen and Ms Bottega—how was their relationship?"

Churchill began to speak, then laughed, a gurgling sound. "Nothing to worry about there, Sergeant. He didn't play around." She saw him writing in his notebook. "And neither did she."

"So there was no one you're aware of that he met, I mean socially, who might have been rubbed up the wrong way?"

"Bound to have been," Churchill said. "That's what I said, didn't I, that he didn't suffer fools?"

He was about to ask another question when she continued, "But not suffering fools doesn't get you killed, does it? I'm not particularly partial to them, either, Sergeant, but look at me—I'm still alive."

"Thank you, Mrs Churchill," he said.

"*Doctor* Churchill, actually," she said. Then she slumped a little. "Sorry. I hope you catch whoever did this terrible thing."

"We will," Brothers said. "We will." He certainly believed it, even if for the life of him he couldn't think of who it might possibly be.

30

AN HOUR LATER HE MET Dr Churchill's husband, Kane, at his office in Carlton, an accounting firm. "You could come to me here," he'd said, "if that's convenient."

Kane Churchill was very tall, with thick dark wavy hair, hunched shoulders producing a slight stoop. Brothers guessed he was in his early forties. Churchill led him to his office, saying, "Will this take long? I've fitted you in. I know it's important. Anything I can do to help. Not sure there is anything. But I have a client meeting shortly." The words came out quickly. He gestured at two chairs across a small table, and they sat down.

"Just a few questions, Mr Churchill—is it Mister?" he asked.

"Yes, that's right. Mister." He suddenly grinned. "Right, right. You got that, did you, from Sally? She can get right irked if people don't realise she's got a doctorate. Says she's a real doctor—and says that's unlike most medicos, who only have a bachelor degree." He paused, looked at Brothers somewhat wistfully. "Like me, for example."

Brothers stared, said nothing.

"And please don't call me *Mister*—Kane will do."

Brothers shook his head and took out his notebook. "Thanks, Kane. As I say, I won't keep you long. How long did you know Dr Chen?"

"How long? How long?" Churchill muttered to himself. "Since I met Sally, I suppose. She's good friends with Lucy."

"And when was that?"

"Oh, let's see. Let's see." He rubbed his chin, still muttering. "Let me see." Then he jerked bolt upright. "Good lord, I'd forgotten," he exclaimed. "Thank God you asked me, Sergeant."

Brothers looked at him in surprise. "You forgot when you met?"

"Our anniversary! Thank God. You're a life saver! It's tomorrow." He beamed at Brothers. "Nine years tomorrow since we married. If you hadn't asked me, I'd really be in the shit." He smiled happily, pulling out a sheet of paper on his desk and jotting down a reminder note. "Whew. What a relief." Then looking back at Brothers, "We've been together about ten years. You married, Sergeant?"

Brothers smiled inwardly. "Yes, as it happens."

"Then you know what I mean." He breathed out deeply and said again, "Whew."

"Er, could we get back to Dr Chen?"

"Sorry, Sergeant. Yes. Let me see. Known them both for about ten years." He slumped. "Knew him, I mean."

"And did he have any enemies?"

"Doug? He certainly could piss people off. Didn't suffer fools. Sally probably told you that. But enemies?" He rubbed his chin again. "None that I know of."

"He didn't suffer fools. How do you mean?"

"He just would, you know, make it really clear, if some idiot was arguing with him."

"Who was arguing with him?'

"Well, Ronnie for one. And anyone who didn't like GM foods."

"Why was that?" Brothers prepared to jot down some more notes.

"It used to infuriate him that people thought he was creating frankenfoods, you know, what some of the Greens are on about. He was working on wheat, but not putting in any poisons or whatever."

"So you knew what he was working on?"

"What? Oh, no. No idea. Apart from improving wheat to give it more protein, or something. No idea how he was doing it." Churchill sat back. "As I understand it," Churchill paused and looked into the distance. "Hmm. Yes, I think I've got this right. Frankenfoods—there are all these sorts of horror stories about what might happen. What *has* happened. Stories spread by the credulous. I mean, some of it might be true. But that's not what Doug was doing. As he made very clear to whoever tried to argue with him." He paused again. "He'd say, everyone *already* eats genetically modified foods. Just that no one knows it. He'd mention seedless watermelons, and things like cauliflower and brussels sprouts, all bred from earlier less interesting primitive versions. You with me?"

Brothers nodded, making more notes.

"He could go on, you know, basically making it clear that whoever believed in frankenfoods was a fuckwit."

"And?"

"In fact, that's the word he often used. So, Sergeant, he didn't suffer fools."

"You mentioned Ronnie. Would that be—"

"Ronnie Manser. But don't get the wrong idea. Ronnie involved with Doug's death? Ridiculous. Ronnie may be passionate, he loves an argument, but he wouldn't hurt a fly."

"So Ronnie never got angry? Didn't harbour a grudge?"

"He might've got angry in the heat of the moment. But we all still kept seeing each other. No grudges, Sergeant. No grudges at all."

"Anyone else you can think of? That got into arguments with Dr Chen?"

Churchill pondered. "No one in particular. Maybe everyone in general!" He laughed. "But you know, it was like water off a duck's back for Doug. I think he enjoyed it. But nothing serious, I mean nothing aggressive," he said.

Brothers glanced at his watch. "Well, I see you'll still have time for your client. Thank you for seeing me." He reached out and shook Churchill's hand.

31

Yasmin Lee regarded Sergeant Brothers with what seemed to him to be indifference. She looked bored, maybe a little irritated that she had to see him. They were at the Lees' home in North Melbourne, a large high-ceilinged 1930s apartment on Chetwynd Street. She was dressed in a dark skirt and white blouse that Brothers saw exposed some cleavage, and he also saw that she had noticed his glance with a flicker of a smile. They were seated in the living room. There were polished boards and a couple of modern rugs, a couch, three arm chairs, a long book case stuffed with books, magazines and DVDs, and a large screen facing the couch. It was pleasantly warm with the occasional sound of the ducted heating as it came on from time to time. He scented a faint perfume wafting from Yasmin.

As with the others, and focusing on her face, he asked her if she knew of any enemies Dr Chen might have had.

"Plenty," she said. It was as if an internal switch had turned on and she had gained energy. She now turned her attention on him.

"Plenty?" Brothers repeated.

"He was very prickly. Very argumentative."

"And?"

"*And*, he really annoyed some people."

Brothers made a note, looked up at her. She had a smile on her face again. Was it a smirk? Her eyes held a gleam. "How did you get on with him, yourself?"

"Oh, fine, fine. He was a very good friend of Simon's. We all got on." Her lips tightened.

Brothers thought he detected some evasiveness in her answer. Yasmin Lee was petite, strikingly attractive and her dark intelligent eyes kept glancing at him from time to time. She momentarily toyed with her blouse.

"He was a good friend of your husband's," Brothers repeated. "What about you? A good friend, too?"

She shrugged. "He was okay. I mean, he did annoy me sometimes, but, yeah, he was okay."

"Annoy? How?"

"I just didn't like the way he'd put people down. People he disagreed with. People he thought were dumb, you know, thought were idiots."

Brothers smiled. "Did he think you were dumb?"

"What? No way." She paused, her eyes sparkling. "He could be condescending. If he was arguing. And by arguing, I mean, laying down the law. He had an arrogance, a certainty. That could be annoying."

He thought she had an arrogance, too. Not necessarily annoying. "What about the others. Did they also find him irritating?"

"How would I know?"

"I mean among your group of friends."

"What? No, we all got along. It was just Doug, you know? That's just who he was." She muttered something to herself.

"Sorry. What was that?"

"Nothing. I shouldn't speak ill of the dead."

Brothers waited. She put a smile on her face. "He could just be a real jerk, sometimes. But so what? We can all be jerks, can't we?'

Brothers couldn't help smiling but made no reply, and instead asked, "So how would you describe your relationship with him?"

"As I said, we were friendly."

"And?"

"Just friends." She looked at him a moment, her face taking on a severe expression. "What are you implying?"

Brothers gazed back at her. Underneath her friendly manner she seemed a tough cookie. "I'm implying nothing. Just asking questions."

She held his gaze, then nodded. "Look, we knew Doug. We knew he was arrogant with people. Not with us, his friends. Or not usually. He was also smart, witty. You just didn't want to get on his wrong side."

"Can you tell me of anyone who got on his wrong side?"

She looked up at the ceiling for a moment, then back at him, smiling weakly. "Not really."

"Hmm," he said, musing.

"Anything else?" she asked, an impish smile on her face.

He gazed at her again. "If there is, I'll call and ask."

32

BROTHERS DROVE TO MEET Simon Lee at his pharmacy in Clarendon Street, South Melbourne. He found a one hour park a few doors down, and looked at the store. There were red and yellow signs advising that prescriptions here were the cheapest, and that real brand perfumes were sold at a discount. The word real was underlined and in red.

He entered and walked down a narrow aisle, crowded with medicines and cosmetics, to the counter, waiting to be served. He saw a man in a white coat behind a windowed-off area, presumably preparing a prescription. The woman in the line in front of him, quite large and with swollen ankles, took her package and proceeded back to the front of the store to pay for it.

He approached the counter and a tall young woman with bleached hair, also in a white coat, said, "Yes?" and looked at him expectantly.

"Is Mr Lee available?" Brothers asked. "I rang earlier and he said he'd see me." He gave his name.

She eyed him speculatively then put her head through the doorway and spoke quietly to the man dispensing the prescription, who emerged and came to the counter. He was in his forties, medium height, slim with thinning black hair.

"Sergeant Brothers? Simon Lee. Let's go where we can talk. Jodie— can you and Sam look after things while I'm gone? Shouldn't be too long."

She nodded, and Lee walked around the counter. He said, "Jodie's a qualified pharmacist," as he shook Brothers' hand and pointed down the aisle. "There's a good place a couple of doors down."

As they left the store Brothers indicated the signage. "You specialise in discount medicine?"

"You have to, unfortunately. It's bloody competitive these days. I'm up against the big chains with their mass market advertising." Lee shrugged. "You've got to be in it to win it." He halted three doors down. "Here we are."

They were outside a place called Cafe Caffè, and they walked in and sat at a table for two besides the wall. There were five other tables, all empty. The glass-fronted cabinets at the counter displayed patisseries, pies, sandwiches and rolls. Music was playing, some 90s song that Brothers vaguely remembered but couldn't identify.

A waiter dressed entirely in black, with stubble and a man bun, approached. "G'day, Simon. How's it going? The usual?"

"Sure, Frank. How's it going with you?"

"Fine, fine. Can't complain." Frank looked at Brothers. "What can I get you?"

"Just a water, please."

"Won't be a jiffy."

As Frank left, Lee looked across the table at Brothers. "How can I help?"

Brothers went through the explanation of how they were talking to Dr Chen's friends and colleagues. "Did you notice anything unusual in recent days, with Dr Chen?"

Lee scratched his chin. "How do you mean?"

"Well, when did you last see him?"

"Oh, yes. We had dinner at their place last week. Friday night."

"Anything different that you noticed?"

"Different? How do you mean?"

"Anything different about Dr Chen."

Lee pondered another moment, then said, "Not really. Can't say I noticed anything."

"Who was at the dinner?"

"The usual gang—the Churchills, Sally and Kane. And Yvonne Wisher and Ronnie Manser, And of course, Yasmin, my wife."

"You've known each other for a while?"

"Oh, yes. I met Doug at university." He wiped his brow. "So terrible. To think he's gone, like that. Do you have any idea why?"

"We're following up some avenues. That's why we're talking to as many people as possible."

Lee nodded. The waiter brought a latte for Lee and a glass of water for each of them.

"How were things between the eight of you? Any tensions?"

"You're not suggesting, I hope, that any of us had anything to do with it?" Lee's voice had raised a little, his face flushing.

"Mr Lee. You understand these are questions I have to ask." He waited, then repeated, "Any tensions?"

"No. Not at all. We've been friends for donkey's years. Nothing at all."

"How about between Yasmin and Dr Chen?"

Lee sat up straight. "What do you mean?"

"What was her relationship with Dr Chen?"

"Relationship? Jesus Christ. So that's what this is about."

Brothers said nothing, waited.

"Look, Sergeant. My wife is a bit of a flirt. You've met her?"

Brothers nodded.

"Well, you know. She's gorgeous. Stunning. Men drool over her." Lee seemed complacent. He glanced at Brothers with a raised eyebrow. "You know what I mean?"

Brothers avoided any reaction.

Lee grinned a little. "Sure she's a flirt. She enjoys doing that. It's a game she plays. But a relationship? Uh uh." He shook his head.

"Are you sure that's all there was, just flirting? How did Dr Chen react to that?"

Again, Lee paused before replying. "Look, Sergeant. Doug could be difficult with people. But not with us. Or not usually." He laughed. "If he wasn't into an argument, he was great. Yas would tease him. But that was that."

"Sorry to ask you this, but do her flirtations ever go more than just flirting?"

Lee laughed. "She's had her moments. What couple doesn't?" He rubbed his throat. "But we don't own each other." He thrust out his jaw.

BROTHERS KNOCKED ON THE DOOR of Lucy Bottega's house. There was no answer, and while he waited a sudden gust of icy air blew up. He rubbed his hands together; was she at home? Then after about a minute he heard footsteps, the door was opened and Bottega looked up at him, her face drawn. She was dressed in dark grey yoga pants and a matching t-shirt. Brothers kept his eyes on her face.

"Oh, hello, Sergeant. Come in," she said. He followed her down the hall to the lounge area. She gestured at a chair and Brothers sat down.

"Do you have any news?"

Brothers shook his head. "Sorry, Ms Bottega. We have some leads that we're following up, but, nothing as yet." He didn't want to raise her hopes with a false sense they were getting anywhere—particularly as they didn't seem to be getting anywhere. "But that's why I've come to see you again."

"Why is that?"

"It seems likely that—Dr Chen was poisoned before he went to his lab. When did you last see him again?"

"As I said before, he was still home when I went to work." She clenched her fists, and stifled a sob. "He told me he'd be working late. That's the last time I saw him."

"That was in the morning?"

"Yes—about 9am."

"Had he eaten breakfast?"

"Yes. His usual. Toast and coffee."

"Did he mention if he was seeing anyone that day?"

"No." She paused and thought. "No. He didn't mention anything. Just said he'd be late and wouldn't be home for dinner."

"Was that usual? I mean him working late?" He repeated the question he'd asked last time.

"Yes." She put her head in her hands for a moment, then looked up. "That's what he often had to do. He'd work through the night if things were going as he wanted. Sometimes he wouldn't get home till late the next day."

"Where would he eat, when he didn't come home?"

"Oh," Bottega grimaced. "He was terrible with his diet—he'd just grab fast food somewhere. I think there's a food court near the Badeker." She smiled wanly at Brothers. "At least here we'd eat good food." She noted his enquiring glance. "I tend to cook. Oh, I work too. It's just I love to cook. And we eat lots of salads and vegetables. Stir fries. Easy on the sugar."

"So you didn't see him after about nine that morning?"

"No." She slumped in her chair. "That's the last time I saw him. I told you that before."

Brothers waited a while, then asked, "What was he like with your friends?"

"How do you mean?"

He checked his notes. "With your group. Yasmin and Simon, Sally and Kane, Yvonne and Ronnie. Anything different recently?"

"What?" Lucy shot him a glance.

"Any changes?"

"No. We just got on the same."

"Could he be a flirt?"

"Who, Doug?" She laughed. "Oh," she said. "You mean with Yasmin?"

Brothers kept his demeanour. "Tell me about that."

"It was nothing. Just …" she trailed off, her eyes looking upwards. "You have to understand. Yas is pretty, well, I suppose you'd say she's stunning, wouldn't you?" She looked at Brothers, who nodded. "She's also a bit of a flirt. Sometimes."

"And she flirted with Dr Chen?"

"I, uh, I think so." She shut her mouth, her lips forming a tight line. She shook her head. "It was nothing. I shouldn't have mentioned it."

"When was this?"

"Oh, as I said, it was nothing. About a couple of months ago."

"What happened?"

"We were over for dinner at the Lees. I went into the kitchen, and Yas had her arm on Doug's shoulder. She was laughing. She saw me and took her arm off straight away. But she is very touchy-feely, so probably nothing in it. As I say, I shouldn't have mentioned it. Nothing happened."

Brothers contemplated her. Sometimes you had to be blunt. "Nothing happened," he repeated. "You're sure about that?"

Bottega shrugged, her face still tight. "Yes," she said. "I'm sure."

"How would you have known if something had happened between them? Did his behaviour change? Did he get a haircut? Start showering more often? Things like that?"

"Of course not—" she began to say, then stopped. "Are you saying he was having an affair with Yasmin?" Her face flushed. "Ridiculous."

"I'm not saying anything, Ms Bottega. Just asking questions."

Nguyen and McTeish arrived at the Badeker just before 11:30, and made their way to level 5. Penrith's assistant was typing at his keyboard and looked up. "Hello."

"Derek, isn't it?" Nguyen asked.

The young man nodded. "Inspector Nguyen. Dr Ostarkie and Mr Robarts are expecting you, in the board room. I'll take you there."

He led them down the corridor and opened a dark wood door, stepping aside to let them enter. The room had a long table with a dozen chairs around it. Ostarkie and Robarts were standing at a window at the far end of the room, looking out at something. They turned on hearing the door open.

"Inspector," Ostarkie said, stepping across to shake his hand. She glanced at McTeish and raised an eyebrow.

"Detective Constable Carol McTeish," McTeish said, shaking both hers and Robarts' hands.

They sat down at the board table, Robarts slouching in one of the chairs, rocking it a little back and forth, Ostarkie sitting with a straight back, her hands clasped in front of her, looking directly at Nguyen and McTeish, an expression of curiosity or expectance on her face. Robarts stared down at the table, drumming the fingers of his right hand on the table top. McTeish took out her notebook and a pen. From the doorway, Derek said, "Would anyone like some water? Or a coffee?"

Nguyen shook his head.

"No thanks, Derek," Ostarkie said. Robarts remained silent.

"If you need anything, you know where I am." Derek shut the door.

Nguyen regarded the two executives. "Thanks for seeing us," he said.

"How can we help?" Robarts spoke for the first time. He scratched his belly with his left hand.

"We've been talking to one of the people protesting outside the labs, a Terry McCauley. He says he's a photographer." He took a photo from his jacket and showed it to them. "Do you know him?"

Ostarkie looked at the photo for a few moments, passed it to Robarts.

"Maybe you know him as Terry Euston?" Nguyen said.

Ostarkie's jaw tightened slightly.

"No," Robarts said. "Don't recognise the face, and haven't heard of either of those names." He resumed drumming his fingers.

"Why the interest in this Euston?" Ostarkie asked, looking from Nguyen to McTeish.

"He's been to Baltimore three times in the last year. You know him?"

Ostarkie frowned a little. "Well, yes, I have met him."

Nguyen thought, now we're getting somewhere. "Is he working for Howarth-Acfield?"

"I'm not sure." She clasped her arms under her breasts.

"You're not sure? Come now, Dr Ostarkie. He's either working for you, or he isn't. Which is it?"

McTeish sat up, jotted in her notebook.

Ostarkie scratched her chin. "I believe he was commissioned to take some photographs for HA. Whether he has finished the job I don't know."

Robarts butted in, "So that's why my colleague isn't sure whether he still works for us, okay?"

Ostarkie made a shushing gesture. "That's okay, Jason," she said to him. And to Nguyen, "That's the long and short of it. He may still have a contract. He may not. I didn't hire him, and I don't know."

McTeish glanced at Nguyen, raising a questioning eyebrow, and he nodded.

"Dr Ostarkie," she said. "Could you explain why Howarth-Acfield would fly a photographer from Melbourne to Baltimore and back, several times, just to take some photos in Melbourne?"

Ostarkie seemed unfazed. "Good question, Constable. You'd have to ask someone back in Baltimore to get an answer to that. As I just said, I didn't hire Mr Euston, and I don't think Jason here did either." She gave him a quick look and he shook his head. "So neither of us hired him. Is that all?"

"Where did you meet him? Was it in Baltimore?" Nguyen asked.

"Yes, we met at our offices there." She sat with a slight smile on her face.

"When was that?"

"Last year." She sat back.

"I gather you didn't meet him?" Nguyen asked Robarts.

"Nope. Didn't meet either a McCauley nor a Euston." Robarts said.

Nguyen turned to Ostarkie. "Who introduced Euston to you?"

Ostarkie didn't answer straight away. She brushed her hand to the side of her head, patting her hair. "Our CEO," she said, and put her hands back together on the table.

"And who is that?"

"Frederick Lovell." She sat as if she were appraising Nguyen. The only sound in the room was the quiet murmur of the air conditioning.

"Hmm," Nguyen said. "And further to Detective Constable McTeish's point, just why exactly would your CEO hire a photographer, fly him to Baltimore, to take photographs at a lab in Melbourne?"

"Outside the labs," Ostarkie said.

"What?"

"I believe he took photos at the protests, which were *outside* the labs."

Nguyen shook his head, trying to clear it. Employed to take photos! As if. So how was McCauley tied to HA? What was the real reason, that called for three trips to Baltimore. "Was this before you, HA, started your relationship with the Badeker?" he said. "Was it before or after you started funding the research?" He wished he'd asked for a glass of water.

Robarts looked up from staring at the table, and Ostarkie nodded to herself. "We had already signed contracts with the Badeker. Well before I met him. Met him in passing, Inspector. Hardly spoke to him. But we've been involved here for more than two years. Very interesting research, the Badeker," she said. She stood up, turned and looked out the window. "Inspector, the work here could change the world." She waved her arm as if to encompass the planet. "And certainly change Howarth-Acfield. I imagine that Fred was covering all bases. Wouldn't you?"

Nguyen looked at both of them. He was getting annoyed. "That still doesn't explain why you wouldn't hire someone directly, here in Melbourne. Why fly him to Baltimore? What aren't you telling us?"

"That's all I know, Inspector." She smiled broadly and sat down again.

"You were introduced to him as Euston, not McCauley?" Nguyen asked.

"Yes."

"What else do you know about him?"

"You'd better ask Frederick." At Nguyen's look, she said, "Frederick Lovell, our CEO."

"Why Frederick Lovell?"

"Euston was about to leave Fred's office when I met him. Briefly."

"I'll call Lovell. Can you please give his phone number to Carol here?"

Robarts opened his mouth, but Ostarkie said, "Sure." And took her phone out, transferred the number to McTeish's phone.

"So," Nguyen said, "you were introduced to him in Baltimore, and that's it? I find that hard to believe."

"That I was introduced to him in Baltimore? Inspector, lots of people get introduced in Baltimore, just as they do in Melbourne."

Nguyen suppressed his annoyance. "We're investigating the murder of Dr Chen Du, here in the labs you're investing in, and you play word games?" He thumped the table. "Why was he introduced to you?"

Ostarkie lost the smug expression on her face. "Sorry, Inspector. Didn't mean to rile you. This guy Euston just happened to be in Fred's office when I walked in one day. That's all I know. We shook hands. He was going to do some photography of the protests. You do understand how much is at stake here? I reckon it's just simple due diligence. Fred was making sure he was covering all bases. Simple as that. I didn't ask any questions, just shook his hand. He was leaving as I was entering. I'm not trying to give you the run around."

"Let me put it this way. And please, Mr Robarts, feel free to answer too," Nguyen said. "Put yourself in my shoes. Do you really expect me to be able to convince my superiors, that Howarth-Acfield would fly a photographer from Melbourne to Baltimore and back, rather than just hiring someone local here? Why the need to travel to Baltimore?" He searched both their faces. "Does that sound reasonable to you?" He waited a moment, but neither spoke. "And therefore, what do you think Terry Euston was really being asked to do?"

"As I say, Inspector," Ostarkie said. "I've told you all I know. You'll have to ask Fred."

Nguyen stood up, and beckoned McTeish. "Well, thank you for your time. Will you please let me or Detective Constable McTeish know if you're considering traveling."

"We're flying home next week," Robarts said.

Nguyen nodded, exasperated. "Understood," he said. "If necessary we can call you."

35

Kosic phoned McTeish and they agreed to meet at the Kino cinema for a 6:15 pm session of *Amélie*, part of the French Film Festival's retrospective screenings. She arrived at ten past, and shortly after that Kosic appeared.

"Hi," he said. They shook hands.

She waited but he said nothing. It was a bit awkward. "Do you have the tickets?" she asked him.

He shook his head. "O, shit. I didn't think …" He looked around, brightened. "I'll get them here." He walked to the counter and presently brought the tickets over and they entered Cinema 2.

In the foyer leaving the cinema, Kosic said. "Are you hungry? We could discuss the movie over a bite."

"Good idea," she said. The arcade areas around the Kino had several quick service cafes. Then she remembered. "I know. Have you eaten at Kenzan? It's just round the corner."

"Good choice." They walked up the stairs to the next level and then to the right and found the restaurant. Kenzan was somewhat dimly lit, but it had a warm, inviting feel to it, and they were able get a table for two. They looked at the menu, and McTeish said, "It's a bit pricey. Are you happy to have miso soup, and then some small dishes?"

Kosic studying the menu, said, "What's that? Oh. Sure. What do you suggest?"

"How about some prawn tempura—"

"Hey, the grilled butterfish comes with miso. Let's have that."

"Good for me. And maybe the custard with seafood and vegetables. Should we have some sake?"

Kosic nodded, and McTeish gave the order to a young Japanese waiter when she came to their table.

"So, what did you think of *Amélie?*" she asked.

Kosic looked at her, and grinned. "I would say you're not like her at all."

"How do you mean?" McTeish took a sip of water.

"Amélie is shy, isn't she? I wouldn't say you were."

The waiter brought their miso soup and the fish dish, and McTeish tucked in before answering. "Yum," she said. "And you're right, I'm not really like her at all."

"You don't try to help people around you?" Kosic said. "My work I hope helps people."

"Well, yes," McTeish said, picking up the bowl and sipping some soup. "I suppose I do at that. But tell me, I've spoken to Terry McCauley, you know, one of the guys who protested outside the Badeker."

"Who's he?"

"Your friends pointed him out. He's a photographer. You don't know him?"

"Sonia may have mentioned him. She said, now I come to think of it, that there was a photographer who seemed a bit different to the others."

"That's this Terry McCauley guy. She didn't say anything else about him?"

Kosic chewed some fish, then said, "That's all I can recall her mentioning. Just that there was a bloke who was a bit different. What's your interest? Is he a photographer?"

"So he says. And he did show me some of the shots he took at the protests." And she couldn't tell him that he was a real odd one. "So you can't tell me anything else about him?"

"No, sorry. Sonia may have mentioned him, as I say. But I'm pretty sure I never met anyone called Terry. But tell me. Do you know how Doug was poisoned? Did it happen in the lab?"

"We're not sure. But it's likely he ingested something before he arrived that evening."

"So you have a list of suspects? Am I one?" Kosic clenched his right hand into a fist, and his mouth tightened.

"We do have a list, and at the moment most people we've talked to seem to be on it."

"Including me?"

McTeish smiled. "Yes, of course."

Kosic whitened. "Why me? That's ridiculous. We were working on what could be a major breakthrough. For a couple of years. Doug's death is the last thing I'd want to happen."

"I'm just saying that because you worked with Dr Chen you have to be on the list. It doesn't mean you're high up on it."

"So you're saying Helena Shildduck is on it too?"

"Yes, and even Dr Penrith." Her eyes gleamed.

"Seriously? Dr Penrith? That's as absurd as me or Helena. We don't have anything to gain. The reverse, actually." Kosic grew heated, spoke emphatically.

"Don't worry. You're not a serious possibility, and nor are Penrith and Shildduck. It just shows that with policing you have to cast a wide net."

Kosic drank the rest of his sake, and stared at her askance, then shook his head. "So seeing the film and eating here is just you casting your police net?"

She nodded, grinning. "But it was a good movie, wasn't it? Thanks for choosing it. And this food is delicious." She saw his face fall. "What?"

"I'd hoped we could become, I don't know, friends. As well as being a suspect, I mean."

She patted his hand as it lay on the table. "We can be friends. But not until the case is resolved. Okay?"

He nodded, his face sulky.

36

Inspector Nguyen remembered it was time to brief Superintendent Forell; much better to take the initiative himself than to wait for her request. He knocked on her door, putting his head in the jamb.

"Come in, John," she said, beckoning with the fingers of her right hand. "What brings you here? Making progress?"

Nguyen thought for a moment. "Yes and no, Super," he said.

Forell rolled her eyes but said nothing. She waved the same hand vaguely in the direction of a chair in front of her desk, and he sat down. She waited.

"We have made some progress—identified a likely, one Terry McCauley, or Euston."

Forell looked at him. "So," she said. "McCauley or Euston?"

"Those seem to be the names he goes by." He told her about the interview at McCauley's home, and that with the Howarth-Acfield representatives. "I think I need to speak to the pharma boss."

"And he's in Baltimore, right?"

Nguyen smiled sheepishly. "It does need to be face to face."

"And you want me to approve the flight?"

"Yes."

Forell placed her hands together on her desk, looked up at the ceiling for a moment. "That'll cut into the travel budget, on what sounds to me like a wild goose chase."

"Ostarkie, the senior Howarth-Acfield exec, has confirmed it was their CEO who hired McCauley."

"Is McCauley American?"

"I don't know. He could be. He could be Australian. Or British. He sounds Australian, but the accent could be put on."

"Tell me again. How did you find out his name was Euston?"

"Our contacts in ASIO." Nguyen shrugged uncomfortably.

"And these contacts of yours couldn't tell you his nationality?"

"We didn't ask."

"Well why don't you get me some more facts, to help me consider the travel request. That okay?"

Nguyen nodded. "Will do."

37

Nguyen called McTeish in. "Forell wants more info on this McCauley character. I don't blame her—I should've thought of that myself. Can you follow up with your mate in the Feds to find out who this Euston or McCauley really is?"

"Ladbroke?" She bit back a retort about him not being a mate. "Sure thing, Boss. Anything else?"

Nguyen regarded her, noting the sparkle in her eyes. "We need to know what if anything ASIO has on him. His nationality for a start. Do you reckon he's an Aussie?"

McTeish sat down in one of the chairs in front of Nguyen's desk. "I hadn't thought about that. He *seemed* Australian. I mean not a bogan or anything." She clasped her hands in front of her. "I suppose he could be a Yank—but if so he's pretty good at the accent. Could he be a Pom?"

"That's what Forell sort of asked, too."

"I'll get on to it." She stood up and looked questioningly at Nguyen, who nodded.

Back at her desk she called Ladbroke, who answered after the first ring. "Constable McTeish! What's up?"

"G'day, Gershon. How are you going?"

"Can't complain. The usual, I suppose. How can I help you? I presume that's why you're calling." He chuckled into the phone.

"You're not wrong. It's about this McCauley character. Or Euston. Any chance you could shake your contacts and find out a little more about him? For example, is he Australian? And why is he on their database in the first place. I should have asked that before."

"Hmm. It could take a little while. I'll do my best."

"Thanks."

"And don't forget that John Nguyen still owes me one. Maybe two, now."

She felt herself blush. "I'll remind him. I'm sure he hasn't forgotten. It's just because we're flat out on this job."

"Not to worry, Carol. Not to worry. All in good time. I'll get back to you as soon as I can, if they've got any more info." He hung up.

McTeish put her phone down and thought about McCauley. Euston. Did his nationality matter? If he's American that makes his being here more suspicious. If he's not, so what? Then again, why couldn't she find anything about him before going to Gershon? And why was he on ASIO's database? And just as importantly, why would a photographer kill a research scientist? Being a photographer could of course just be a cover. It did seem likely. But then, why would he want to kill Chen? Why would anyone?

She went back to Nguyen's office, and shared her concerns with him.

He smiled at her, in a friendly way. "That's how a detective should be thinking. Why indeed would anyone want to kill Dr Chen? Have we forgotten that question? It's the most important one—who gains from his death?" He scratched his left cheek. "Graham hasn't talked to Chen's friends yet, has he?"

"I think he's doing that today, or last night."

"That might surface some domestic issue." Nguyen put his head in his hands for a moment, then sat upright. "It's either a domestic, or there's something fishy about the research stuff. And certainly we need to do more about Mr Euston and HA. They certainly give off an odd aroma, don't they?" He smiled up at McTeish. "But we can't rule out some personal upheaval."

At that moment Brothers knocked on the door.

"Graham! Just the man I need to see." McTeish started to get up. "No, Carol. Stay for this." And to Brothers, "Have you got anything about Chen's friends?"

"Certainly have, Boss. You wouldn't believe it!" He sat down heavily in the chair next to McTeish's, grinning.

"Well, spit it out," Nguyen said.

"Seems there's some bad blood between Chen and one of his so-called mates. Was bad blood," Brothers corrected himself.

"How do you mean?" Nguyen asked.

"I'm not positive, but one of his friends, a Yasmin Lee, might have been having it off with him."

McTeish said with a grin, "Why would that be bad blood?"

"Well, Chen's partner, Lucy, won't say if anything happened. But she certainly seemed uncomfortable when I questioned her. So if they did get up to something I reckon her husband, Simon, would not have liked it."

"What did he have to say for himself, then? Nguyen asked.

"He's a bit vague—says he doesn't own her. Says she's a flirt, but I don't think he believes she was having an affair."

"Graham," Nguyen said. "Just because we're trying to find motives, don't read too much into things."

"What me, Boss?" he laughed. "Just reporting what's what. Not reading anything into anything. But judging by Yasmin and Lucy, something was certainly up."

"Any sense this might have happened at his work as well?" Nguyen said. "We need to talk to some of the women who worked with him at the Badeker."

"We've talked with Dr Shildduck and Tamas Kosic. There were no other women on his team."

"Yes, but because we've focused on the photographer, McCauley—"

"Euston," McTeish interjected.

Nguyen looked at her for a moment, then continued. "The photographer, we need to check what other women work there. Just because they're not on his team doesn't mean there can't be relationships." He paused. "What about that other fellow's team? Robertson's. Any women working there?"

McTeish shut her eyes in a momentary grimace. "I haven't followed that up yet. Will do." She made a note in her phone.

Nguyen looked at the whiteboard display in his office. "We have three groups of people. Maybe four. So far." He sighed. "One: Dr Chen, his partner and friends. Two: Dr Chen's work colleagues. Three: The Green protesters. Four: The HA people. Maybe they're part of Two, the work group." He paused, glancing at Brothers and McTeish. "Any others?"

After a moment both shook their heads.

"So do we have any possible suspects?" He counted on his fingers of his right hand. "We have a suspicious photographer. We have a possible affair. We have an odd group of big pharma investors. And we have the Greenies." He shook his head. "None very promising, so far. Is there enough to justify me flying to Baltimore?" He rubbed his jaw. "Certainly this Euston character raises a lot of questions." He regarded the two again. McTeish was sitting upright on a chair, her hands holding her notebook and a pen. Brothers had stood up and now lounged against the desk, a buttock perched on the corner, staring at the whiteboard. "Any suggestions?"

"Well," McTeish said, when Brothers remained silent. "We need to find out more about Dr Chen's relationships." She glanced at her notebook. "I can check out things with Tamas, er Dr Kosic, and with Dr Schildduck, as well as with Dr Robertson's team." She stared at the whiteboard. "Boss, I think you do need to go to Baltimore."

"You looking for a trip, Carol?" Brothers said.

"No, no. I just said what I could do. It's just that Euston, or McCauley, really is an odd bod. It doesn't make sense."

Nguyen nodded, arms across his chest.

Brothers said, "I need to finish looking for possible personal enemies outside Chen's work. I don't think his friends are being completely open."

Nguyen raised an eyebrow.

"Oh, they are trying to give the impression that all is hunky dory, apart from Chen's ability to be snarky. For example, Lucy Bottega said when I first interviewed her—" Brothers flipped through some pages of his notebook—"*He was a bit of a loner, but he got on with everyone. He didn't even have arguments.* That's certainly not what everyone's saying now." He glanced at Nguyen and McTeish. "Of course, that doesn't necessarily mean much. As you say, Winner, the photographer could be the best bet. Will the Super buy it?"

"We're lucky the media aren't hounding us."

"Lucky he wasn't a sports person, or a movie star. Or embezzled a million bucks," Brothers said.

"Unfortunately the Greenies angle will get them interested at some stage," Nguyen said. He sat pondering for a moment, then said, "On the other hand, a bit of media pressure might help us. Okay, Carol, you take on the lab people, Graham keep on the friends, and I'll try Forell about a little trip."

"Boss, I could talk to Kosic about Dr Chen's friends, too," McTeish said.

"Just keep Graham in the loop."

"Of course."

38

SHE DECIDED TO SPEAK to Kosic first and was about to call him when her phone rang. She didn't recognise the number.

"Constable McTeish. Can we meet?" She heard the voice of Terry Euston.

"Is that Mr McCauley?"

"Yes. Terry here."

"Or Mr Euston?"

There was a pause.

"Well, well, well. Didn't I say you were the clever one?"

She heard a chuckle. What next? she wondered.

"Constable McTeish?"

She waited a moment longer, then said, "Yes?"

"I'm ringing to see if we can get together."

Again McTeish waited a moment. She wanted to provoke him.

"Constable?"

She sighed. "Yes. I'm still here."

"I want, er, to discuss my brief."

"Your brief?"

"From Howarth-Acfield"

"I see." She paused again, her thoughts running wild. Was this a breakthrough? "When would you like to meet?"

"Do you have time today? This afternoon?"

For some reason she checked her watch, then looked at her diary. "Yes. I could fit you in. How about 3 pm. Can you come here to the station?"

Now there was a pause on the other end.

"I'd prefer not."

"Well, I don't have time to travel out to see you." That was bold. She grimaced. Would it backfire?

"Very well." His voice had taken on a sulky tone. "I'll come in."

She gave him details, and hung up. She felt shaky, even though she was sitting down. She sped over to Winner's office. He was at his desk, writing. She knocked and entered, and Nguyen looked up, smiled.

"Euston rang," she burst out, eyes glowing. "He's coming here!"

Nguyen gazed calmly at her. "What time?"

"Three o'clock. He wants to discuss his "brief" as he calls it, his brief from Howarth-Acfield." Nguyen maintained his impassive expression. Why wasn't he excited?

"Good. Good." He smiled and rubbed his hands together. "Good work! We'll put him in one of the better interview rooms. Three o'clock, you say?"

She nodded.

"Good." He resumed writing.

McTeish went back to her desk, idly handling her notebook. She glanced down. Kosic. She had to set up a meeting with him. She shook her head, picked up her phone and he answered after no more than a couple of seconds.

"Carol—er, Detective. How are you?"

"Hi, Tamas. Look, I wonder if we could meet up again."

"Of course! When?" She detected a rise in energy in his voice.

"Are you free today?"

"Let's see. It's 9:40 now. We could meet for coffee, later this morning. I don't need to be at the lab."

That suited McTeish and they arranged to meet at 11 am at a coffee shop that was part of the Badeker complex. McTeish calculated it would take her fifteen minutes at most to get there. She grinned and formed a fist as if to pump it in a gesture of "Yes!", then she saw what she was doing and stopped herself.

Instead, she stood up, put her head into Winner's office and told him she was meeting Kosic at 11.

He didn't look up, but said, "Good," and went on writing.
She shook her head, snorted quietly and went back to her cubicle.

39

AT A FEW MINUTES to eleven she parked and walked past the Badeker into a small mall, and entered Con and Sue's Coffee, and sat waiting for Kosic. A stylish waiter dressed in black came over.

"Are you Con?" she asked.

"Yes. That's me." He held up his pad and pen and looked at her. "What would you like?"

McTeish introduced herself. He seemed indifferent to the fact she was a detective. "Have you been open long?"

"About a year. Sue and I signed the lease, let me see, fourteen months ago."

"Did the Badeker people come here for coffee?" she asked.

"Of course. And people from all the other offices around here."

"So did you get to know them?"

"Well. By face of course. And quite a few I know the names. We do have the odd chat."

"So did you know Dr Chen Du?"

Con stood up a little straighter. "Doug? Yes. I mean not personally. But we did speak occasionally. So sad. So sad," he added.

"What was he like?"

"Well, I don't know. He was a customer. I mean he was fine." Con shrugged.

"No problems with him?"

"Problems?" Con looked puzzled. "No, no problems."

At that point Tamas Kosic turned up. "Hello, Carol," he said, and sat down opposite her. "Have you ordered yet?"

She shook her head. "A latte, please."

Kosic ordered too, and Con returned to the counter to prepare them.

"So," Kosic said, eyebrows raised. "You wanted to see me?"

"Yes," McTeish said. She grinned inwardly. She would have to make sure she didn't inadvertently encourage him. "It's about Dr Chen. We've heard he could often get very prickly, and argue and so on. You never mentioned that." She looked calmly at him.

"You didn't ask me," he said.

"Well, was he?" She smiled at him, then remembered and switched it off.

"He could certainly lose it, sometimes. Is that what you mean?"

She nodded. "But was he rude to people as well?"

Kosic hesitated. "Is this important?"

"It's just one more element in helping us understand what happened."

"Okay, then," he said. "Yes, he could be rude. He was brilliant, but he really knew how to put you down. Make you feel this small." He held his right thumb and forefinger an inch apart. He gave a short laugh. "Sorry. Got a bit carried away there."

"So he made you angry. Was he rude to others as well?"

"Of course. To everyone. Except Dr Penrith, of course. He was never rude to those he needed to help him."

"What about his friends? Did you know them?"

"Well I met his partner, of course. And I suppose I might have met some of his friends. Maybe over drinks. But he tended to keep his work life separate. We all do, I suppose."

"Was he rude with his friends?"

Kosic looked puzzled. "Not that I noticed. I mean I only met them socially. You know, he could argue when he wanted to. Could be biting. But I didn't notice that with Lucy. Or the others."

"Were there many others?"

"I don't know." He shifted in his chair. "I didn't get to know them. I don't think I even went to his house."

McTeish thought for a moment. "So what about Dr Shildduck? You said he could be rude to her. Did she get upset?"

Kosic sat back and rubbed his chin. "I suppose she did, but she hid it. She's a professional." He looked at her again for moment. "You must know how it is. If your boss let fly from time to time, would you let it get to you? Or just put it down to pressure, and get on with whatever you're doing?"

McTeish nodded, opened her notebook and made a note. "What about other colleagues. Was he rude to anyone else in your team?"

"There were just three of us in the team. Just Helen and me left."

"Were there others that you worked with, from time to time? That he was rude to? What about others at the Institute?"

"He was an equal-opportunity abuser." Kosic smiled, looking up at her. "Anyone and everyone, particularly if he was under the pump. And, you know, he was under pressure. Enormous pressure."

She raised her eyebrows.

At her expression he nodded and said, "Pressure to get results. And he pressured himself, too. So we usually didn't mind when he cracked the shits."

McTeish made a note.

Con arrived with the coffees, and placed them down in front of them, then returned with two glasses and a brown glass bottle of water.

"You said, you *usually* didn't mind," McTeish said when the waiter had left. "Meaning there were times you did mind. Or people did?"

"Yes, yes," he said. He flopped his hands face down on the table, then sipped his coffee. "Doug could be pretty cutting."

McTeish made another note.

"Did he upset Dr Shildduck, too?"

"He could be pretty mean." He breathed out in a heavy sigh.

"And anyone else?"

"Look. It wasn't often. It sort of goes with the territory, you know. When we have to produce, produce, produce. So yes, I'm sure there'd be a few others."

"Thanks, Tamas."

He lifted his head, gazed at her. "It's not how I want to remember him."

40

Back at the station McTeish reviewed her notes, then knocked on Nguyen's door to remind him of Euston.

"He should be here in five. How do you want to do this?'

"He rang you," Nguyen said. "So you lead the interview. I'll chip in when necessary. Have you let Reception know to expect him?"

She nodded, and they took the lift to Level 1 to the interview rooms.

"You go down to meet him, and bring him up," Nguyen said.

"Okay." She stayed in the lift and waited at the ground floor reception area, behind the wall in front of the reception desk, so she could appear once Euston arrived.

At two minutes to three, McTeish through the one-way glass window saw Terry Euston enter the lobby and walk up to Reception. She opened the door and walked up to him.

"Mr Euston."

"Hello, Constable." He shook her hand. The grip was firm, and brief enough, before he gave a quick squeeze and let her hand go.

"You want to talk?" McTeish asked.

He nodded.

"Come this way." She led him to the lifts and to the interview room, McTeish ushering him in before her.

"Detective," Euston called out when he saw Nguyen. "A not unexpected pleasure." He approached and shook Nguyen's hand. "Where would you like me to sit?"

Nguyen indicated the empty chair opposite him. McTeish sat at right angles, so it wasn't two against one.

"Constable McTeish tells me you have something to say," Nguyen said.

"Yes indeed. As I mentioned on the phone, it's about my brief." He glanced at McTeish. "Not briefs!" He chuckled.

McTeish maintained a stony expression.

"My brief from Howarth-Acfield," he said, looking now at Nguyen.

Nguyen waited.

"I thought since our last meeting that you may have got the wrong idea about me. Silly, I know." He chuckled, looking from one to the other. "So I thought if I talked to you, I could answer any questions you might have." He waited a moment, and when neither Nguyen nor McTeish said anything, he continued. "In a nutshell, and I imagine this won't be a great surprise to you, they tasked me with taking photos of the protesters."

"Yes. I don't think that's news to us. Why you, Mr Euston? And why the false name?" McTeish said.

"I'll come to that, if I may."

When neither McTeish nor Nguyen said anything, he continued. "I happened to be in Baltimore on business. And I happen to know some of the HA people, so I got the job."

"Why wouldn't they hire someone local, here in Melbourne?" McTeish asked.

"Perhaps they did. Perhaps they didn't. Who knows? All I know is they asked me to do the job. You'll have to ask them why they chose me."

"And the name change?"

"Well—" Euston smiled in a deprecatory manner, and shot his shirt cuffs. "I have to be careful, you know. For my own protection."

"You do know that using a false name to enter the country is an illegal act?"

"I do know that. But did I? I mean enter illegally? Which name is false, Constable? McCauley or Euston?" He grinned.

"You tell us. No doubt our intelligence sources will let us know." Nguyen said.

"That's for me to know and you to find out. I do like a bit of ambiguity, Detective. Don't you? And Constable?" He looked at both in turn.

"Our job is to cut through the ambiguities, and get to what really is the case," Nguyen said. "So I'm sure we'll establish your real name in due course. But that's not the main thing at the moment. Who gave you the brief in Baltimore?"

Euston sat back. "Why the CEO. Mr Lovell."

"Isn't that odd?" McTeish asked. "For the CEO to hire you as a photographer?"

"We go back a ways. I've done work for Mr Lovell before."

"And he wanted you to photograph some protesters?"

"That's it. Spot on."

"And what else?"

"Eh?" Euston smiled. "I of course sent photos back, if that's what you mean."

"Was Howarth-Acfield interested in who the protesters were? Did Mr Lovell ask you to send information on them back to him?"

"He may have asked for rough numbers. You know, the size of the protests. Were they big or were they small."

"Did he say why?"

"Constable McTeish. Don't you think he might have been concerned about his investments in the Badeker?"

McTeish bit her lip. "So your job was simply to take photographs and let Mr Lovell know the size of the protests?"

"That's about it."

"You photographed the protesters. Did any of them seem odd to you?"

"They *were* protesters, you know, Constable. So doesn't that make them odd?"

"Did any seem to know Dr Chen? I recall you asked them who he was."

Euston paused. "Well, they certainly knew who he was. That's one of the reasons they were protesting. But I don't think any of them knew him personally, if that's what you mean."

"Okay. Anything else?"

"Are you any closer to finding out who did it?"

"Did wh—" McTeish snapped her mouth shut.

"Our enquiries are progressing," Nguyen said calmly.

"I'll take that as a 'no', shall I?"

When neither spoke, Euston said, "Do you need me any more?" He emphasised the word 'need', staring at McTeish.

"You're the one who rang wanting to talk," McTeish said. "So have you anything further to say to us?"

Euston sat back, put his hands face down on the table.

"For example, why did you fly three times to Baltimore?" she asked.

Euston blinked, then smiled, his eyes cold. "If you recall, I think I already told you of the wonders of Baltimore. If you like music, well David Byrne, Cab Calloway and Mama Cass all hail from that fine town. And Larry Adler, too."

"That'll be all," Nguyen said. "Thank you for coming in. If you have any more information, please let us know."

McTeish walked Euston to the elevator, to go down to Reception. As its doors closed, she said, "Why'd you really come here, Mr Euston?"

"Terry, please." He smiled at her, clasped his hands together in front of his stomach and flexed his fingers.

"You told us almost nothing. So—?" She looked at him in the eye. He winked at her. "What's that supposed to mean?"

"It means the real reason I came here was…" He paused, gave a sort of smirk. "I came here to see you." He waited a moment. "There. I've said it."

"What do you mean, to see—" She broke off. Of all the nerve. She suddenly felt furious and her face reddened. "To see me? To see me? What the hell are you on about." Her voice was raised as the doors opened on the ground floor.

"Now, now, Constable," Euston said. "What's so surprising? Look at you. You're smart."

Her mouth hung open.

"Don't tell me no one has ever told you that. Cute, too."

"And half your age," McTeish said with a snarl. "You've got to be joking." She spluttered in disbelief.

"No joke, Constable. No joke at all. Age is just a state of mind, didn't someone say? Hmm." He put his right forefinger to his cheek. "Ah yes. Mark Twain, wasn't it? *Age is a case of mind over matter; if you don't mind it, it doesn't matter!*" He waved a hand and walked out towards the front entrance.

"Well I do mind," McTeish muttered to his back. She stood there stony faced, her anger grown cold. The thought of that creep fancying her. Ugh. —Hang on a sec, she told herself. Was he just winding me up? Trying to get under my skin? She shook her head. If that was his plan, he had succeeded. She relaxed a little, smiled ruefully. The question, she asked herself, is why?

She returned to the meeting room, where Nguyen waited.

"What did you make of that?" he asked. He looked calmly at her.

McTeish shrugged and sat down. Should she say what Euston had said to her? "I'm not sure why he came in. He didn't say much we didn't know. But he did try to wind me up."

"How do you mean?"

McTeish bit her tongue, then told him of the exchange.

Nguyen gave a chuckle. "I'm sure you've dealt with worse things. You do look a little out of sorts, though. Forget about it."

"Already forgotten, Boss."

"He was trying to allay our suspicions, probably." Nguyen smiled again. "If anything, it had the reverse effect. Do you agree?"

"I think so," McTeish said. "Surely Lovell must have wanted him to do something else. Not just take photos. But if so, what?"

"I'm sure we'll find out. Particularly if I can get the Super to okay a Baltimore trip. In the meantime—can you lean on your friend Sergeant Ladbroke. See if he can get something out of ASIO on him? Okay?"

So, it seems she would be stuck with Ladbroke as her 'friend'. She nodded. "By the way, who's Larry Adler? Does that mean anything?" she said.,

"He was a harmonica player." Nguyen grinned. "A pretty good one, too. But I doubt he has anything to do with our case."

Nguyen knocked on Forell's door and entered at her command of "Come!"

"John. Sit down." She pointed at the chair in front of her desk. "This about Baltimore?"

Nguyen cut short a sigh. "Exactly," he said. "We've established that Euston used that name when he travelled to the US and back. And that he used McCauley with the GOCH protesters. He went three times to Baltimore in the past year. Claims he makes pilgrimages there, and he quoted several celebrities to us."

"Phillip Glass? Billie Holiday? John Barth?" Forell asked.

"Are they from Baltimore? How do you know that?"

"Forget it. That's not enough to justify a trip."

"Hang on. He visited the pharma Company, Howarth-Acfield, we think three times. And was commissioned by their CEO to take photos here in Melbourne, at the Badeker." He paused, looking at Forell.

She waited, expressionless.

"I think the only way to find out why is to meet him in the flesh. They're investing in the Badeker, so yes they could be interested in what's happening, in terms of protests. That I understand. But why would the CEO of a major pharma fly a photographer from Melbourne to Baltimore, three times, rather than getting someone here to hire him? What else is going on?"

"Hmm." Forell said. "I see what you mean." Then he saw a glint in her eye. "You know Baltimore is one of the most crime-ridden cities in the States, don't you?"

Nguyen nodded. "Homicide rates are pretty high."

"What is it? Eight times the US average?"

Nguyen nodded again, though he had no idea whether that was the correct ratio.

"Any idea why that is so?" Forrell waited a moment then answered her own question. "Drugs." She smiled. "Funny about that, isn't it? The very business of your Howarth-Acfield."

"What? Not those sort of drugs," Nguyen said.

"Maybe not. But we good guys are finally getting the message that drugs are much of a muchness. Our political masters are starting to realise that it's the whole criminalising of some drugs that's created the problems."

Nguyen nodded again. "Sure. Making them illegal gives a huge kick to the dealers, the mafia, the bikies." He remembered the bribery stories, and not just of his fellow officers. A whole industry thrived from the fact drugs were illegal. Including tv shows about it all. "And all the jurisdictions that are decriminalising are seeing a drop off in street crime, not to mention drug deaths and prison populations." He stopped. Why had Forell brought this up?"

"Yes," she said. "The sooner our government sees this is a medical and social problem, and not a legal one, the sooner we can focus on more important things. Like whether Howarth-Acfield is approaching the legal grey zone from the opposite direction. What are they up to with this McCauley? Any news on why he uses the second name? Any help from then Feds?"

"Still waiting to hear back on that. Euston claims he uses the McCauley name for his own protection."

"A likely story."

"Exactly. But he doesn't seem to have broken any laws yet—none that we know about, anyway." He thought of McCauley. What a smart arse. Had he broken any laws? The sooner they heard back from ASIO the better.

"And what about other lines of inquiry?" Forell asked. "You mentioned you're checking Chen's personal relationships."

"As I said, we're exploring that possibility. It seems Chen made a few enemies. Apparently he didn't tolerate fools, and he regarded anyone who questioned him as a fool. Including work colleagues."

"How so?" Forell asked.

"By putting people down. The more we talked to his friends and colleagues, the more he seemed to be a very prickly specimen."

"Was he a bully?"

"It seems he could be. And, Supe, it's also possible he was having an affair."

Forell raised her eyebrows.

"With one of his friends, or his partner's friends. Yasmin Lee. Not sure yet if it was just a flirtation, or whether there was more to it."

"Good." Forell leaned back in her chair. "I like options to be kept open." She sat up straight again. "What about professional jealousy? You said another team was also working on wheat. Was there competition to get the results first?"

"That's still possible, I suppose, but there's nothing to support that idea." Noting the slight tightening of Forell's mouth, Nguyen added, "But we're not discounting it. In fact we're interviewing his team to see what that might throw up. Whoever gets there first would get a huge boost to their reputation. "

"Hmm." She considered Nguyen for a moment or two. "About Baltimore. I'm inclined to agree with you that that needs further investigation. But you might like to check first what else Howarth-Acfield are doing at the Badeker before you go. It could give you more ammunition." Then she added, "Can the Baltimore police help you? Do you really need to go yourself?"

Nguyen had prepared himself for this question. "The locals won't have a clue who we are and won't understand our problems. Why would they care about a photographer being hired by one of their major companies? How could we get someone there to find the time to help us? Think of all the pressures they're under at the moment—you know, including the crime rate problems you mentioned, and the political shenanigans they're going through." He saw that Forell had a slight smile on her lips. "They might be able to help us, but we won't be a priority. We need answers pretty quickly."

"How much time will you need there?"

So she'd given him the go ahead after all. He repressed a smile. "Shouldn't take long. Two or three days, perhaps. No more than a week including travel time."

"Do we have any contacts with Baltimore's finest?" she asked.

"We'll check it out."

43

Back in the office Nguyen called Brothers and McTeish together. "We've got the go ahead for Baltimore," He said, then paused, waited for reactions.

"Great, Winner," said Brothers.

"You don't need a handbag, do you?" said McTeish.

"I'd like to take you both—but the budget won't go that far. More importantly, we've got to talk to the rest of the Badeker scientists, and question Chen's friends a bit more." His eyes sparkled. "Need that to be done while I'm away."

Brothers laughed, and then so did McTeish.

"You got it, Winner," Brothers said, and McTeish nodded.

"The challenge will be to get the HA president, Fred Lovell, to talk to me," Nguyen said. "The Baltimore Special Investigations team may have some advice. See if I can get them to ask him to meet me, if I get the run around."

"Get them to lean on him? How?" Brothers said.

Nguyen tapped his chin with a finger. "We know he met personally with this Euston guy," he said. "I think the fact Euston is on our security people's radar will help. Also, this is a murder investigation. I suspect Lovell won't want to appear to be obstructing that. So I'll see if I can get the Baltimore people to ask him to meet me. It's worth a try. No point travelling all that way if he won't see me. By the same token, if I've flown all that way, it just might make him curious. A bit different to saying no to a local." He stood up. "Carol, can you get me the contact details of the head of the Baltimore Special Investigations team? Our admin people should have them.

44

Nguyen emailed Major Janne Fleischer, the head of Baltimore's Special Investigations department, outlining briefly the murder inquiry and seeking to speak via zoom. A time was arranged for 8:30am Melbourne time, which was 4:30pm in Baltimore.

"Detective Inspector Nguyen," she said. Fleischer was in her 50s, handsome with long blond shoulder length hair, astute eyes that regarded him through the camera. "This is sure some surprise. You're in Melbourne, Australia, is that right? By the way, I visited you folks at one time. Sydney. Saw the Opera House and your bridge. I didn't get to Melbourne. And forget the Major business. I answer to Janne, or Fleischer, or some other names I won't bother you with." Her voice was alto and though friendly he could discern a no-nonsense element in the tone.

"Thanks, Janne. And call me John." He paused a moment, then continued. "We've got a tricky situation. A senior scientist has been murdered, as I outlined in my email, and he worked in a lab with funding by one of your pharma companies, Howarth-Acfield."

"Howarth-Acfield. They're investing in Australia? And how is HA linked to your case?"

"Well, we're not sure they are." Nguyen rubbed his forehead.

"You're not?" She raised her eyebrows.

"Well, they could be. Their CEO personally hired a guy who says he's a photographer. An Australian guy, who turned up at protests outside the lab. But this photographer, if that's all he is, flew to Baltimore a few times to meet him. Pretty unusual, we think. So I want to have a word with him."

"That's a long way to come to have a word," Fleischer said. You couldn't zoom like we are?"

"Well, Janne, you know face to face is best. If it was just a simple case of HA hiring someone to photograph the protests, I wouldn't need to be bothering you."

She raised an eyebrow again but said nothing.

"The photographer, a Terry Euston, also uses the name McCauley, and our security services have him on their radar. It could be that HA has nothing to do with any of this except at a tangent."

"You think there's more to it," she said.

"I do. It just doesn't add up. If you're wanting to protect an investment, surely some middle manager would hire a photographer, not the CEO. And not have him fly to Baltimore. I should mention that this Euston is what we Aussies call a smart arse. Full of himself. Thinks he's trying to play games with us. What you might call a wise guy."

"Smart arse. I like that. We just call them assholes. That what you mean?"

Nguyen laughed. "Yeah, that's about right. Anyhow, this Euston asshole is up to something much more than taking photos. And I need to talk to Frederick Lovell. He's the CEO. Do you know anything about him?"

Fleischer sat thinking for a time. "Freddie, eh? He knows the Commissioner, and the Governor and the Mayor," she said. "HA makes donations to our Front Line Club and the Blue Donors, and he and his wife go to the usual society events. So take it from me, he's well connected."

Nguyen's ears pricked up at the mention of the Front Line Club. "The Front Line Club," he began. "We have Bluespace and a veterans support body. Is that like—?"

"The Front Line Club supports our people who went down in the line of duty." She nodded, as if confirming a thought. "Lovell will take my call."

Nguyen breathed out. "Thanks."

"What should I say to him? He'll be intrigued that an Australian has come all the way to Baltimore." She laughed a little. "I don't mean that coming to Baltimore will intrigue him. He'll expect anyone would want to come to our fair city."

"You mean the city of Billie Holliday and John Waters?"

"Exactly. And many more. You've done your homework." She smiled. "We do have our fair share of celebrities. But he'll be surprised you've flown all that distance from Australia. So what should I tell him?" She sat back.

"Maybe don't tell him he's the reason I'm coming to Baltimore. Just that seeing I'll be in town, and I have this case, I'd appreciate a few minutes of his time."

"What reason will I tell him for you coming here, if not this case?"

"Tell him—" Nguyen thought—"tell him I'm meeting up with colleagues to share policing. You're bringing the crime rate down, aren't you?"

"Well, we were." She shrugged. "It's sort of stabilised."

"We're learning from each other. Next time, you can come to Melbourne." He grinned.

"Hmm. Not a bad idea. I'll tell you what, I'll assign a couple of my people to meet you and show you around. When do you want to come?"

"Soon as I can get a flight booked. With luck I should be able to get in this Sunday evening."

"Okay. Leave it with me and I'll get back to you. Nice meeting you, John."

"Nice meeting you, Janne. I look forward to meeting you in the flesh."

"And you, too, John."

45

WHILE NGUYEN'S FLIGHT LANDED at 6:19 pm on Sunday, it took almost a quarter of an hour for the plane to taxi to the terminal and start to let passengers disembark. It then took a further 40 minutes to go through Customs, by which time his bag was waiting on the carousel. He emerged into the public area a little after 7:30 pm. He scanned the crowd, and saw two police in dark blue scanning the arrivals, one a tall woman with bleached blond curly hair, the other a man with short black hair, both young and both with smiles on their faces when they saw him approach.

"Detective Nguyen?" the woman asked. "I'm Laila Billings—they call me Bill—and this is Sergeant Frank Kapper, but don't call him Cap!" They shook hands.

"So, this what an Aussie cop looks like?" Kapper said, with a gravelly voice.

"Got me there," Nguyen said. "They all look the same as me. And are you what Baltimore cops look like?" He grinned.

"Bill" Billings had a creamy skin and was, Nguyen decided, simply gorgeous. Frank Kapper, a shade shorter than Billings, was clean shaven and looked out of central casting for a twenty something white male cop. "Thanks for meeting me here. Did you have to wait long?"

"No problem," Billings said. "Not every day we get to meet a fellow officer from down under."

"Let's get you to your hotel," Kapper said, grabbing Nguyen's bag before he could stop him. "Where are you staying?"

"The Marriott Delta on East Elwood Street." Nguyen said.

"Close to us. Good thinking," Billings said. "The Major says you're working a murder case. Care to fill us in while we drive?"

"Sure. I think I'm meeting Major Fleischer tomorrow morning. Will you guys be there?"

"I sure do hope so," Billings said. She glanced at Kapper, who grinned. "Seeing as we'll be delivering you to her."

"Right. Right," Nguyen said, and they walked to the car park, Kapper dragging Nguyen's case and Nguyen rolling his smaller cabin one. Billings led the way to a white Ford Interceptor, and Kapper stowed the bags and they got in, Billings driving.

Nguyen briefly summarised what he knew about Chen's murder. "Save your questions till we're with your boss," he said.

It took about 25 minutes, and Billings pulled up outside the Delta. "Here we are, John. Can we buy you dinner?"

"Look, I'd love that. But could we do that tomorrow? I won't be good company right now. I think I'll just get a shower and hit the sack. But thanks for asking."

"Understood," Billings said. "I'm free tomorrow. Frank—how about you?"

"Yes. Can do. We'll treat you to some prime Baltimore steak," Kapper said. "You do eat steak?"

"Love it," Nguyen said. "Really appreciate you guys picking me up."

"Great. Sounds like a plan. You okay if we call by for you tomorrow morning, around 8:30?" Billings said.

"Sure. That's very kind of you." Nguyen's meeting with Fleischer was at nine.

"We'll have time to give you a quick look over our offices."

"Thank you, Bill, Frank." He jumped out and took his bags from the trunk, waved them goodbye. The car drove off.

Nguyen took his bags to reception and checked in, took his key and headed to his room. On the wall of the elevator he noticed the hotel restaurant was called Pho Viet. He shook his head; what a coincidence. Maybe he'd have time to check it out.

46

Nguyen ate a quick breakfast at the buffet and was in the lobby at 8:25. Five minutes later Billings and Kapper drew up at the kerb.

"How'd you sleep? Any jet lag?" were Kapper's first words.

"I woke at about 2 am, and I must have got back to sleep cause my alarm woke me at seven," Nguyen said.

"Are you ready for the Major?" Billings asked, a grin on her face.

"Janne and I are like this," Nguyen said, holding up two crossed fingers. Then he separated them and laughed. "You mean she's hard going?"

"Nah. Nah. Just joshing," Billings said. They were quiet in the few minutes it took until they parked under Police Headquarters and headed for the elevators.

"I'll come up with you," Billings said.

"You're not joining us?" Nguyen asked Kapper.

"I'll catch you later. I've got something else on." He shook hands before leaving on Level 6. They continued riding up to Level 14, and Billings led the way, knocking on the door of Major Fleischer's office.

"Come in," Fleischer's voice rang out. Billings urged him in.

"Ah, John. I see you arrived in one piece. Good to meet in the flesh. I've asked Bill here to join us for a reason, which I'll come to shortly. Take a seat."

"Thanks, Janne," Nguyen said. She was a big woman. He momentarily wondered how like his boss Superintendent Forell she was; they both had a commanding presence. He looked around. "This is some office."

The office was large, with a glassed-in bookcase along one wall, two framed certificates alongside it, and a view towards the harbour behind her desk. Very smart to have the view behind her, Nguyen thought: she won't be distracted by staring out the window. And her visitors might be. They sat at a table with four chairs around it.

"Now," Fleischer said. "About your case." She listened intently without interrupting as Nguyen outlined the situation.

"And so you see, we need to talk to Fred Lovell," Nguyen said.

"I can see why you have questions. Particularly about this Euston guy. I didn't know too much about Lovell, beyond what I told you, you know, his support for our charities, but I've asked around. Seems he's got a pretty big ego—no surprise there. His support for the Blue Line Club is part of it. Don't get me wrong. We sure appreciate the support. These guys have the usual motives for their supposed good works. Not just the tax breaks. Know what I mean?"

Nguyen nodded. "If something crops up and he needs help, you're happy to oblige. We get the same thing." He chuckled. "Can be tricky."

"You said it—and something else. I'm told Howarth-Acfield's investment in FC Group brings in the giant share of their revenue since Covid, when they missed out on the vaccine business. So their pharma business is not doing so well."

Nguyen pricked up his ears. McTeish's research had thrown up that HA's subsidiary FC Group was a major seller of fertilisers to Australian farmers. "Yeah, they're not just investing in our research, but also selling to our farmers."

"Is that so?" Fleischer said. "Anyway, I have confirmation for your appointment with him this morning." She glanced at her watch. "At 10:30." She looked at both of them, a smile playing on her lips. "I had to call in a few favours, but it's lined up. And that's where Bill comes in."

Nguyen waited, raised his eyebrows.

"She'll drive you there. Also—" Fleischer paused, her face expressionless, then sighed and resumed. "This may not sound professional, but Lovell is renowned in this town for having an eye for the ladies." She gestured at Billings. "Having Bill with you should grease the wheels, so to speak. He's likely to loosen up, try to impress."

"But," Bill said, "You know I play for the other team."

"I know. I know." Fleischer said. "But he doesn't know that, does he?"

47

MᴄTᴇɪsʜ ʜᴀᴅ ᴀʀʀᴀɴɢᴇᴅ ᴛᴏ ᴍᴇᴇᴛ Dr Helene Shildduck in her office. There was the slightest lab tang of ammonia in the air. As she sat down she noticed a vase on a credenza against the wall, with pink roses wilting in it.

Shildduck saw the glance. "Hmph. They need replacing. They were fresh the day before Doug died. I haven't got round to getting new ones."

"Understandable," McTeish said.

"What do you mean?"

"Well, with what's happened here. The fact that your boss died on this same floor …"

If this was a concern to Shildduck, there was no trace at all of it in her manner. "What? No, I've just been busy," she said. "Now, what do you want to ask me?"

Her voice held a no-nonsense quality. She was direct and, McTeish sensed, not given to tolerating fools.

"Thanks for seeing me."

"We have a choice?"

McTeish stifled a gasp and ignored the comment. "Was there anything you noticed different about Dr Chen in recent weeks? Anything out of the ordinary?"

Shildduck said, "Out of the ordinary? What do you call ordinary?"

McTeish drew in a deep breath. "Well, there must be some sort of routine, I imagine—"

"Routine? We're scientists. What do you mean routine?" Shildduck halted whatever she was going to say. "Sorry." Her lips formed a smile of sorts. "Of course there was routine. But our routine is often full of ups and downs, depending how the work is going. So often the unexpected happens. And add to that Doug's prickliness. But yes, I suppose we had a routine."

"Did anything unusual happen recently? Outside the, er, ups and downs?"

Shildduck frowned, put her hands on the desk, picked up a pen, then put it down again. "There was something," she said.

McTeish waited.

"No. Not worth mentioning, in the scheme of things."

"What's not worth mentioning?"

"You'll probably read too much into it. Take it out of context."

McTeish said nothing, waited.

"Doug discovered there were attempts to make some sort of recreational drugs in our labs," Shildduck said. "I suppose that was outside the normal routine."

"Recreational drugs? Like what? Did Dr Chen know who did it?" McTeish sat back, her eyes wide.

"Some sort of psychedelic stuff. He thought it was Tamas. You know, going off on some sort of a frolic."

"And was he?"

"Well, yes. Of course he was. You've talked to Tamas?"

McTeish decided she needed to talk to him again. Soon. "I have. I didn't realise he was into things like that."

Shildduck looked at McTeish, shook her head. "He's thirty. Who isn't at that age. Or indeed any age?"

McTeish stared back at her, her mouth open.

"Come on, Constable. Do you mean you've never smoked, or had E at a rave?"

"Smoked? You mean dope?"

"Tobacco contains one of the most addictive drugs known to man—nicotine. Dope has some mood enhancers." She folded her hands in front of stomach, a smile playing on her lips. "And alcohol is one of the most dangerous drugs we know of. I shouldn't have to tell you, a policewoman, that. You lot have to deal with the aftermaths. It just so happens that cigarettes and booze are legal, and so-called recreational drugs aren't—yet. That's changing. The biggest problem with illegal drugs is that they are illegal. Why do you think people use them?"

She answered her own question. "Because they're either self-medicating, deadening pain, or simply having a bit of fun. If drugs were legalised, you'd cut out all the pushers, the bribery, the burglaries, the cramming of our prisons. Instead, people could get medical help."

McTeish kept a straight face. "Did Dr Chen share that view?"

"Do you mean did he think drugs shouldn't be a legal problem? I doubt it. He was very old school."

McTeish regarded Shildduck. She was in her fifties, conservatively dressed in a dark blue suit with white blouse, and did not look like a druggie. And it sounded like she had made that little speech before.

"How did he react?"

"Dr Chen, or Tamas?"

"Dr Chen."

"He didn't like it, Dr Chen. Not at all. In fact, he was angry."

"Did he do anything? I mean, to show his anger?"

"He certainly did. He called a team meeting. Said this sort of thing was not on. It could undermine the research. Did I say he was angry? More like furious. You know what he was like." She eyed McTeish. "Sorry. Of course you don't know. Didn't know him." She corrected herself. "Anyhow, he could be prickly and angry. And sometimes just angry. Then it'd be gone. Till the next time he was under pressure."

"Did he do anything else apart from the team meeting? Did he report it to anyone?"

Shildduck inverted her hands and flexed them. "I'm not sure. He certainly gave me the impression he was going to."

"How so?"

"He said he was going to."

"And how did Tamas react?"

"He didn't. Not in the meeting. Didn't say a word. Waited till Doug calmed down." Shildduck sighed. "Well, he did go a bit pale, I suppose."

McTeish waited, but Shildduck said no more. "When did all this happen? When was the team meeting?"

"Um." Shildduck gulped. "Two days before he died."

McTeish restrained a gasp of excitement. "I'll talk to Mr Kosic again."

"It's Dr Kosic."

McTeish winced. These scientists were so touchy. "Thank you, *Doctor* Shildduck." A thought occurred to her. "Is Dr Kosic here today?"

Shildduck stood up. "Yes. He'll be in his room on the other side of the lab." She stopped, seemed to be arguing with herself. "Please don't mention I told you this."

McTeish also stood up. "Would that be a problem?"

"Of course it'd be a problem. He'll think he's a suspect."

"Why would he think that?"

"Come on, Constable. If Doug had reported Tamas, that could finish his work here." She held out her hand, and McTeish shook it. "If you let him know I told you this, he'll also think that *I* think he's a suspect. Which I don't. Not at all. He's not. Tamas would never, *could* never do something like that."

"Okay," she said. "I don't share what interviewees say, anyhow. So no need to worry. But if what you say is true, it does mean we can't rule Ta—any person out, yet."

Tamas, she thought as she left. Could he have done it? Despite herself, she found she liked him. She pushed that idea away. She'd maintain her professionalism.

48

Dr Tamas Kosic was in his office when McTeish knocked on the open door. He was sitting at his desk, reading a magazine, and looked up. A beaming smile formed when he saw her. "Hi Carol, er, Detective. How are you? Come in." He stood up and came around from behind the desk.

"Hi Tamas. I need to follow up a couple of things. Have you got time now?"

"Always have time for you." Tamas' grin faltered. "Sorry. That came out a bit cheesy. I mean, yes, we can do it now." He grimaced. "Talk now."

"Okay. Shall we—" she indicated the chairs.

"Er, yes. Yes. Right." He sat down on one of the two chairs beside a small coffee table. He immediately stood again and cleared some papers and a book from the table.

McTeish sat opposite. She decided to ask the same question she'd asked Dr Shildduck. She leant forward. "Was there anything you noticed different about Dr Chen in recent weeks? Anything out of the ordinary?"

"Out of the ordinary? In what way?" Tamas wrinkled his brow.

"Anything different crop up? Possibly not work-related?"

"Not work related?" Kosic reddened. "There was something," he mumbled.

"What was that, Tamas?" She deliberately used his first name.

He put his head in his hands. "I, er, did something stupid." He sat up. "I did a little lab work of my own."

"What sort of lab work?"

"In psychedelics, if you must know."

She nodded. "And?"

"Well, when Doug found out he hit the roof. He said he was going to report me."

"Did he report you?"

"I don't know. Oh." He shuddered. "He couldn't have once, once that happened." He folded his arms across his chest. "Oh, no," he muttered. He looked her in the eye. "You don't think—no, there's no way."

"What do you mean?"

"He said he was going to report me. But if you knew Doug, he often said things in the heat of the moment. It doesn't mean he would have actually reported me."

"So what don't I think?"

His face was pale. "I didn't poison him!"

"Okay. Okay. I didn't say you did. But you must realise I have to follow it up."

He brushed his hair from his forehead. "I suppose so." He slumped, then brightened. "Actually, that's good. Yes, please do follow it up. You'll see there's nothing to it." He sat up straighter. "Yes. I'm glad you know about it, it's out in the open. It was a stupid thing to do, and Doug was right to be upset. But really, psychedelics are the future for mental health treatment."

"And you were researching them? Come off it, Tamas."

"I never said that. Many people micro dose. I was just wanting to get some, I mean unadulterated." He stopped. "It was stupid. I don't think Doug would have been too worried, once he thought about it."

McTeish made a note. "Anything else you want to tell me? Anything else Dr Chen was doing differently?"

Kosic sat back, rubbed his chin. "No. Nothing else I can think of."

49

AFTER A DRIVE OF about fifteen minutes in light traffic Billings pulled up outside the tall Howarth-Acfield building, in the former Eli Lilly centre on Belvedere Avenue. They entered the lobby, and were registered at the desk by a large middle-aged man, who rang and confirmed their appointment and issued them with visitor passes.

"The fifteenth floor, Officer," he said to Billings. "Mr Lovell's secretary will meet you."

On the fifteenth floor the doors opened onto a large area, with green plants lining the sides, the whole lit by translucent panels in the ceiling, providing a pleasant slightly yellow light. A young woman with dreadlocks sat at a desk with a computer and keyboard, and no paper in sight.

She stood up when they left the elevator and greeted them. "Detective Nguyen and Officer Billings?"

Billings responded for both of them. "That's us," she said.

"Please come in. Mr Lovell is expecting you." She knocked on a door between two large rubber plants and immediately entered.

A man in his fifties in a pale blue shirt with silver cufflinks came towards them, and shook their hands. He was tall with a barrel chest, chin leading out. Nguyen noticed he had a full head of dark hair with grey streaks that somehow didn't quite match the hair around his ears. The office had a minimalist look, bare of decoration or furnishings apart from a set of chairs and two settees around a large dark wooden coffee table.

"Thank you, Roni. Welcome to Howarth-Acfield, Detective Inspector, and Officer."

"Nice to meet you," Nguyen said.

Lovell held on to Billings' hand for a little longer than necessary, beaming at her. "Please be seated. Roni—" he looked up at his assistant—"have you asked our guests if they'd like refreshments?" She in turn looked questioningly at them both.

"Just water for me, please," Nguyen said.

"I'm good," Billings said.

Roni left, shutting the door behind her.

"Now. How can I help you? Major Fleischer has piqued my curiosity." Before Nguyen could respond, Lovell added, "It's a long way to come all the way from Australia to Baltimore. How long was the flight?" Under his pleasant baritone Nguyen could detect a restrained aggression.

"Just a bit over twenty hours. And thanks for agreeing to see me. As Major Fleischer said, I'm leading an investigation in Australia on the murder of a research scientist in a lab at the Badeker Institute, in Melbourne."

"Yes, that's what she said. And you—" he leaned forward towards Billings. "How are you involved? Indeed, how am I involved, now I come to think of it."

"Mr Lovell," Billings said.

"Fred, please," Lovell said.

"I'm here to provide any assistance Inspector Nguyen needs," she said. "Or any assistance you need from the Baltimore police." She smiled at him. "I'm sure the inspector can explain whatever involvement there might be."

"Howarth-Acfield's involvement is through your funding of research at the Badeker," Nguyen said.

"Ah yes, the Badeker. I've checked our records. We do support a Dr Felix Robertson and his team there. But it wasn't Dr Robertson who was murdered, was it? Or have I been misinformed?"

Nguyen shook his head. "No, as far as I know he's still alive and kicking. It was a colleague of Dr Robertson's—Dr Chen Du. You know of him? He was poisoned in his lab."

"I've heard of Dr Chen. Very sad. Very sad." Lovell took out a handkerchief and dabbed his eyes, put the handkerchief back in his pocket. He stared at Nguyen. "And you think Howarth-Acfield was involved?"

There was a knock on the door and a young man in black shirt and trousers with a white apron entered, bearing a black tray with two glasses of water. He offered one to Nguyen and the other to Lovell, then withdrew.

"What was I saying? Ah yes. What has all this to do with Howarth-Acfield? How does this involve us?"

"Well, you are involved, if only through your investments. We've talked with your colleagues who are currently in Melbourne, Dr Ostarkie and Mr Robarts."

"Our funding is public knowledge. Glad you could talk with Sheila and Frank. I trust they were helpful?"

Nguyen nodded.

"Then, if they were helpful, why come here? Would you normally fly all this way just because a company has put money into a research project?"

"As you would appreciate, this is a serious case. I'm sure you understand my job is to follow up on all sorts of details. And you're right. I wouldn't normally fly to the States for a Melbourne murder." Nguyen paused.

Lovell waited.

"The odd thing is, and this is why I'm checking things out here, is that you employed a Terry Euston, who somehow seems to be involved in all this," Nguyen said.

"Euston?" Lovell sat up in his chair.

"You know him?" Nguyen also sat up. "He says he's a photographer."

"The name does ring a bell."

"Euston says you, Fred, personally hired him, and flew him here from Australia. Three times. Is that so?"

Lovell opened his mouth, shut it, opened it again. "Well ... yes, I do know Mr Euston."

"Would you mind telling me why you employed him?"

"Why, to take photographs." Lovell seemed to relax. "You just said he was a photographer."

"Mr Lovell," Billings said.

Lovell looked at her, smiled. "Fred, please, Officer."

"Fred. I think we'd both of us like to know why you flew this Euston out here three times. Inspector Nguyen has told us there's a lot of suspicious activity he may be involved in, which is why we may have an interest here, too." She smiled at him, eyes wide. Nguyen thought, did she actually flutter her eyelashes at Lovell, or had he imagined it?

"Three times, you say?" Lovell said. "We do use Mr Euston on a range of work. He's very reliable. That's why we use him." He folded his hands across his belly, leaned back.

"What other work does Howarth-Acfield have in Melbourne? I mean, do you involve Euston in other work?" Nguyen said.

"We're not just a pharmaceutical company, Inspector. By no means. We're also one of the largest in the fertiliser business, through our subsidiary FC. You heard of the FC Group?"

"I have heard of FC. What do they do in Australia?"

"We sell a sh—huge load to your farmers. Nitrates and phosphates. Very important for grains and vegetables. We're pioneering stuff that even the organic people use. You could say we're a pharma that deals with farmers." He smiled at them, more like a smirk, Nguyen thought; he clearly had used the line before. "And oddly, contrary to what the uninformed may think, our fertiliser business is far bigger than our pharmaceuticals. Fertiliser is almost a 200 billion dollar industry."

"So CF is bigger than HA, even with the pandemic?" Billings asked.

"The pandemic." Lovell's mouth twisted with displeasure. He leant forward, hands on his knees. "Officer, I don't know how much you know about what goes on in the Swamp—" he paused, looked inquisitively at both Billings and Nguyen. Billings nodded but Nguyen looked blankly at him.

"The Swamp?" Nguyen said.

"Washington." Lovell sighed. "Hasn't been drained yet. Never going to be, either. Give you good odds on that not happening." He stretched back in his chair, put his hands behind his head, a picture of complacency. "Yes, Covid. Let's just say that, for whatever reasons, our candidates for the vaccines weren't given the green light." The complacency had turned to bitterness. "So, no, the pandemic didn't help us, unlike some of our competitors. Of course, if Dr Robertson does what we hope he'll do, then that's another matter. And I still don't understand why you've had to travel here to Baltimore. I mean, why your bosses have paid for you to come here."

"Very simple, Fred. Euston may be the key to Dr Chen's murder."

"In what way? Look, Inspector, I've been very patient. I don't have to talk to you. I'm a very busy man, and you come in here, tell me one of our contractors is the key to a murder? Really." Lovell's tone had become strident.

"The fact is, Fred, you met with this Euston several times. I'm not suggesting you know what he's doing or what he's done, outside what you asked him. But we have to work out what exactly he's been doing. Is that unreasonable?"

Lovell glowered, then in a switch of mood breathed out, smiled, and said, "Of course, Inspector. Not unreasonable. But I think I've helped you as much as I can."

"Thank you for your time," Nguyen said. "But I wonder ..."

Lovell looked at him, his eyes narrowing. "You wonder?"

"I wonder whether you could have someone show me around? I've never been to a pharmaceutical corporation before."

Lovell kept his eyes on Nguyen for a moment or two. "Sure," he said. "Sure. Why not? It'll be my pleasure." He stood up. "I'll get my assistant to make arrangements. Through Officer Billings. Is that okay?"

"Did Euston have dealings with anyone else here at HA?" Billings said.

Lovell rubbed his chin. "Not that I'm aware of. You see, he's an old friend of mine. Someone I trust. That's why I saw him."

"Before, you said the name Euston rang a bell," Billings said. "Now you say he's an old friend. Doesn't that seem strange?"

Lovell glared at her for a moment, then relaxed and said, "I'd have thought it'd be even stranger if a friend's name didn't ring a bell."

"You know what I mean."

Nguyen stood up. "Thank you for your time, Fred," he said. "I'm in town until Thursday, so that'll be great if your assistant can line up a time to see the business. And if I think of some other questions, can I see you before I go?"

Lovell looked up at him, then across at Billings. "I'll get my assistant to make sure I can fit you both in," he said, standing as well. He glanced at Billings again. "You know what?" he said. "I think I'll guide you myself." He beamed at them both.

"Well, thank you. What's a good time for you?" Nguyen asked. "As I said, I'm here till Thursday."

Lovell turned and pressed a button on his desk. A few moments later his assistant entered the room. "Roni—how's my diary? Can I fit in a time tomorrow to show these good people around the place? Say an hour?"

"Just a sec, Mr Lovell." She looked at her phone for a few moments, then looked up. "You could do it at three tomorrow afternoon. I can move a meeting."

"Good. Does that suit you both?" Lovell said.

"Fine by me," Nguyen said.

Billings thought for a moment. "Yes, I can do that," she said.

In the elevator going down, Billings said, "Was that helpful? He didn't seem to give out much info." She glanced at him, grinning. "Was it worth the trip from Australia?"

"Well, it makes me wonder." Nguyen paused, then shrugged. "Why the photographer? What do you think he hired this Euston to do? Could he have paid him to take out Dr Chen? But if so, why? Surely he'd want to keep him alive, if he's investing in the research. How could he or HA benefit from Chen's death?"

"He said their agribusiness is doing better than the pharma side," Billings said. The doors of the elevator opened and they walked to Billings' car.

"Would Chen's research affect the fertiliser business?" Nguyen mused.

"How do you mean?"

"Probably nothing. Ridiculous. But …"

Billings opened the driver's door and got in. "Ridiculous? How so?"

"Nothing." Nguyen got in.

"Back to our office?"

"Thanks."

Billings drove off.

Major Fleischer greeted them at the door—she was leaving as they arrived, but stopped and ushered them in. "Where's Frank?" she asked.

"I'll text him. He's working on the Kansas job, and couldn't join us at HA." Billings keyed her cell phone, while they were sitting down. There was a ping. "He'll join us shortly."

"Good. Let's wait a moment 'till he gets here."

That surprised Nguyen. Commander Forell would wait for no man. No one, in fact.

A moment later, Frank Kapper knocked and entered. "Sorry—I was caught up."

Fleischer indicated a chair for him to sit on, and said, "Well? Get what you want? I must admit I'm now a little bit more curious about your man Lovell."

"There's something going on, that's for sure," Nguyen said. "He knows this guy Euston, says he's a friend, in fact. But it doesn't add up."

"He's taking us on a tour of HA tomorrow afternoon," Billings said.

"He's taking you himself? Not some underling?" Fleischer asked, eyebrows raised.

"Think we have Bill here to thank for that," Nguyen said. "He was about to get someone to do it, but I saw him eyeing Bill. Could almost see his mind ticking over."

"His mind?" Fleischer said with a grin.

"Well, that, too. Anyway, he's taking us at three tomorrow. I asked if we could get to see how it all works."

"Anything else you got from the meeting?"

"Well. He's across the detail of the company's investment in the research lab in Melbourne. Not sure if the President would normally know the names of some of the researchers. But he does."

"And he finally said he paid for this Euston to fly to Baltimore three times," Billings said. "After initially pretending not to know who he was, now he says he's an old friend."

"Hmm," Fleischer murmured.

"Should I come tomorrow?" Kapper said.

Nguyen looked at Fleischer.

"Your call," she said.

"Look, if we want to have Lovell distracted by Bill here, it's probably best you don't come, Frank. But I'll take you up on that offer of dinner tonight, if that's still on the cards."

"You bet. Major, will you join us?"

Fleischer glanced at her desk, shook her head. "Sorry. Can't tonight. Maybe another time." Then to Nguyen, "How long are you here in our fair city? Is it Friday? Saturday?"

"I fly back Friday," Nguyen said.

"Okay. Maybe we can do something Wednesday."

A thought occurred to Nguyen. "By the way, Janne. Maybe I should also get in touch with the FBI. I wonder if they have anything on this Euston or McCauley."

Fleischer stood and gazed out her window across Baltimore, stretching her arms backwards. "My back's a bit stiff," she said. "Standing helps. You think he might be on their radar?"

"Our security people have him in their database. Maybe the FBI does, too. I met a very helpful guy in New York, Harry Brownovski. But that was to do with the mafia."

"The mafia? Are they in Australia?" Fleischer turned from the window and looked at Nguyen.

"They're everywhere, as far as I know. And they sent out a couple of goons on a billion-dollar money skimming scam."

"A billion-dollar scam?"

"I helped put them away," he said.

"Tell us about it," Kapper said.

Nguyen grinned. "With pleasure. Over dinner tonight. Who do you suggest I talk to at the FBI?"

"Let me see," Fleischer said. "It could be to do with Homeland Security if it's just a passport issue—you said he used two different names. Or if it's something else, we can see if the Bureau has anything on him. You could ask your contact in New York. But I'll call Tricia Rooney. She's an assistant SAC."

"SAC?" Nguyen asked.

"Special Agent in Charge—she's one of their seniors here in Maryland. She'll know who's who in the zoo, who you should talk to." Fleischer sat down again. "You must have calls to make. You want a desk to work at?"

"Well, thanks. I was thinking of going back to the hotel. But if you can spare a spot for me, that'd be great."

"Bill. Can you and Frank look after John?" She stood up.

"Thanks, Janne," he said. "I'll keep you to Wednesday night."

"What? Oh yeah. Dinner. Okay."

Billings and Kapper led Nguyen out of Fleischer's office. "We'll take you down to our level," Billings said as they waited for the elevator.

On level four they walked through an open plan section, with small meeting rooms set against the walls. The carpet was dark blue, almost the same colour as the Baltimore Police uniform, and the walls were off-white. The overhead fluorescent lights reminded Nguyen of his building back home.

Kapper said, "We're due to have the lights replaced with LEDs."

"Yeah. Like two years ago," Billings said. "It'll happen—when hell freezes over." She grinned. "Here. You can use this room." She opened a door to a small room with a table, a credenza with a printer on it, and swept a swag of papers off the table and put them on the credenza.

"Here you are. Frank and I are over there. Yell out if you need anything."

"Can I take you guys out for a meal? What time do you eat lunch?"

"I usually just grab a burger or Chinese." He patted his stomach. "Bill on the other hand is picky."

"That's why—" she patted her midriff as Kapper had done—"why I keep healthy."

"And I'm not healthy?" Kapper frowned, then relaxed. "Nah. You're right. I could lose a few pounds."

Nguyen smiled. "Frank, if you think you need to lose a few pounds, you should see some of my colleagues. I don't mean they're ..." He paused. Thought better of what he was about to say. "Let's just say they're not the slim fit things they were when they signed up. You two have nothing to worry about." He had a thought. "Bill, thinking about our tour tomorrow. Would you mind giving Lovell's assistant a call, to confirm arrangements? It's one thing for them to make a time for us, but it would be good to confirm it. Are we meeting at the same building? It'd be better coming from you, don't you think?"

Billings stared at Nguyen for a moment. "You didn't come down in the last shower, did you?"

"What do you mean?" Kapper said.

"I reckon," Nguyen said, "that Roni—that's her name, isn't it?—might attract the same sort of attention from Lovell that Bill here seems to."

Billings grinned. "Roni Peron. I've got her card."

Nguyen returned the grin. "So see if you can have a coffee with her. Who knows what you might learn."

"What?" Kapper said. "What? Oh. Yeah. Yeah."

Billings pinked. "Get with the program, Frank," she said, extracting the card from her wallet.

Kapper said, "You didn't come down in the last shower, either!"

Billings rolled her eyes. "We'll come by in an hour or so."

Billings rang Roni Peron and after confirming the details for the meeting tomorrow at the labs she asked whether she might be free to meet for a coffee.

"You want to meet up?"

"Sure. I want to get up to speed on Howarth-Acfield before we see the labs tomorrow. I thought you might be able to fill me in a bit, so I know what's what."

There was a momentary silence. "Mr Lovell is away from the office tomorrow from about ten till lunch time," she said. "So would eleven suit you?"

"Eleven is good. Thank you. That's so helpful." Billings gave a thumbs up to Kapper and Nguyen.

"You know Blue Moon Too?" Peron said. "It's on Light and Poultney—not far from either of us."

"I know it. Good choice. Funky, hey? See you tomorrow at eleven."

52

"Where should we take John to eat?" Billings asked Kapper.

"I thought you were the gourmet here," Kapper said. "But seeing you're asking, what about …Hang on." He tilted his head towards Nguyen. "Do you want to eat Vietnamese?"

"Whatever. I'm easy. I wouldn't mind seeing what Baltimore does in the way of Pho at some stage. So, I'll shout you another time, if you can recommend something else."

"Shout?" Kapper said.

"An Aussie expression. Means, my treat."

"Shout, eh?" Billings echoed. "Then it's our shout tonight. Is that what you'd say?"

Nguyen nodded.

"If you want Asian, there's a nice place called Ekiben," Kapper said. "But why don't we try Peter's Pour House?"

Billings grinned. "Good idea. You wanna sample some good ol' USA food?"

"Sounds good to me. Why's it called poor house? Is that some local thing? Feeding the poor underpaid police?"

"Spelt P O U R. And they do a good line in beer. Even if it's on Water Street! You gotta try their House Draft. And it's got great burgers and seafood. You like shrimp? Crab?"

"Beer, shrimp and crab will hit the spot," Nguyen said, suddenly feeling famished.

"Okay, Peter's Pour House it is. I'll drive," Kapper said. "One of Baltimore's closely guarded secrets."

✳

Peter's Pour House had polished wood floors, tables with simple wood chairs, and was crowded, with a friendly buzz. They found a table against the wall near the bar, and Kapper went over and ordered the beer. "They're called House Drafts," he said.

Nguyen's eyes widened when three House Drafts arrived: they were 32 oz each. "That … that's a beer, all right!" he said.

"To getting to the bottom of this Howarth-Acfield stuff!" Billings said, raising her glass,

"I'll drink to that," Nguyen said. They clinked their beers and he took a deep mouthful.

After perusing the menu, Nguyen ordered the Jumbo Delight over a Caesar salad, Billings the Sword Fish Platter with a garden salad and Kapper the hot Roast Beef. They ordered a separate serving of fries.

"You both originally from Baltimore?" Nguyen asked.

"Born and bred," Billings said.

"My mom, yes," Kapper said. "My dad, he's a Scot. Came out here as a backpacker, and stayed. Suspect my mom had something to do with that." Kapper's mouth creased in a smile. "Not someone you want to mess with."

"A Scot," Billings guffawed. "You never told me that!"

"Och, I nae had reason to," Kapper said in an unmistakable Scots accent.

"Frank!" Billings' eyes gleamed in delight. "Can you say more like that?"

"I wouldna want to," he said.

"Love it! Oh, wait till the guys hear about this."

"Dinna fash yersel." He broke off. "It's a long time since I've done that," he said in his regular Baltimore twang. "Let's keep this to ourselves, eh, Bill?"

She laughed, her cheeks dimpling. "You do learn something new every day." She coughed. "Hang on—Kapper doesn't sound particularly Scottish," she said.

"Dad went to live there as a kid."

"Right. Right. So he became a sort of Scot? And you, John?" she said, containing her humour. "You grew up in Melbourne?"

Nguyen regarded the two with amusement. Billings even more sparkling, Kapper a picture of suavity, both stifling grins. "Yep. My folks were boat people from Vietnam." Billings and Kapper simultaneously gave a muffled "Oh!" And simultaneously shut their mouths.

"They arrived in Australia in 1980. Don't worry," he said, seeing their expressions of concern, "This was before the huge fear of refugees was stirred up. In fact, they must have been amongst the last to come by boat. Those that survived, I mean. After that, most of the rest came by plane. So my folks, arriving by boat—it's a sort of badge of honour." He sipped his beer, thinking about it. "Yes, they had me, once they arrived. I was born and went to school in Melbourne."

"And joined the police? How did that happen?" Billings asked.

Nguyen regarded the two of them. "I suppose the usual sort of thing." He sighed. "One time, when I was a teenager, maybe thirteen, maybe fourteen, me and some mates were getting a bit of stick from a few skips, er Aussie boys. You know, telling us gooks to get back where we came from—with the help of some fists. Pretty amusing, when you think about it. The kids were probably balts or wogs."

"Balts or wogs?" Billings said.

Both she and Kapper were frowning, eyes wide in puzzlement.

"People from Europe," Nguyen said. "Balts were from the Baltic states, Latvia, Lithuania, and the wogs were from Italy or Greece. Aussie slang. What used to be called New Australians. It was funny they, the New Australians, were abusing me, the newer Australian. I'm sure you both know what I'm talking about—copping abuse from people."

They nodded. Kapper shook his head, sighed.

"Anyhow, these guys were taking it a bit too far—did I mention fists? And the odd boot? Fortunately for me a cop turned up, maybe middle-aged. He gave them an earful, and a bit of their own stick back. From what my parents said, that's not what police in the home country would've done, you know? Anyhow, it sowed the seed. I wanted to be like him, like that cop." He drank some more beer, shook his head, and looked into their eyes, one to the other. "How long have you guys been in the force?" he asked.

"Five years for me," Billing said.

"Same," Frank said. "We trained together."

"And now you work together, a team?"

"Not always, but the last year." They both glanced at each other.

"What?" Nguyen saw the exchange.

"Bill gets some flak from a few of the unreconstructed chauvinists. I've got her back."

"Frank! I can look after myself," she growled.

"Course you can. Just sayin'." Kapper drank some beer.

"Hmmph."

"Speaking of which, how did Ms Roni sound, when you called her?" Nguyen asked, his lips twitching.

Billings glared at him for a moment, then she softened into a grudging smile. "You Aussies don't miss much, do you?"

"Some of us don't. Some of my colleagues down under—" he shook his head. "Uh uh. Some of 'em are pretty unreconstructed too."

Billings sighed. The three sat for a moment, sipping their beers. Billings looked up, put her glass down, her eyes now sparkling again. "Tell us about this billion-dollar mafia job you mentioned,"

And Nguyen outlined the Y2K issue. "You're both too young to remember, but in 1999 people feared that banks would collapse, planes fall out of the sky. Because the old computer code had the year in the last two digits only, so no one knew what would happen when January1, 2000 came around. Would the computers switch to 2000, or 1900?" Seeing their expressions, Nguyen said, "True! Everyone was worried. Nothing happened, of course. But that's because all the IT guys worked flat out to fix the computer code. And that's where the scam came in."

Nguyen took another mouthful of beer. "A clever coder working for a bank devised a little side hustle. With the code revisions he set it up so for every transaction including less than a cent, the fraction of a cent was skimmed off to another account. Who would notice? It seems that no one did. With hundreds of thousands of transactions a day, over twenty years more than a billion dollars was creamed off. That's what got the mafia interested."

Billings and Kapper sat wide-eyed.

"And you were involved in this?" Billings said.

"We had a murder mystery. An unknown dead guy, who turned out to be the key to what we called The Millennium Job, back in Oz." Nguyen went on to describe the case.

"Wow," Kappa said. "You must be a bit of a hero. No wonder you got okayed to fly here."

"Well, actually, the whole thing was sort of kept under wraps. There were a few embarrassing aspects, you understand. So not much actually hit the media."

Their food arrived, and they fell to eating.

"Know much about Baltimore? I mean before you came?" Kapper asked.

"I watched *The Wire*," Nguyen said. "One of my colleagues did mention a few famous names to me, like Billie Holliday, who came from Baltimore. How accurate was *The Wire*? Did that, does that, sort of stuff still happen here?"

"I think I can confidently say we're still close to being the crime capital of America," Kappa said with a lopsided grin. "And *The Wire* was right about one thing—the street people were just the foot soldiers. It went right up to the highest levels."

"Hey. The force is pretty clean, now," Billings said. "Well, as clean as any police force can be. *The Wire* got people talking. Actually helped fix a lot of things. But as my grandma says, where there's opportunity, there's always people to profit from it. Like maybe our friend Fred Lovell."

"You say you saw *The Wire*," Kapper said. "I'm a bit of a film buff. Did you ever see *Serial Mom*—with Kathleen Turner? That's also set in

Baltimore. Or *12 Monkeys?* Or *Hairspray?* Hitchcock's *Marnie? Sleepless in Seattle?* All Baltimore."

"Jesus, Frank. Isn't *Sleepless in Seattle* set in—Seattle?" Billings said.

"Yeah, but Annie Reed, the love interest, works on the *Baltimore Sun*." He sat back, sipping his beer and picking up some fries.

"I could mention some films set in Melbourne," Nguyen said.

"Would anyone know them outside Australia?" Billings asked, a twinkle in her eye.

"How about *On The Beach?*"

"Hey, that's the one about the end of the world, isn't it?" Kapper said. "With Fred Astaire and Ava Gardner, after some nuclear accident, or war. The apocalypse. Didn't it also have Gregory Peck and that guy in Psycho, Anthony Perkins?"

"That's the one. There's a story that Ava Gardner said Melbourne was the best place to set a film about the end of the world. Turns out, though, she never said it. Made up by some Aussie journo."

"What, he put down his own town?" Billings said.

"It got what he was after—he got his interview published. In fact, it turns out Ava Gardner didn't even do the interview. He made it all up." He drank some more beer. "Have you heard of *Romper Stomper*, or *Animal Kingdom* or *Kenny?*"

Kapper shook his head.

"*Romper Stomper* was one of Russell Crowe's first movies. Put him on the map. What about *Mad Max*, then?"

"Even I've seen *Mad Max*," Billings said.

"Wait a minute," Kapper squinted in thought. "Come on. Isn't it set in a desert?"

"Well, yes, of course. But it was actually shot in Melbourne. But you're right, there's a host of Aussie movies set in Melbourne that no one knows outside Australia." Nguyen took another sip of his beer. Almost ready for a second one. "Did you know Melbourne was the heart of film making in Australia? The first feature ever made, anywhere, was made in Melbourne." He sat back, finishing his glass.

"That'd be *The Story of the Kelly Gang*, wouldn't it? Made in 1906." Kapper said.

Billings looked at Kapper in amazement. "No way. How the fuck do you know that?"

"Did film studies before deciding to join up." Kapper formed a loose fist with his right hand and blew across the knuckles.

Billings turned to Nguyen. "Jesus, are you a film buff too?"

"Not at all," Nguyen said, shaking his head. "I do watch the odd movie though. Wouldn't call me a buff. Not like Frank here." He picked up his glass. "Anyone want another?"

53

Promptly at eleven Billings entered Blue Moon Too, and saw Roni Peron already seated. She looked up and waved at her.

"Hello, Bill," she said in a low mellow voice. "How can I help?" She was maybe ten years older than her, and her dreadlocks framed a face with a broad smile.

"Thanks for coming out to see me," Billings said. "Your boss doesn't mind you leaving the office?"

Peron gave a slight frown, just for a split second, then relaxed. "What he don't know he won't worry about. And I'm always in touch." She held up her phone.

Billings decided to be direct. "I noticed he paid particular attention to me, yesterday. He's partial to the ladies?"

Peron blinked. "Now, Officer, how can you expect me to comment on a statement like that? I will say that there are certain men you gotta be careful around. You and anyone else halfway attractive. Know what I mean?" She grinned broadly. "But you surely didn't ask to see me to ask about the peccadilloes of Mr Lovell."

"Seems to me he was trying to peck a—trying to be nice and friendly with me, yesterday. And you being particularly striking yourself, I thought you might have a few tips for me."

Peron burst out laughing. "Anything in a skirt can arouse a certain reaction in some types of men, as I'm sure you know as well as me. Note, I don't saying nothing 'gainst Mr Lovell. He can look after hisself. As I'm sure you can, too." She rolled her eyes. "A few of my predecessors maybe had to learn—the hard way." She chuckled. "Me? I don't take nothing from nobody. You'd surely know, too, being a police, that with a bully—and mind, I'm talking generally, woman to woman, not mentioning anyone in particular—the only way to deal with a bullying type is to stand up to them. Man or woman, makes no difference." She broke off. "We order at the bar. "What'll you have? A coffee?"

"I'll get it," Billings said.

"No way, Bill. It's on HA."

Billings nodded. "You sure? Thanks. With a drop of cream. No sugar."

Peron went over and ordered for them, returned and sat down. "They'll bring them over. Now where were we?"

"I was going to ask you about Howarth-Acfield, but first check you weren't getting any untoward attention." She twitched her lips. "You've made that situation clear."

Peron grimaced. "I know how to look after myself."

"How long have you been working with Mr Lovell?"

Peron thought a moment. "Just over a year. Now, what's it about HA you want to ask? What's the interest, anyways?"

"The cop from down under, Inspector Nguyen, who brought me along yesterday. He's investigating a murder back in Australia."

Peron gasped. "A murder? What in all that's holy has that got to do with Baltimore, and what's a murder got to do with us at HA?"

"Seems HA invested in a research lab—where the murder took place. So Inspector Nguyen's following up. And I'm providing whatever help he needs."

A young man with shaved sides to his head brought their coffees. "Anything else," he said, "just order at the counter."

"Thanks," Peron said, then turned to Billings. "Seems a long bow," she said, taking a sip. "I mean, to come all the way here, from Australia. You do know HA invests all over the world."

"Yes, but there's a particular reason. There could be a connection with a guy your boss employed, a bit of a shady character, it seems. He could be somehow associated with the whole business."

Peron sat up straight. "Shady character? Who's that?"

"A guy name of Euston. Know anything about him?" Billings tasted her coffee. Her eyes sparkled. "This is good stuff!"

"Ah, Terry Euston," Peron sighed. "The boss deals with him." She broke off, then grinned. "Shady character is right. He's a bit of a sleaze, too. But murder? How's he fit in with murder?"

"He's a person of interest. He was photographing protests outside the lab, the one in Australia where the scientist got poisoned."

"Protests? Why would there be protests about a science lab? And what's that got to do with HA?"

Billings thought a moment about what John Nguyen had said. "The protests were about GM food. Seems the scientist was researching about that. And Mr Euston was photographing it all—for Mr Lovell."

"Well." Peron took a deep breath. "That's news to me. How did Mr Lovell take it when you all talked to him?"

"He seemed to brush it off." Billings sipped and set her cup down. "And to tell the truth, there might be nothing in it. It may be pure coincidence. But as I'm sure you know, we police always take an interest in coincidences."

"So," Peron drawled, lengthening the word. "You want to grill me about my boss?" Her face was expressionless.

Billings shook her head. "No way. Nothing like that, Roni. I just wanted to know if you knew anything about this Euston guy. Or why Mr Lovell would want him to photograph protests in Melbourne."

Peron sat quietly for a while. "Can't say I can help you there," she finally said.

"Could you at least let me know if Euston crops up again? Even if he phones or e-mails?"

Peron sat still.

"As I say, he's a person of interest," Billings said. "And it would be helping the investigation. For all we know whatever Euston did in Melbourne has nothing to do with HA—apart from taking photos. And maybe nothing to do with the murder." Billings looked Peron in the eye. "But if Euston is involved, it's him we're interested in. You would be helping protect Mr Lovell." She finished her coffee.

"So, you want me to let you know if Euston calls."

"That's it. No need to do anything else. And, let's keep this just between us, if that's okay."

"You mean not tell Mr Lovell?"

"Look, because he's friendly with Euston, it's best not to mention this to him—he'd just as likely get upset. Of course, if we discover Euston *is* involved, that's different." She regarded Peron, who after a moment shrugged.

"Okay, I guess," she said.

Billings thought she'd try another tack. "You know, Roni. You need to think of yourself, too."

"How do you mean?" Peron fidgeted with her hands.

"What if your boss, Mr Lovell, and I'm just saying what if. But what if there is more going on? That there is something that Euston is doing that's, shall we say, not completely above board."

"I don't know what you mean," Peron muttered.

"I'm just saying you need to look after yourself. In case things go pear-shaped. For instance, is there anything you can tell me or find out about what HA is doing with wheat, and how that relates to HA's fertiliser business?"

"The fertiliser business?"

"Mr Lovell did mention that since HA missed out on some Covid contracts, the fertiliser business is now more important than the pharmaceutical side."

"Well, yes. If that's what he said. But I can't talk about company business. You know that."

"I'm not asking you to. Just to keep an eye out on anything to do with Euston that seems suss. As I said, it might have nothing to do with your boss, and it could protect him. Or if it does have anything to do with him, you need to protect yourself."

Peron looked steadily at Billings, then smiled. "Understood. I'll let you know if Euston calls. Or if I hear anything."

Billings smiled back. "Feel like a drink some time? I mean after work?"

Peron raised her hand to her mouth, then lowered it to reveal a grin. "Sure. When do you suggest?"

"Whenever it suits. Give me a call."

54

On Tuesday morning Nguyen decided to call Melbourne. He checked his watch: 11:44 am. It would be 9:44 pm in Melbourne. Never mind. Nguyen sat down at the table, took out his phone and called McTeish. The phone rang twice.

"Boss? What's happening?"

"I was about to ask you the same thing. I haven't woken you up, have I?"

"Just making some notes. Had an interesting talk with the research guy, Tamas. But, how was your flight? Have you gone to Howarth-Acfield yet?"

"The flight was okay. Even got a bit of sleep. And I met up with Fred Lovell yesterday morning, helped by a young policewoman a bit like you." He outlined how Lovell had finally admitted he and Euston were friends. "Major Fleischer is checking with an FBI contact to see if they know anything about him. Which reminds me—have you heard back from the Feds about him?"

"Not yet." McTeish clicked her tongue.

"And your interview?"

"Yeah. Tamas wasn't quite as open as I thought he'd been. Seems he'd had an altercation with Dr Chen."

"About what?"

"About an illegal drugs lab or something." McTeish laughed. "An amateur lab. Seems Dr Chen discovered Tamas had brewed himself a little concoction."

"Jesus!" Nguyen said. "He was making drugs?"

"Strictly for his own use, he said."

"That throws a different light on things."

"Do you think that could be a reason to knock Chen off?" she asked.

"It's possible. You'd have to keep him on the suspects list."

"But, I dunno, I'm not sure. He doesn't seem the type."

"The type?" Nguyen smiled. "Carol, you'll learn there's no such thing as a type, when it comes to murder. Anyone, if pushed, can do it. Hulking brutes, little old ladies. Kids, geriatrics." He stopped. "Don't let Hollywood influence your judgement."

McTeish was silent for a moment, then said, "Sorry, Boss. I just didn't think …"

"Yeah, well the force is littered with 'didn't thinks'." He paused, sensing McTeish being mortified. "Don't worry. We've all done that."

"Even—" she started to say, then shut up.

"Yes, even me." He thought of a moment. "It goes with another bias we're prone to—when you're sure one suspect is the guilty party, you focus on that, and ignore other leads that could have taken you to the real killer. Again, we've all been guilty of that."

"So you think Kosic could be the killer? That he poisoned his boss, Dr Chen?"

"No so fast, Carol. He could be. He might not be. Let's not rule him out just yet, okay?"

"Got it, boss. Does that also mean you're not ruling out Lovell, or Euston?"

Nguyen smiled. "You've got it." He thought a moment. "Let's set up a zoom meeting with Brothers. I want to hear where you've got to."

"Sure thing. Early tomorrow morning will be good. Graham was talking to Lucy Bottega, so he'll be able to update you."

"Thanks, Carol." Nguyen hung up.

55

On Tuesday afternoon Nguyen experienced Fred Lovell in tour guide mode, showing Billings and him HA's facilities in Baltimore. He strode ahead of them, with his assistant Roni bringing up the rear, recording on her phone any notes he wanted.

There were a series of labs, each much like the others, all brightly lit, full of benches, computers, sinks and devices that looked a little like domestic washing machines, all with a low-level background hum, and a whiff of some sort of detergent in the air. Clearly Lovell hadn't been there for a while, in that he asked the lab managers what they were doing, then stood back, usually next to Billings.

One lab was researching mRNA delivery systems, he said. The lab manager, who Lovell introduced after peering at her name tag, was Dr Sevara Usmanova, a tall slender woman in regulation white coat. "Tell them about mRNA," Lovell said.

Usmanova sighed, her attitude long-suffering, as if she had to demean herself to explain scientific complexities to civilians.

"Is your family originally Ukrainian?" Nguyen asked.

Usmanova looked at him directly for the first time, then sighed again. "Yes. So?" She paused, took a breath and looked around the lab. "About the mRNA, the m stands for messenger, and RNA is, well, RNA."

"Ribonucleic Acid," Nguyen and Billings said simultaneously.

"You know it?" She frowned.

"Well of course. We are police, you know. We do DNA tests, and increasingly RNA is a factor," Nguyen said.

"What do *you* do with the mRNA?" Billings asked.

"Well, mRNA is a single stranded molecule of RNA." She paused.

They nodded.

"It corresponds to the genetic sequence of a gene. The m or messenger is a way of transferring the desired proteins in a vaccine, for example, into the appropriate part of the body."

"Let's not get too technical, uh, Sevara," Lovell interrupted.

"Very well." She stopped, turned on her heel. Lovell nodded and led the way out of the lab.

The next lab was testing eye drops on white mice. The next was experimenting on refining prednisolone. "We're well known for our cortisone range," Lovell said. "It's a glucocorticoid medication." The term rolled off his tongue. He was looking at Billings as he said it, clearly expecting some puzzled question. "But you have to be careful using it. It does tend to suppress the immune system."

"I thought it was an anti-inflammatory," Billings said. "I got prescribed it for a sprained ankle."

"Anti-inflammatory, it certainly is. But it helps with many, many things. Asthma, for example."

They took a lift to the next floor, and into another brightly-lit lab humming with background noise. A large vat fed a line of vials slowly moving along a conveyor. Lovell introduced Dr Travis Curtis, a stocky man with a large beard, also in white coat.

"This is for clinical trials," Curtis said. "We mix the particular medicine we're researching in the vat, then it's sucked up and injected into the vials. Sometimes it's just a placebo in the vat."

"It's great for a clinical trial," Lovell interjected. "Not for mass production, though. We have that done in China."

"What's the reason you're investing in wheat?" Billings asked. "It seems a lot different to what you've shown us."

"Oh, this is just a small part of what we do."

"But, wheat?"

"We do have a substantial business in fertilisers. Very substantial." He eyed Billings with a raised eyebrow. "Wheat fits in there."

"How do you mean?"

"That lab down under, where that scientist was killed. They were researching how to make wheat more productive. And our fertiliser business is about the same thing. How to make farmers more productive with the wheat and other grains they grow."

After they returned to police headquarters, Nguyen bowed out of any evening activity, pleading jetlag.

56

OSTARKIE CALLED OLGA PENRITH and arranged to meet with Kosic and Shildduck, at their lab at the Badeker. After they'd made their way there Ostarkie and Robarts halted briefly outside the lab beforehand. "We need to sign these guys up," Ostarkie said.

Robarts blinked. "You think they'll go against what Dr Chen wanted?"

"My bet is they'll want to keep working. Olga made it plain it would be too hard to apply for new research funding from their national body. Apparently it'd take at least a year. The Badeker can't afford to carry them both for that time."

"You mean Chen's funding died with him?"

"No. Not at all. His money's there for a time, but if they're serious, the work will need to go on longer. They'll need us, if they think about it. And that's why our offer should prove attractive."

Robarts shook his head. "I hope you're right," he said.

"Of course I'm right. Now," she paused a moment. "How about you get Dr Shildduck to explain the research a bit—get her energised. Then I'll put the offer."

He nodded. "Okay."

She opened the door and they entered. She looked around; there was no one in the lab. "Strange," she muttered. She checked her watch. It was 10:30 am.

At that moment Dr Shildduck put her head out of her office. "Ms Ostarkie? Mr Robarts?" she said.

"Dr Ostarkie." Robarts nodded.

"Please come in." She indicated her office. "Dr Kosic is here, too."

They entered Shildduck's office. Kosic stood up and shook their hands. Both scientists wore white lab coats. They all sat around the coffee table.

"Sorry it's a bit cramped," Shildduck said. "How can we help?"

Ostarkie cleared her throat. "Thanks for seeing us so promptly," she said. "We want to talk to you both about funding. Howarth-Acfield would like to see your research continue."

Robarts sat back, watching the two scientists as Ostarkie spoke.

"Of course we're continuing our research," Shildduck said. "We have the funding from Dr Chen's grant."

"But that will run out, won't it?" Ostarkie eyed the two. "We want to offer you something along the lines we currently fund Dr Robertson's team."

"You do know," Kosic said, "that Dr Chen didn't want to be tied to you, or to any pharma? He wanted the IP to be available for everyone."

"A reasonable point of view," Ostarkie said. "But as you both know, regardless of whether the IP is in the public domain or privately held, the big question is who pays for putting the research into practice. If we help fund you, you have the backing of HA."

"All very well and good," Shildduck said. "Why should we change what our late leader agreed?"

"That's what we'd like to discuss." She paused and watched them as they sat there, Shildduck relaxed but with a calculating look in her eyes, and Kosic with his arms across his chest. "We know your approach is different to Felix's team. Who knows who will prove successful? HA shares your vision, Dr Chen's vision. We want to make sure that more productive wheat is produced.

"So you're saying our funding will run out?"

"You both know that national research council grants run for a specific time. We can both supplement the existing money. Plus we can extend it."

At the mention of the word supplement Kosic sat up. "How do you mean?" he said.

Shildduck said, "Relax, Tamas. They'll tell us." She grinned. "Won't you?"

"We will if you're interested. If you're not—" she shrugged. "Your bad luck. Entirely up to you."

"Could I ask a question," Robarts said. "I'm Vice President of Research at HA. Could you tell me a little of where you're at?"

"That will depend whether we want to discuss your offer further. And," Shildduck smiled again, "we don't really have an offer to discuss, do we? Just some generalities."

"That's right," Ostarkie said. "Would it make it easier if we signed an NDA? If your work ends up in the public domain, we'll know about it then, anyway. If you agree to fill us in with some detail, we'll be able to give a much more specific offer for you to consider." She paused, then continued. "For example, we envisage that you, Dr Shildduck, will take over as lead. Do you have enough resources? Do you need to hire anyone else? Another scientist, I mean? Do you need more computing power? These are all things HA can help you with."

Shildduck and Kosic exchanged glances.

"An NDA would be useful," Shildduck said.

Robarts produced papers from a folder and passed them across the table. "Have a read of this. Sign it later once you've had a chance to read it, if you're happy with it. No pressure."

"An NDA is well enough—but what if what we tell you enables you to get someone else to do our work?"

Robarts let out a hiss of exasperation. Ostarkie intervened before he could speak. "Of course—but wouldn't that mean we'd just have to find some other researchers? Much easier to fund you."

Now it was Shildduck's turn to voice exasperation. "That's true—if we decide to accept your funding. If we don't. You'll have some knowledge, to point some other researcher in the direction we're exploring."

Robarts blew out his lips. "Okay. Point taken." He grimaced. "That's why we much prefer to go with you lot." He stared intently at

Shildduck. "Are you sure, in this great wide world we inhabit, there's not some other researchers doing just what you're trying to do?"

Shildduck shrugged. "Anything's possible."

"Look—we know from what Olga's told us, and our work with Dr Robertson, and indeed our earlier discussions with Dr Chen, that you're looking at the wheat genome," Robarts said. A thought seemed to occur to him. "That's why the Greenies are protesting, isn't it? They know you're trying to do something with wheat. In fact, I seem to recall that Dr Chen, and Dr Robertson, told them exactly that."

"Well, of course," Shildduck said.

"We're not asking for all the nitty gritty—that can wait till after you decide to go with us. Just an indication."

"Well," Shildduck said again, then paused a moment. "It *is* common knowledge—at least among people like us—that plants developed photosynthesis by somehow taking over the mechanism bacteria use, and they've been doing that for more than a billion years. You know the British magazine *New Scientist*? It had a piece more than a decade ago that put it well, and I remember it because that is what Doug said led him to his work. It was about how, for all the complexity that plants have evolved since then, they are still powered by the same engine they've had from that time a billion years ago. It made the comparison of building a modern aircraft carrier and powering it with a Victorian steam engine. So what we're doing is updating that motor, if you like."

Robarts twitched his lips. "Yes, yes. That much we certainly do know. And you're working on the mechanism the cyanobacteria evolved, the mechanism that is so much more productive than photosynthesis, trying to put that mechanism into wheat. As is Dr Robertson and his team."

"Yes, exactly." Shildduck nodded. "We'll read the NDA. If we agree, we can then go into the detail of our particular approach. As you know, it's quite different to what Dr Robertson is doing." She picked up one of the copies of the NDA. "When do you want us to get back to you?"

"How much time do you need?" Ostarkie said.

"Tamas and I will discuss this." She glanced at Kosic, who gave a thumbs up. "I'll give you a call later today."

AFTER OSTARKIE AND ROBARTS had left, Shildduck skimmed through the NDA. "This all looks pretty straightforward," she said to Kosic, "but we'll need to read it in detail later."

"Sure," Kosic said.

"The important thing is, what do we do? What do you think? Should we sign it?"

"Ah…"

"Should we accept more funding?" Shildduck interrupted. "Should we let HA own our IP?"

"Doesn't the Badeker already own a chunk, even if it became publicly available?" Kosic said. "And we do, too. I mean I've only got 0.5 percent, and you must have a bit more. Where does Doug's share go now? To his partner? I suppose if the IP is in the public domain, available to anyone, then none of us gets anything."

"Sorry, I interrupted you before. What do you reckon about HA?"

"I … my impulse is to go with it."

"Same," Shildduck said. "But we should get some advice."

"Leslie Smithson?"

Shildduck laughed. "You've got to be joking. He would just represent the Badeker."

Kosic nodded. "Right. Right. Do you know anyone we can talk to?"

"The uni has a good lawyer. He advised Doug and me a couple of years ago, when we were negotiating with the Badeker. What was his name? Reynolds, I think. I hope he's still there."

"Shouldn't we work out what we want to do before we talk to a lawyer? What do you want?"

Shildduck sighed. She rubbed her eyes. "You know what? If everything lines up, I think I'd go with Howarth-Acfield. At least in the short term we'd get more money, now, if that is part of what they're offering. Plus if HA licences the work—I know that's getting ahead of ourselves, but assuming we pull this off, that it all works out, we should also be able to get a share of royalties." She folded her hands in her lap, looked across at Kosic. "Still—it's a long way off. Could be three to four years. And Dr Chen's grant won't last that long. So any extra money will not only be welcome, but probably essential if we're to keep going." She scratched her wrist, gazing at the table, then looked up at Kosic. "And you?"

"I'll go with whatever you decide. Some extra money now wouldn't go astray. And extra royalties—do you think that's possible?"

"That's where the lawyer should help us."

57

Brothers knocked on Lucy Bottega's door, and before he could finish a second rap it opened. Bottega had a coat on, white with large red spots. She didn't smile, but her eyes widened in recognition.

"Hello, Sergeant." She shook his hand. "I was just going out. What brings you here?"

"I have a couple of questions," Brothers said. "Do you have a moment to talk now?"

She appeared indecisive, then smiled with her mouth, almost a grimace. "Yes, of course. Come in. I was just going to the shops. That can wait." She paused, gazing at him for a time. "What's happened? Do you have any news?" She stood to one side and ushered him in down the hall to the living room, and they sat.

"I'm just following up on a few things."

"Yes?" She looked at him, leaning forward in her chair. "Oh. Excuse me. Would you like a glass of water, or a cup of tea?"

"No. I'm good." Brothers opened his note book. "Look, I want to make sure I understand a couple of things." He flipped back some pages. "Ah, here we are." He looked up; Bottega sat waiting, her mouth slightly open. "You said earlier that Dr Chen wasn't argumentative. But from people we've talked to, it seems that wasn't true, was it? Clearly he was very prickly. And argumentative."

Bottega sat back, her shoulders slumping. After a moment she said in a small voice, "He wasn't argumentative with me. Just with others." She glanced at him taking notes. "Only argumentative if he disagreed with them."

"So, he *was* argumentative?"

"He didn't really mean anything by it. I just didn't want to paint a bad picture of him. I'm sorry if I misled you."

"That's okay." He flipped back through some more pages, and looked up at her. "And you said you didn't think he was having an affair."

"An affair?" Her face froze.

"With Yasmin."

"It was just flirting." She folded her arms across her chest.

Brothers said nothing for a while, just looked at her, then said, "It wasn't just flirting, was it, Ms Botttega? Did you discuss it with Dr Chen?"

Bottega opened her mouth, seemingly about to say something, then closed it. She sighed, her mouth sagging. "Oh, you may as well know. We had a flaming row about it."

"Argumentative?"

"No," she said loudly. "Not argumentative. A row. A fight. Almost." She sat back. "He said he'd stop."

"And did he?"

"Did he what?" Her face was ashen.

"Stop the affair."

She heaved a sigh, shrugged her shoulders. "Yes," she muttered. "He said he'd stopped it."

"What was that?" Brothers said.

"He said he'd stopped!" Bottega cried out. She put a hand to her mouth, sat up straight.

Brothers made another note. He looked up. "When was this?"

She wiped her eyes. "Let me see." She gritted her teeth. "A week before he died."

Brothers wrote some more in his notebook, then asked, just above a murmur, "Did you talk to Yasmin about it?"

"No." She sat up straight. "I didn't see her before—" she broke off, took a deep breath, shut her mouth tight, sighed again. "Before he died. There was no point mentioning it afterwards."

58

Back at the station Brothers and McTeish compared notes, sitting at their adjoining desks. McTeish set up the Zoom meeting and Nguyen joined them. He was seated at a desk in an office—he could have been in Melbourne.

"G'day," Nguyen said.

"How are things in Baltimore?" Brothers asked.

"Good, good. Very helpful, the Baltimore police. As Carol has probably told you, they helped me meet with the Howarth-Acfield CEO yesterday morning."

"Any joy?" Brothers asked.

"Not a great deal yet. But certainly confirmed there's something really suss about the Euston guy—Carol, you were going to chase up the Feds about him?"

"I've put in a call to Gershon. He said he'd get back when he could," she said

"Well, it's clear Euston is well-known to Lovell, the CEO, who by the way I saw again this afternoon. Got a guided tour of some of the HA labs." Nguyen stretched his arms behind his back. "How's the team going?"

"The team's going well," Brothers said. "Looks like our good Dr Chen was a bit of a naughty boy. He *was* having an affair with Yasmin Lee. And Lucy Bottega was pretty angry about it."

"Mmm," Nguyen said. "I wonder what her partner, I mean Yasmin's partner, thought of that? It's Simon, isn't it?"

"Simon Lee." Brothers rubbed his chin. "He seemed a bit dismissive when he talked to me about it. Said she was just flirting, that Yasmin is a flirt. Does it with everyone." He paused a moment.

Nguyen asked, "Is that how Lucy described it? Just flirting?"

"Yes, more or less—well at first. Then she admitted they had a..." Brothers consulted his notebook, "*a flaming row. A fight.* And this was a week before he was killed."

"So, what about Simon Lee?" McTeish said. "He didn't mind at all?"

There was silence as the implication sank in.

"Good one, Carol. Good point," Nguyen said. "Graham, can you speak to Lee again? Maybe he's the jealous hubby. That could be enough to make him want to get his nibs out of the picture, eh?"

"Could well be a motive," Brothers said.

"Can't rule him out," McTeish said.

"Speaking of which," Nguyen said. "What about our Dr Kosic? Have you had time to let Graham know?"

"No—I thought we'd discuss it now. Not sure if it makes him a likely. But certainly keeps him on the list."

"Oh?" Brothers raised an eyebrow. "What's he done?"

McTeish quirked her lips. "Tamas was also a bit of a naughty boy. He was concocting some psychedelics in the lab, and Dr Chen found out."

"Jesus."

"Threatened to report him. And this was a day before he was poisoned."

"Well." Brothers shook his head, rubbed his eyes. "That certainly gives us a motive, too."

"It does. But I wonder," McTeish said. "Agreed he stays on the list." She thought of Nguyen's comment to her earlier: *He could be. He might not be. Let's not rule him out just yet.* "It's just..." She broke off.

"Just?" Nguyen said.

"Nothing. You're right. What you said last night on the phone, Boss. You're right. What was I thinking? He's on the list."

"So," Nguyen said. "We can add him with Euston. And Simon Lee. And Lucy Bottega."

"Bottega?" Brothers said. "Of course. Jealous wife, er, partner. Yes, she can't be ruled out either. So, what's that…" He counted on his fingers. "Four suspects—so far." He grinned, eyes gleaming. "It's all starting to come together."

"Come together?" McTeish said in a sort of squeak. "Seems it's going everywhere. Instead of just that creep Terry McCauley, or Euston, or whatever name he's going under now. How is that coming together?"

"Instead of having no clue whatsoever, we now have a list we can narrow down." Nguyen's face on the monitor broke into a grin. "Anything else?" He waited a moment, and neither Brothers nor McTeish spoke. "Okay, then. Why don't the two of you follow up with Dr Kosic and Simon Lee. And maybe talk to Yasmin again. And taking Carol with you might get more information from Lucy Bottega. All good?"

They both nodded.

"Talk soon." He left the meeting.

At which point McTeish's phone rang; she glanced at it. Her mother. She flicked a "can't talk now" message.

Brothers raised a questioning eyebrow.

"My mother. She can wait."

"Ah, mothers," he said. "The best of times, the worst of times, eh?" He laughed. Seeing her expression, he said, "Tolstoy, isn't it?"

"Dickens," McTeish said. "And not about mothers."

"Jesus, Carol. Who cares who wrote it? Still applies, though, doesn't it?"

"You've met my mother?" She tried not to grin.

Brothers surveyed her for a moment. "You'd better call her. In my experience—limited I know to just one mother—it's best to bite the bullet. Save you a heap of misunderstandings and trouble."

McTeish looked at her phone, nodded, and dialled.

"Darling," she heard her mother's typical insincere gush. "When will I see you?"

McTeish frowned. "Didn't we have dinner last week? Remember, I bought fish and chips?"

"Of course, dear. But it was so nice—are you free this evening?"

"You want me to cook for you, don't you?"

"Don't be such a silly! I'm ordering take in—from a new app that has gourmet restaurants. I thought we'd try it out."

When McTeish made no reply, she said, "Darling? Or have you got a date with your boyfriend?"

"Mum, I told you, I don't have a boyfriend."

"Or boyfriends."

"Mum." She thought about it. Gourmet food didn't sound bad. "What time?"

"I dunno. About seven? That okay?"

"Okay. See you at seven." She hung up, looked up and saw Brothers studying her. "What?"

"Told you it's best to…"

"Yes, yes." She laughed. "You were right."

"How are we going to do this, these new interviews?"

"I'll set them up," McTeish said. "How's your diary?"

"My diary? My diary?" Brothers snorted. "Nothing on in the next couple of days that I can't move for Dr Chen."

59

McTeish drove by a supermarket and bought a bottle of Prosecco chilled from the wine-fridge to bring to her mother's, and arrived in Elwood just after seven. She rang the bell, and waited, thinking that at least they'd enjoy some good food. A moment later the door opened.

"Come in, come in," her mother said, taking the wine from her and led her down the hallway. She was dressed up in a cocktail dress. "What's this, eh?"

"I thought a Prosecco would be good. Have you ordered yet?"

Her mother stopped and half-turned. "No. Thought I'd wait till you were here. And there's someone I want you to meet." He eyes sparkled.

McTeish froze. "Mum. You never mentioned—you know I don't like meeting your boyfriends."

"Oh, shush." She turned and continued into the lounge area. "Darling, this is my friend, Terry."

Terry McCauley was sitting, grinning widely, arms spread out on her mother's couch. He jumped to his feet to greet her. "Hello, Constable. Or can I call you Carol now?"

McTeish stared in horror. "Mr Euston?" she gasped.

"Euston, McCauley. Whatever. As the bard said, a rose by any name would smell as sweet." He moved to kiss her cheek, and McTeish backed away, holding her hands up.

"Mum! Do you know who this is?" she cried out.

"Of course I do, darling. This is Terry. My good friend Terry." She winked. Did she actually *wink*?

"How do you know him?"

"We met ... do I ask you how you meet your boyfriends?"

"Boyfriends? What boyfriends?" McTeish took a deep breath. "Mum. I can't stay. This man is part of my case. My murder case."

"Now, come on, Carol," Euston said. "What's the harm in a quick bite to eat? Nothing ventured, nothing gained, I say. And I must say, Claire is as fascinating as you are." He put an arm around her mother's shoulder, and moved his lips into a smile. His eyes remained cold, staring at her. "Let's all get to know each other a bit better." He turned to her mother. "Have you decided what we should order?"

"Fancy Italian, dear?" Her mother smirked as McTeish reddened in embarrassment.

"Mum. Sorry. I've got to go." McTeish backed up and rushed out the front door, ran to her car and drove off.

60

As McTeish drove back to her flat her phone rang, cutting off her radio that was playing Taylor Swift's *I Knew You Were Trouble*. Her mother calling her? She glanced at the screen. No, it was Tamas Kosic. She pressed a button and answered, "Hi Tamas." Her voice was tight.

"Hi, er, Carol." His voice faded out.

"Yes?" she snapped. Calm down, she told herself. Don't let her mother and her disastrous fucking boyfriends get to you. She breathed slowly, waiting for whatever Kosic was going to say.

"I just … " Again he stopped.

She waited.

"Can we meet up? I need to talk to you." His voice held a plaintive tone.

"Do you know what time it is?"

"What? About 7:30. Why?"

Only seven thirty? God, the encounter with Euston and her mother had completely thrown her.

"Have you eaten yet?" he asked.

She realised she was very hungry, but also that she should be careful. "No. What do you suggest?"

"Care to have a bite? Somewhere casual? I need to talk to you."

"You said that. What about?" She tried to keep her voice impersonal.

"About my stupidity. Please?"

She thought a moment. Maybe there would be an opportunity to find out more. "Where do you suggest?"

"How about Eis, in Albert Park."

"Ace? What's that?"

"It's a Japanese restaurant, in Bridport Street."

She drummed her fingers on the steering wheel, then made a decision. "Okay. I'm in my car at the moment. Meet you there in fifteen? What's the address again?"

She kept driving from Elwood and soon arrived in Albert Park. She saw the restaurant. Ah, it was *Eis*. She entered; it was small, narrow, dimly lit in a comforting way, and she sat down at a table for two, facing the door. She was the only customer. A middle-aged Japanese man brought a menu.

"I'm waiting for a friend," she said.

"Okay." He turned and brought a second menu and two glasses with a bottle of water.

The door opened and four people entered, two couples in their twenties. They walked past her and sat towards the rear of the restaurant.

While she waited for Kosic she pondered what she should tell Inspector Nguyen. She glanced at her watch: it was quarter to eight. What was that in Baltimore? She checked her phone. Far too early— 5:45 am. She'd call him after the meal. It was so embarrassing. Maybe she should call Brothers? She dismissed the idea. It had to be Winner. He'd know what she should do.

The door opened and Kosic walked in, saw her and smiled, sat down. "Thanks for seeing me at short notice."

She nodded, moved one of the menus across to him. "What's this about?"

"Um." He reddened, took a deep breath. "Look, I know I was stupid, doing that stuff in the lab."

She looked at him, saying nothing.

"You know, the psychedelics. I just wanted to say to you I didn't do anything to Dr Chen. I'd never do anything like that. Harm someone, anyone, particularly Dr Chen. I'm not that sort of person." He gazed at her.

"So?"

Before he could answer the waiter reappeared, pen and notebook in hand.

"Hang on a sec," McTeish said. She perused the menu. "What do you recommend?" she asked Kosic.

"Can I order for us both? Anything you don't like?"

"Yes, you choose. Anything'll be fine." One less decision to make on this disastrous evening. "Not too much, please."

"Sake, wine, beer?"

"Sake, please."

Kosic ordered edamame, gyoza, fresh crab meat dumplings and chicken teriyaki with vegetables. "That should do us," he shut the menu. The waiter nodded and took it.

"You were saying?" McTeish said, folding her arms.

"I wanted to clear the air. I know you'll have to investigate, and I know you have to think I might've, could've, done it, that I'm a suspect. But I didn't. I need you to know it wasn't me." He took a sip of water. "Doug had his faults, of course, but he was brilliant, really smart. I was lucky to work for him. And we were getting close to a breakthrough. Whoever killed him did a terrible, terrible thing. Not just killing him, of course." He squirmed. "It sabotaged the project."

"You mean you and Dr Shildduck can't continue it?"

"Of course we can. It's just—it won't be the same. And also..." his voice lightened and he gazed at her.

"Also?" McTeish said.

"I ... like you. I want to see you."

Fuck, she thought. She felt like screaming. Not only my mum has a completely inappropriate boyfriend, but now ...She shut her eyes, held her head in her hands and took a deep breath. She let it out slowly. "Tamas. Tamas. I told you, I'm working this case. Once it's over, assuming you're in the clear—"

"Of course you'll see I'm in the clear!"

"Assuming you're in the clear,"she continued in a stern voice, "*then* we can see what may happen. But not now."

"But—"

"No buts."

"You said we can see what happens." He had brightened.

"Tamas!"

The waiter brought a bottle of sake and two small ceramic cups.

She sighed, glancing at him. He was now despondent and slouched in his chair. She considered him. Tamas *was* interesting, if a bit of a fool. But not now. She steeled herself. "Let's drink to the successful resolution of this case." She poured a little sake in each cup.

Kosic raised his eyes and his cup and they clinked them, and drank.

The food arrived, and as she scented the aromas, she thought, what can we talk about over this dinner? I should never have agreed to seeing him. What was I thinking—he's part of the case. That gave her an idea. It might help get things back on track. "Tell me more about the research," she said.

Kovacs sat up, energised, a smile forming on his lips. "Well," he said. "This is all confidential, as you know." He held his hand up when McTeish was about to speak. "I know, I know, it's a murder investigation, and you're police, not scientists. And you'll keep it confidential. But, what the hell. I'll give you an overview. And please, please, keep it to yourself. Or at least just to Detective Nguyen." He tilted his head, his eyes focused in the distance, then shook his head as if clearing it. "You know how plants convert nitrogen into food, using photosynthesis?"

McTeish nodded.

"Well, they do that using machinery they stole from bacteria a billion years ago. I say stole. I mean they incorporated the bacteria. All plants have the same stuff. The bacteria that were incorporated are now sort of built in—they've lost their independence—and they now form the engine of plant cells. The technical name for what they've become is chloroplast."

"Chloroplast," McTeish echoed.

"Yes, chloroplast. They're like a mini solar power station, inside the cell."

A light went on in McTeish's head. "Solar power? Converting light into …?"

"Food. Protein."

McTeish nodded again. Kovacs had lost his awkwardness and his speech was fluent.

"Before your eyes glaze over, there's another thing about this key building block I should mention—it's a cyanobacterium. It's the one that formed the basis of all chloroplasts. They all come from one ancient cyanobacterium. But in the world outside plants, other bacteria evolved and developed much more efficient ways to turn carbon dioxide into food, and many now make their own nitrogen fertiliser. That's what we're trying to put into wheat—putting the whole carbon-concentrating mechanism of modern cyanobacteria into the chloroplasts in wheat."

"To make the wheat more efficient, at producing protein?"

"Yes. Exactly."

"But if other bacteria evolved, as you say, why didn't the cyano …" McTeish stumbled over the word.

"Cyanobacterium."

"Yes. Why didn't they evolve too? I mean those in the chloroplasts."

"That's the trick. Think of the sea. It's full of cyanobacteria. Huge numbers of them. They're blue-green algae. They reproduce very quickly. If one of them mutates and improves photosynthesis, it'll also reproduce quickly, and its descendants will become the dominant variety. Very quickly. But in a plant, if the cyanobacterium in a chloroplast mutates, the whole plant probably won't. The mutation mightn't be good for the chloroplast. Or, it could be in a leaf that drops to the ground, and dies. And also, another obstacle, the life cycle of a plant is so much longer than a bacterium's." Kosic took a sip of sake. "So we're trying to inject the speed of mutation in the sea into a wheat chloroplast." He sat back, his eyes gleaming. "And, if we can help plants get nitrogen directly from the air, as many bacteria do, that will eliminate the need for most fertilisers. Peas and beans do that already, of course. But the whole thing's incredibly complex, and we're trying to understand the number of genes and how and why they might need to be affected. That will be the breakthrough."

"And was Dr Chen close to breaking through?" McTeish asked. "And you and Dr Shildduck, of course."

"We're getting there. But it's a slow process. Could be a year or two away." He took another drink, smiled at her. "Anyhow, please forget I said any of this, will you? We don't want to give a clue to other researchers."

It *was* worth meeting him tonight, she thought. Was this research the grounds for Dr Chen's murder?

"What happens to you and Dr Shildduck, now?" she asked.

"How do you mean?" Kosic regarded her steadily.

"Does your work continue? Surely it's too important not to. What will the Badeker do about it?"

"Of course we all want it to continue." He paused a moment. "Funding is the thing. I think Dr Penrith is talking to Howarth-Acfield. They're already funding other work here at their Institute."

"You don't have the same problem that Dr Chen had? He didn't accept their money."

"I'm just a lowly post-doc. I can't afford to worry about where the money comes from."

61

AFTER SHE GOT HOME McTeish decided to take a shower, and after it felt a little more human. Now, to call Winner. She steeled herself and checked the time. It was a little after ten thirty, or half past eight in the morning Baltimore time.

"Hi Carol. What's up? It must be late at night, Melbourne time." Nguyen said.

"I … there's a problem," she said. She managed to keep her voice level and calm.

Nguyen waited.

"I went to see my mum, er mother—"

"That's good. Families are important. Wish I could see mine." Nguyen's mother had died four years previously. "What's the problem?"

"When I got there, she had a new boyfriend. Did I tell you she has boyfriends from time to time? They don't usually last long."

Again, Nguyen waited.

"It was Euston," she burst out, then fell silent, waiting for his response.

"Euston, as in McCauley? That Euston?"

"That Euston."

"What did you do?"

"It was awful. I left straight away." She stopped herself from sobbing.

"Hmm."

McTeish waited but that was all Nguyen said.

"What should I do?"

"Carol. Keep calm. Let's think about this. Did you mother know Euston before this case? I doubt it. So it's likely he deliberately found her. Probably to get to you. *He* would have approached *her*. Not the other way around." He paused for a moment. "Don't take this the wrong way, but you said your mum has had several boyfriends…?"

"Yes."

"So, let's think. We know Euston is, I dunno, able to flatter."

"Yes." McTeish realised she was being monosyllabic.

"You know, Carol, this is actually helpful, don't you think?"

"Helpful? It's horrific." She felt like screaming.

"Think about it. Why would he want to get to you? Doesn't that confirm how suss he is?"

"I suppose."

"Of course, he may just have been taken with you. Or your mum."

"Boss!" she gasped.

"But given what he seems like, he's trying something on."

"Trying what on?" She felt panicky.

"That's for us to find out, Carol." His voice was a calm as ever.

"But that's not all," she managed to get out.

"How do you mean?"

"Tamas, er Dr Kosic, took me out to dinner this evening."

"Tamas, eh?" She could imagine Nguyen smiling.

"He said he likes me. I told him straight away that that was not on. I tried to get him to talk about his research, instead." She waited.

"Yes?"

"And that gave me an idea."

Nguyen was silent.

"If Dr Chen and his team were trying to find a way to get wheat to have more protein, then why wouldn't HA have funded his research?"

"Hang on. Didn't Olga Penrith say they wanted to, but Chen wasn't interested?"

"Yes, but —oh, you're right. Forget it."

"Look on the bright side. We have Euston who seems increasingly likely to be hooked up into all this. Of course we have to find out what he's up to."

"How do we do that?"

"For a start, see if you can talk to your mother, without Euston. Find out how they met."

That she could do. "I'll call her tomorrow."

"*And*," Nguyen said. "Now we have three other possibles in the frame. As well as Euston, what about Simon Lee, Kosic and Lucy Bottega? I've been thinking about it. What do three of the four of them have in common?"

McTeish thought, but her mind was a blank. "What?"

"Access to poisons. Euston works for a big pharma, so he'd have access to poisons. Lee's a chemist, so he would have access, too. And Kosic works in a lab, so he also could get hold of stuff. The only one who might have had difficulty finding the poison would be Bottega. Unless, of course, she was in cahoots with Simon Lee."

McTeish's jaw dropped. "That's right! They all could have got hold of the poison." Then she slumped. "Hang on. Can you really see Dr Chen's partner teaming up with his mistress's husband?" She thought some more. "Has Forensics made any more progress in identifying exactly what poison was used?"

"That's something you can chase up with Sue Gossiter while I'm away."

62

McTeish got out of bed and put on oats to make porridge for breakfast. While it was heating up she turned on the espresso machine and made herself a coffee, all the time thinking, how should she approach her mother? There was no doubt she had to talk to her. Maybe warn her about Euston? That would go down like a ton of bricks. She sipped her coffee, spooned porridge into a bowl and added yogurt before eating it. She checked the time. Seven sixteen. Too early to call. Or was it? She stifled the nasty thought. Okay. She'd wait till—eight? Eight thirty? She'd call from the office, she decided. And having made that decision she showered and dressed.

Brothers was there when she arrived, and she bit the bullet and told him about her evening. About Euston being with her mum, and eating with Kovacs, and her call to Nguyen. Broad brush, without too many details.

To her relief Brothers just listened, and asked no questions, simply shook his head and waited. She stared at him.

"No, Carol," he said. "Nothing I can add at this stage. You did say the boss wants you to call your mum? I'll wait, and when that's done and dusted we can talk. If you want. I would like to talk about the Lees, though. And you can fill me in on Kovacs. But call your mum, okay?"

"Okay. I will. There's nothing much to report on Kovacs. My gut tells me he wasn't involved, but I know that's not necessarily reliable."

"Wait till you've got a gut," Brothers said, patting his paunch. "Comes with experience, and too many beers."

She grinned, felt her tension ease. "Okay. Project Mumma!"

She stood and went into Nguyen's office and shut the door.

Her mother answered straightaway. "Darling! What happened to you? You ruined a perfectly good dinner! And don't tell me you don't like the company I keep."

McTeish shook her head in frustration. "You know I don't like your boyfriends."

"None of them?"

"Look. Forget all that. This is different." She took a gulp of air.

"Different? Why yes, I suppose Terry is different, isn't he? Certainly not a toy boy!" Her mother chuckled. "But he is charming."

"That's what I'm ringing about, Mum. He may be charming, but I don't think he's a prince."

"Oh, you're just jealous. I suppose *your* boyfriend is?"

"I don't have a boyfriend."

"Who was that you went to last night, then?" She could imagine her mother's insinuating sly glance.

"What do you mean?" McTeish tried to keep her voice from rising.

"I'm sure after you abandoned us you would still have been hungry. So, it doesn't take Einstein to think you had dinner. So, who'd you eat with? Admit you've got a boyfriend!"

Her mother's knack of getting under her skin had not declined in the slightest. She took another deep breath. "Let's talk about Terry. He's involved in a case I'm working on."

"Oh, I know, dear. He told me, after you left so suddenly. Said he'd met you, and thought you were a lovely young woman."

A lovely young woman. McTeish almost exploded. She clenched her jaw, then tried to relax. "How did you meet him?" she said through gritted teeth.

Her mother laughed. "Where else, but at the gym! I was trying to lift some weights, and he came over and helped me. So thoughtful. And we got chatting, as you do. Or maybe that's something you need to learn to do, darling."

"What's that?"

"Chatting. Getting to know people."

McTeish thought of the succession of men her mother had been with, and shuddered. "So you chatted. And then?"

"Well, dear, one thing leads to another. We talked a bit about each other, and I discovered he'd already met you. Fancy that! He said some very nice things about your interview techniques."

"My interview techniques?" she burst out. "He's a suspect in a murder investigation, for Christ's sake."

"Oh, I know, dear. He told me about that. Stuff and nonsense. He said he hoped he was helpful to you. Said you were really impressive, that I should be proud of you."

What? Her mother proud of her?

"Of course, he doesn't really know you," her mother continued, "but it was nice of him to say that. And he seems taken with a certain someone, too." She gave a girlish giggle. "So when are the three of us going to get together? How many times have I told you you've got to face up to things? Terry didn't seem upset that you scarpered last night. I was furious, but he said something like, girls will be girls, or some such."

"Mum," she said, then paused, calmed herself down. "It's not a good idea for me to meet him—outside of official work, of course."

"Oh, don't be a nervous Nellie. By the way," she said, in a different tone of voice, "Why don't you come clean? How's *your* boyfriend? Ready to introduce him to me? Or are you too ashamed of me?"

"Mum. For Pete's sake. I don't have a boyfriend. How many times do I have to tell you?"

"So those calls you get are just work, are they? Come on, be honest. You can tell me."

"Bye, Mum." McTeish hung up. She sat for a moment, then went back to her desk.

Brothers looked up. "How did that go?"

She shook her head. "*He* told *her* about me. Can you believe it?"

Brothers regarded her for a moment, then said. "You're a bit too close to all this. Maybe I should have a chat with him. Or Winner should."

McTeish thought about it. Brothers was right. And maybe Euston had nothing to do with the murder at all, apart from being employed by HA to take photos. Still, he creeped her out. And could she help it if he seemed to be infatuated with her family? She cleared her desk, and switched on her computer. "You're welcome to him. But let's discuss this with the Boss, first. Okay?"

He nodded. "It'll be early evening in Baltimore. Why don't you call him?"

Before she could reply, her phone rang. She glanced at it. Her mother again. She debated with herself of a moment before answering. "Hi Mum."

"It's not your mum. It's me," the voice of Terry Euston said. "Claire wants you to come over. Now!"

McTeish blanched. Putting the call on speaker and muting her microphone, she said to Brothers, "It's Euston. He wants me to go to my mum's place, now." She felt her heart beat faster. "What should I do?"

"Ask to speak to her."

She unmuted her phone. "Can I speak to her, please?"

"She can't come to the phone right now." The voice was flat. "She wants you to come over."

"Why?"

"She'll tell you when you get here."

McTeish pressed mute again. "What should I do?"

Brothers raised an eyebrow. "Tell him you can't get away for another hour."

She unmuted the phone. "Mr Euston. I can't just come from work out of the blue. I might be able to leave in an hour or so. What's the problem?"

"No problem." Euston chuckled. "No problem—yet. See you in an hour." He hung up.

"When we get the phone records we'll be able to see if he's been talking to Baltimore," McTeish said. "We should get them today."

"And whether the others have been speaking to manufacturing chemists or whatever," Brothers said. "As you said, it could be this bozo has nothing to do with the poisoning, and we have to look at Lee, Kosic or Bottega." He rubbed his chin, looking down at some notes on his desk. He looked up. "Let's call the Boss." He picked up his phone, put it on speaker, and soon Nguyen answered.

"You got me at a good time. I'm just about to go eat with Major Fleischer."

McTeish filled him in on the call from Euston.

"So, he already told your mother he knew you through the case. And now he's back there, and your mother didn't come to the phone?"

"I spoke to her earlier, and I thought she was ringing again. But it was Euston." McTeish's heart was pounding; she took a deep breath. "Could he have done something to her?"

"Well, you've got an hour." Nguyen paused. "I wonder if he's been talking to Lovell at HA, and if so, how often?"

"We expect to get the phone records today for Euston." Brothers said. As he spoke there was a ping on his phone. He glanced at it. "Speak of the devil. It's just come in." He clicked on the link on his computer and pulled up the document. "Hang on a sec." He perused it. "There you go. He made a call yesterday to Baltimore. I presume it's to HA. We can check that later. And three other calls to Baltimore since the murder. Plus a call on Monday from Baltimore to him." He looked up and grinned. "They're pretty good—this is up to date as of last night."

"Pull him in for questioning," Nguyen said. "And Graham, go with Carol to her mother's."

"Of course," Brothers said.

"Anything else? I need to get down to meet the Major."

"Enjoy your dinner," Brothers said.

"Thanks, Boss," McTeish said.

63

McTeish drove Brothers to Elwood and they parked outside her mother's house.

"You go first," Brothers said.

She led the way and knocked on the door.

A moment later it was opened, and Euston stood there. A smile on his face slipped for moment when he saw Brothers. Then he greeted McTeish. "Ah, Constable. Glad to see you. And," he raised his left arm and inspected his watch, "you're here just under an hour. Congratulations on your time management. Very important for a rising—shall we say star? And I see you've brought reinforcements." He eyed Brothers. "I'm Terry Euston, as I'm sure Carol, er, Constable McTeish has told you. Do come in. Do come in."

"This is Detective Sergeant Brothers," McTeish said.

Brothers said nothing and they followed Euston into the lounge room, which was empty.

"Where's my mother?" McTeish asked.

"Why here, darling." Her mother strolled from her bedroom, fussing with her hair.

"Where were you earlier? Why couldn't I speak to you?" McTeish asked.

"We did speak, darling—I rang you, remember? And who's this, dear?"

"This is Detective Sergeant Brothers."

Claire McTeish looked Brothers up and down and almost imperceptibly sniffed. "He doesn't look boyfriend material," she said.

"Mother! And I mean earlier, when you rang back. When Mr Euston rang back. Why didn't you speak to me then?"

"I was otherwise occupied, darling," she said, gesturing with a slow movement of her right arm towards the bathroom. "I'd already spoken to you, hadn't I? Remember? And I knew you'd be coming here. So what's the big deal?"

"Terry Euston?" Brothers said, interrupting.

"Yes, Sergeant?" Euston's lips formed a smile; his eyes stayed focused on McTeish.

"Please come with us. We'd like you to come to the station, for questioning."

"What? Questioning me? You've already questioned me. Twice. Or rather, not you, but Constable McTeish and Detective Inspector Nguyen. Now you? What on earth for? For forming a friendship with Carol's mother? I must say Claire is as delightful as I am sure Carol is."

"Mr Euston. Cut the crap. We're going to the station."

"As I said before, Sergeant, in one word, why?"

"On suspicion of involvement in murder," Brothers replied.

"Murder? Me? You must be out of your mind." Euston glared at Brothers, turned to McTeish and snarled, "What else can you possibly want to know?"

"Yes," Claire McTeish said. "Why question Terry, darling? He told me he's been most co-operative with you."

"Mum, we have information that shows Mr Euston has not been as co-operative as he should have been."

"Not as co-operative as I should have been?" Euston snapped. "In what possible way, may I ask? Or rather, I *am* asking!"

"Enough of this," Brothers said. He remained calm, looked steadily at Euston. "Don't make matters worse for yourself."

Euston grabbed Claire McTeish and stood behind her. "Careful what you're doing, Sergeant," he said.

"Let her go, Euston. You'll only make things worse for yourself."

"Worse for myself, Sergeant?" Euston said. "I'd say I'll make things worse for you!"

He bundled Claire into the bedroom and slammed the door.

McTeish rushed to the door and tried to open it. The door was locked.

"What do we do now?" McTeish turned to Brothers, her face ashen.

"We take him down to the station. In handcuffs."

"But what about mum? My mother?" McTeish said.

At that moment the bedroom door opened and Euston appeared, behind Claire McTeish, with a revolver in his right hand. Her mother had lost her girlish manner, and Euston pushed her forward. "Now folks," he said. "If you would be so good as to open the front door." He waved his gun in that direction.

"Jesus, Euston," Brothers said, rolling his eyes. "No matter what you do, in the end there's only one outcome. You know that. Or you would, if you thought about it. Don't be stupid."

"Stupid. Stupid. Stupid, eh? I could say the same thing about you two." He twisted Claire McTeish's arm, and she cried out. "Open the front door!"

McTeish ran and opened it.

Euston waved his gun. "Stand over there, so I can see you both."

Brothers and McTeish moved into the kitchen. Euston backed out behind Claire McTeish and out the front door, slamming it as they left.

McTeish dashed and opened the door. Euston was putting Claire into a car, and climbed in himself. They drove away.

McTeish jotted down the number plate, and phoned it in.

64

Billings was back at her desk when her phone rang.

"Bill? This is Roni." Her voice was the same low drawl she had heard that morning. Billings smiled to herself.

"Hi there." She leant back in her chair.

"Feel like that drink we talked about? This evening?"

"Of course." She sat up and said, "Where do you suggest?"

"You know the Drinkery?"

"Yes." Billings restrained herself from pumping her fist in the air. The Drinkery was one of Baltimore's better gay bars. "What time?"

"How about six thirty. Does that work for you?"

"Six thirty is fine. That's ... kind of quick." Hastily she added, "I'm not complaining."

"I have some news. See you there." She hung up.

Billings sat at the back bar at the Drinkery; she'd changed into a simple black dress and arrived a few minutes early. The lighting was dim, and the music playing from a juke box was Kylie Minogue's *Tension*. As it finished Taylor Swift's *Love Story* came on, and she saw Peron enter, dressed in her office suit. Perfect timing, she thought. She stood to greet Peron, who leant in and bussed her cheek.

"Hi there. Thanks for meeting at short notice." She put her hands lightly on Billings shoulders and inspected her at arm's length for a moment.

Billings widened her eyes but tried to be nonchalant. "What can I get you," she asked, a smile playing on her face.

"What are you having?" Peron looked at the drink on the bar. "Is that a margarita?"

Billings nodded and they seated themselves.

"Same, please."

Billings signalled the bar keep, a young woman with spiky hair and enough metal to set off an airport detector, who rubbed a wide brimmed glass into a dish of salt before adding tequila and lime juice.

"Good to see you again," Billings said, her face cocked to one side. "You said you had some news?"

"An excuse to—but yes, I do have some news. That guy you mentioned, Euston. He called Mr Lovell. I heard some of it—Lordy, seems he's worried he might get caught up in something, what with your Australian colleague here in town. I thought I'd pass that on." She sipped her drink.

"Thanks." Billings looked at Peron. "What did Euston say?"

"Not so much what he said. I couldn't hear all that much. More the tone of voice—he was cross. Said he needed Lovell to take care of things. Sounded like he was under pressure."

"What's that mean? Take care of things?"

Peron smiled. "Beats me. That's all I picked up." She swirled her drink in the glass. "Good enough reason to meet up?"

Billings nodded, took her hand.

65

On Wednesday evening Nguyen and Fleischer ate at the Charleston, an elegant restaurant with starched white tablecloths and red chairs, in Little Italy. Two walls were framed in wood painted the same red as the chairs, behind which were housed an impressive range of bottles of wine.

"It's a mixture of French and South Carolina cooking," Fleischer said, as they perused the menus. "Let's order the three-course option. Fortunately they come with specific wines, so we won't have to worry about this." She picked up the wine list, a hefty sixty pages, and put it back on the table. "Is that okay with you?"

"No worries," Nguyen said, then raised his eyebrows when he saw the prices.

"What?" Fleischer said. "I do have an expense account, you know."

They both ordered soup—fresh artichoke; Nguyen ordered the Pan-Roasted Hudson Valley Magret of Duck and Fleischer the Grilled Creekstone Farms Beef Tenderloin. They decided to choose a dessert later.

"Anything to drink for the moment?" the waiter asked.

Fleischer looked at Nguyen, who shook his head.

"Water will be fine, thanks."

As they sipped, Fleischer said, "How did you get that nickname, 'Winner'?"

"Well …" Nguyen paused, grimaced, then shook his head. "You don't want to know."

"Sure I do. Cause it sort of rhymes with Nguyen?"

"Well yes, there's that." Nguyen broke off. After a moment he took a deep breath. "Okay," he said. "We Aussies have a way with nicknames. For us a redhead is typically called Bluey. A tall guy is called Shorty. So when I was first called Winner, at police academy, they meant I was a loser." He shrugged his shoulders. His face was tight. "There was the odd bit of racism in the force back then. Maybe there still is." Nguyen stared at Fleischer, who looked back without comment. "I had to work extra hard to turn that around." He kept a straight face.

"Jesus," Fleischer said, breaking into a grin. "Does that mean I should have been called 'Skinny'?"

"I think 'Slim' was the term, back then." Nguyen laughed. "It's not about what you're called, though, is it? That says more about the caller. It's how you react that matters."

"Right. Right."

Their soups arrived with small glasses of white wine, and they supped quietly for a moment.

"By the way, Tricia Rooney phoned me back," Fleischer said.

"Rooney? Oh. With the FBI. The Special—SAC?" Nguyen said.

"Yes. She said she'd spoken to you. Was she helpful?" Fleischer said.

"Sure. Said she'd check out Euston. But I told her I'd be speaking to my New York FBI contact, Harry Brownovski, and she said she didn't want to cross lines with him, and that in any case he'd be better placed to follow up on Euston. I sent him some photos of Euston."

"Did Brownovski say when he'd get back?"

Before he could answer, the soups were cleared away and the duck and beef were brought out, this time with glasses of a Tuscan red.

"You know those guys. He was helpful, but couldn't give me a timeline. Last time he was very quick, so it could be tomorrow. I mentioned your name and said how you'd put me on to Agent Rooney."

"Thanks." Fleischer took a mouthful of grilled beef tenderloin, chewed and swallowed. "Rooney dropped a little info in my ear. Seems your Mr Lovell is in a bit of a hole."

Nguyen looked up. "In a hole? How so?"

"HA is just hanging on—thanks to its fertiliser business, FC Group."

"What, HA is being propped up by FC? Lovell did sort of hint at that. He talked about HA missing out on the Covid vaccine contracts." Nguyen thought for a moment. "He must be hoping the wheat research pays off, to get HA back on its feet."

"Here's the thing, John. The wheat research might not be so good after all. It might be good for HA. Not so good for FC."

Nguyen thought about it. "How so?" he asked again.

"If the new strain of wheat doesn't need fertiliser, it'll fuck FC's business model. The demand for fertiliser will drop off. Not immediately. But over time."

Nguyen rubbed his chin. "That sounds like an incentive to stop the research. Or at least to own and control it."

"Like the auto companies did with mass transit?"

"Is that what happened?" Nguyen sat up. He put his knife and fork down and studied Fleischer.

"I thought it was an urban myth, but apparently back in the day General Motors was convicted of conspiracy to acquire control of a number of transit companies, to form a transportation monopoly. I think they worked with tire manufacturers and big oil. They were systematically buying streetcar lines and then shutting them down, so people would buy their autos. It happened here in Baltimore. GM through its National Bus Company bought up most of Baltimore's streetcar lines. Is that what you mean?"

"Something like that. We in Melbourne somehow managed to keep our trams. But consider this. The scientists at the Badeker are trying to develop a wheat that doesn't need fertilisers. That would be a threat to all the fertiliser manufacturers, wouldn't it? And if HA owns the Badeker research, then if it threatens their fertiliser business they could just sit on it."

"That would be ..." Fleischer broke off. "You're serious?"

"There are two research projects at the Badeker. HA has a contract with one of them, but not the other—not with Dr Chen's. That gives HA a motive to get rid of him." Nguyen sat back, his brow knitted into a frown. "That could be why they hired Euston. Not just to take photographs." He reached for his phone, then put it down. "And another thing. Your young officer, Bill, rang me an hour ago to say that her contact at HA, Roni Peron, Lovell's assistant, told her that Euston had rung again, and that she heard Lovell telling him to be careful."

Fleischer took a sip of wine. "Seems your visit to him has stirred a few things."

Nguyen picked up his phone. "Would you excuse me while I make a quick call?"

Fleischer nodded, a smile playing on her lips.

He dialled Graham Brothers and set up a zoom meeting with him and McTeish. "We need to keep a closer eye on Euston," he said. "Get a search warrant. In fact, bring him in for questioning."

66

McTeish's phone rang as she sat at her desk at the station, and she checked the screen. It was her mother.

"Hello, mum," she said.

"Constable McTeish. How pleasant."

She felt her heart sink on hearing Euston's supercilious voice.

"Where are you?" she said without thinking. "Is my mother all right?"

"Claire is just dandy," Euston said. "Are you?"

"Why have you taken her?"

"Your Sergeant, what's his name? Brothers? He was *bothering* me."

"Where have you taken her?"

"That's for me to know and you to find out."

She heard a chuckle. Or was it a snigger? She ground her teeth and thought, we can find out where the phone is. She knew it would take time to get the information. She had to keep him talking.

"What are you up to, Mr Euston?" she asked him. While she talked to Euston, she picked up the desk handset and dialled Brothers.

"It's Mr Euston, now, is it? Call me Terry."

"Mr Euston—"

"Terry! Or I'll hang up."

"Okay. Terry."

"That's better."

At that moment Brothers answered her landline. "Carol? What's up?"

She muted her mobile phone before responding. "Sarge, I've got Euston on my mobile. He's calling from my mother's phone."

"Jesus. We can we find out where they are. How long will it take? I'll put in an urgent request. What's the number?"

She told him the number.

"We can check which tower her phone's close to."

"Carol. Are you there?" Euston spoke calmly. "Because if you're not, you know what'll happen to your mother?"

"I'm listening," McTeish said into her mobile after unmuting it. "What will happen to my mother?"

"Nothing, if you do as I say."

McTeish took a deep breath and let it out slowly. "I asked before what you are up to. Why are you doing this? Why involve my mother?"

Euston chuckled. "This a delicate situation, Carol. Your mother, lovely woman that she is, is just a means to an end. She could almost be your big sister." His voice took on a harsh quality. "You and Detective Nguyen have put me in this … situation. You understand, surely, that I want to protect myself. I mean, *have* to protect myself."

"Where are you?" McTeish said. "Can I come and meet you? Surely you don't need my mother."

"Hmm," Euston said. "That is what I had in mind. Are you a mind reader, Carol?"

McTeish with an effort kept her voice calm. "Where should I go? To meet you both?"

There was silence from Euston.

"Carol," Brothers said on the landline. "I'll hang up and come back to the office. Okay?"

McTeish muted her mobile. "Sure, Sarge. I just don't know what this fucknut wants." She bit back tears. "Or what he'll do."

"It's a good sign he's talking. Keep him on the line, if you can. See you soon." Brothers hung up.

She unmuted her mobile. Euston was still silent. "Terry—"

"Right. Good start, Carol. Now we're getting somewhere. But we have a problem, don't we?"

"Of course we have a problem. You abducted my mother."

"That's a very big call, abduction. That implies the abductee is not willing, doesn't it? I wouldn't say *that's* the problem. Or rather, it's not *my* problem."

"So?" McTeish replaced the desk handset in its cradle.

Euston sighed theatrically. "Constable. Constable. You're a smart one, aren't you? *This* is the problem: if you come here, you'll no doubt let your colleagues know. And then where will we be? I might be forced to do something drastic. In fact, I *would* be forced to do something drastic."

"Why would you want to do anything like that? Let's be reasonable." Reasonable! She almost laughed at herself.

"Reasonable is as reasonable does."

"I asked you what you want. Why have you called me?"

"A *reasonable* question, Carol. I want an exchange. Your mother for—" there was a pause.

"For what?"

"For you and your friends—I should say colleagues—to leave me alone. I don't know why you've taken this interest in me—or rather I know why *you* might be interested. But Detective Nguyen, or Sergeant Brothers? My friend in Baltimore has told me your precious detective inspector is over there. I just want to get on with my life. And maybe get to know you as well as I've got to know Claire."

McTeish did not reply, but thought to herself, how much longer does the Sarge need?

"Carol?" Euston's voice was querulous. "You there?"

"Yes, I'm here. You're willing to release mum, my mother. And want us to forget about you. Right?"

"Right. Good girl!"

"The only reason we're interested in you is because of Dr Chen's murder. You understand?"

"How many times do I have to tell you? I had nothing to do with it!"

Yeah, right. "If you had nothing to do with it, then why this over-reaction?"

"If you think this is an over-reaction, then you don't know me. Hang on—"

McTeish heard her mother's voice, muffled, and then the phone was muted.

"Hello?" What was he doing? She waited, and after a few seconds she heard, "Carol? Sorry about that. Where were we?" Euston's voice was back to its calm fake sincerity.

"You were saying you'll release my mother."

"Ah yes. But we have another problem. She now says she doesn't want to be released."

"Can I speak to her, please?"

"Of course you *can* speak to her. The correct term is, *may* I speak to her. And I'm not so sure I want you to do that just yet."

"If I can't speak to her, how do I know she's safe. Or that she doesn't want to be released."

"Released implies she's being held."

"You drove her away in your car. I saw you do it with my own eyes."

"Well, yes, you've got me there. Always the observant one, aren't you?" He chuckled. "But now she's quite happy to stay with me."

"Let me hear her say that."

"I think you've got the wrong idea about me."

"Just put my mother on."

"All in good time, Carol."

She shuddered at the way he spoke her name, a sort of purring of the syllables.

"Patience, they say, is a virtue," Euston said. "Though I must say if you had only a few seconds to escape an incoming tidal wave, I doubt patience would be a virtue, at all. But don't let me get side-tracked."

"You said you'd put my mother on."

"Did I say that? I don't think I did. But I will, I will. Just be … patient."

"You say you'll release mum if you're left alone. Is that right?"

"Now the horse is galloping! Exactly right."

"But how will you trust us to leave you alone? What can we do? Is that your problem?"

"Again, exactly right."

She could imagine him leering, and repeated. "How can you be convinced?"

There was silence, and she waited.

"Let me get back to you on that," he finally said.

"Then let her speak to me. Please."

"Oh, very well. Here—"

"Hello darling." Her mother's breathy voice came on. "What did you want to say?"

"Mum! Are you okay?"

"Of course I'm okay. You're not thinking of that little kerfuffle last night, are you? It's all fine. All worked out."

"So you see, Carol." Euston's voice came on, "there's no need to worry."

But hadn't her mum sounded anxious, under it all? She must know she couldn't say anything in front of Euston. "When can I see her?"

"Soon enough, soon enough."

McTeish looked up: Brothers had arrived. He looked questioningly at her, and she muted her phone. "We've got the location of your mother's phone. It's in Windsor," he said.

"That's where he lives. Where Winner and I visited him." McTeish felt her hopes rise. "Let's go there now." She unmuted her phone. "Terry?"

"I said, soon enough. Is that not soon enough for you?" He chuckled.

"I'll speak to you soon." She hung up.

Brothers nodded, and they left.

67

THE DAY WAS OVERCAST and there was a sprinkle of light rain as McTeish drove to Windsor with Brothers. She said, "I got the feeling my mum was under pressure. She said she was fine, but …"

"What did she say?" Brothers asked.

McTeish tried to remember the exact words. "She said, 'I'm okay' and then 'It's all fine. All worked out.' But I got the feeling that with Euston there she couldn't speak freely."

Brothers nodded. "The fact that your mother said she's okay doesn't mean anything. She could be frightened. She might not. She might be okay. She might not." He checked his revolver, then replaced it in his shoulder holster. "Hopefully it won't come to this. We'll find out soon enough," he said. "When we get there, the important thing is to reduce the risk of triggering any violent reaction from Euston. So no sudden movements."

McTeish sighed. "Of course. I suppose I should be the one to knock on the door. After all, I'm the one he wants to see. Is that okay?"

"Sure. These situations can go simply and easily, or blow up in your face. How well do we know this Euston? Is he stable? Does he seem to be a nutter? He certainly acted like one yesterday."

"He gives me the creeps. For some reason he wants to get to know me. And he's cunning, I think. Why would he grab my mum like that?"

Brothers folded his hands in his lap. "He could've panicked, I suppose. For my money it puts him in the frame for Dr Chen's murderer." He glanced across at McTeish, who was grasping the steering wheel tightly, her knuckles white. "I know we still have to consider Kosic and Lee, but—" he shrugged. "Let's just be careful."

They arrived and she parked. The rain had lifted. They walked through the unkempt garden to the door of Euston's house.

"Maybe you should stand to one side, so he doesn't see you when he opens the door," McTeish said. "Then if it looks safe we can go in." she glanced at Brothers, took a deep breath, and knocked on the door.

There was silence from within. Then she heard footsteps, and the door opened. Euston peered out, saw McTeish and grinned. "Carol! You should have let me know you were coming—I'd've baked a cake! Or at least put the kettle on."

"Terry. I've come to see my mother."

"Of course you have."

Brothers stepped into view, "And we still need to interview you."

"Sergeant," Euston said. He shook his head. "Never rains but it pours. The more the merrier, I suppose." He stepped aside and they entered. "This way," he said.

As they reached the living room, McTeish saw her mother sitting on a chair. "Mum," she called out, and ran to her, wrapping her arms around her in a hug.

"Darling, what are you doing here?" Her mother stood stiffly and disengaged herself. "That's very ... demonstrative. What's got into you?"

"I've come to get you."

"Whatever for?" Her mother smiled. "Why, hullo, Sergeant. What brings you here, too?"

"Good question, Claire," Euston said. "Why have you both come? I mean, Carol, you're most welcome."

Brothers looked around, saw that Euston did not appear to be armed, and said, "I'm arresting you for kidnaping Mrs McTeish." He reached for his handcuffs.

"Kidnaping, Sergeant?" Claire McTeish said. "I already told Carol that that was all a misunderstanding."

Brothers blinked. "We saw you being forced into the car, at gunpoint."

"Rubbish. It may have seemed like that, but that was just Terry trying to get me away."

"Funny how there're two expressions to do with poultry, aren't there, Sergeant?" Euston said. "Don't count your chickens before they're hatched. And what was the other one? Oh, yes. Something about them coming home to roost. I think they both might apply to you."

"What the hell are you on about?" Brothers said. He took the handcuffs and approached Euston, who put out his hands and Brothers clicked them on.

"See, Sergeant? I'm cooperative. Most cooperative."

"Carol," her mother called out. "Can't you stop this nonsense? I'm here because I want to be here."

Brothers stopped. He scratched his head. "You want to be here? You weren't kidnaped?"

"That's what I'm trying to say." She looked him up and down. "You don't need to do this. How can there be a crime? Who was kidnaped?"

"Mum," McTeish called out. She stared into her mother's eyes. "Is this one of your games?"

"I doubt it's a game, Claire," Euston said. "They have just jumped to the wrong conclusion." There was a sneer on his face.

McTeish's face whitened. Her anxiety for her mother, the stress of not knowing she was safe, had got her heart racing. Now she felt adrift. She turned to Brothers, who was staring at both Euston and Claire McTeish.

"If I take these off, will you come to the station with me?" he asked.

Euston held his hands out. "I suppose I have to. As I keep trying to tell you, I want to be cooperative."

"Then why did you pull a gun and take off with Mrs McTeish?"

"The streaker's defence,' Euston said. "It seemed a good idea at the time." He smirked. "I admit, I was a little out of order. What's that expression, Sergeant? Nothing ventured, nothing gained?" He waved his hands forward towards Brothers. "And most importantly, no harm done. You heard the lady." He moved his arms towards Claire McTeish. "The lady's not for turning—nor complaining. Are you, sweetie?"

Claire McTeish nodded.

Brothers took the key from his pocket and undid the handcuffs, then led Euston out to the car.

McTeish clasped her mother's hands, and gazed into her eyes. "Are you sure you're all right?" she asked.

"Darling, of course I'm all right." Her eyes sparkled. "I did get a little concerned at first, I must admit. But what's life for if there's no excitement? Have I said that to you before?"

McTeish nodded, still holding her mother's hands. It was her mother's favourite response after she had pointed out the inadequacies of her men friends upon the endings of several of her relationships.

"Okay, Mum. I ... look, I'll go in with Sergeant Brothers. But please—this is not just excitement. This is serious. A man has been killed and your...new boyfriend needs to answer some questions."

"Okay, darling. Whatever. You never listen to me, anyway." She flounced her head and disengaged her hands. "Here, come closer." She brought her mouth to McTeish's ear. "He told me it'd be a lark. And it was!"

68

McTeish drove, with Brothers beside her and Euston in the back seat. McTeish sat silent, fuming. Euston whistled tunelessly, then stopped. Brothers glanced back at him, said nothing.

"Carol, Sergeant," Euston said. "As a matter of interest, how did Dr Chen get poisoned?"

Neither spoke.

"I mean, you somehow want to put me in the frame, here, don't you?" He waited, but when both remained silent continued. "So, being my own devil's advocate for a moment, if I may. If you think I poisoned him—which clearly you do—how did I do it?" He chuckled. "I mean, get a life! Looking back, you'll agree I *have* been a bit mischievous." He waited. "No response? Never mind. You've somehow got it into your heads that I must have done it. But how? And, more importantly, why?"

"Let's wait till we get to the station, eh?" Brothers said.

"Don't mind me," Euston said. "I'm just speaking out loud. Clearing my head. You have to admit, though, there isn't even a skerrick of evidence to involve me. So," Euston paused, and chuckled again. "You mustn't have anyone else, have you, so you're determined to get me nice and lined up. But let me tell you, and I'm really disappointed in you, Carol, not you Sergeant so much, but Constable McTeish here is smart. Or at least I thought so. But are you that desperate? Admittedly I teased you with my little stunt with Claire—"

"Shut up!" McTeish snapped. "As the Sergeant said, wait till we get to the station. You can say as much as you want there. But not now. Let me concentrate on my driving."

"Hmm. Have I touched a nerve? Very well." Euston stopped speaking.

McTeish drove to the basement and parked the car. They got out and, still silent, walked to the lift, took Eston up to interview room 3.

"Take a seat," Brothers said, and left, shutting and locking the door behind him. He leant back against the wall of the corridor and sighed. "Let's let him stew for a while." He shrugged and gave a weak smile.

McTeish was stony faced. She glanced at her watch. It was just before 10 am. "Let's give the Boss a call," she said, "before we talk further to—" she made a moue of distaste. "It'll be early evening there." Without waiting she walked along the corridor, out of potential earshot of the room, and dialled his number, and Nguyen answered a few seconds later.

"Carol. What's up?"

"We've got Euston here in interview room 3."

"What's he done?"

"He took my mother. Abducted her. Last night." McTeish suppressed the urge to laugh hysterically as she told him this. "Only when we got to them, it turns out she was okay with it all. It wasn't an abduction. He was playing games with us." It all came out in a rush. "Sorry," she said. "Is everything going okay with you?"

"Yes, all good here. In fact with a little help from my new Baltimore friend Major Janne, it seems Howarth-Acfield may have had a reason to shut down Chen's research. And that's where Euston comes in. So tell me again, you've got him locked up because … he went off with your mother?"

"Yes." She related how she and Brothers had found out Euston's whereabouts and had gone there, only to have the rug pulled out from under their feet, with her mother denying she'd been in any danger. On mentioning Brothers, she glanced at him. He was standing watching her, an expression of irritation on his face. She put the phone on speaker.

"G'day, Winner," Brothers said. "Euston still claims he had nothing to do with Dr Chen's death. Reckons we've got no evidence to link him."

"Did he say that, about the evidence?"

"I think his words were, 'not a skerrick of evidence'," McTeish put in.

"Would he say that if he was innocent?" Nguyen asked. "Sounds suspicious to me. Though given what an arsehole he is, maybe he would. But as I was saying, I think HA might have had a good reason to shut down Chen's research. It could threaten their more important business. It could be that their investment in the Badeker isn't to reap the results of the research, but rather to suppress it."

"But I thought Dr Chen hadn't signed up," McTeish said, relieved they were no longer talking about her mother. "So how could they suppress his work?"

"That's the point, Carol. If he'd signed up, they wouldn't have had a problem. But he didn't."

"And therefore he wasn't under their control," McTeish finished the sentence.

"Motive," Brothers said. "Opportunity? Euston was here."

"I'll get back in a day or so. In the meantime, make sure you question him about his movements on the day of Dr Chen's death. And don't release him. Keep him for however long you need."

"A reasonable time?" Brothers said.

"Exactly," Nguyen said. "It's not specified, but given the seriousness of this case—the murder, the abduction, or pretend abduction. Keep him overnight. And speak to me again if you are thinking of releasing him.

There was a pause while Brothers and McTeish made quick notes, both grimacing.

"But we need also to check on the other suspects," Nguyen continued. "Have you talked to Sue Gossiter yet? Forensics should have confirmed the poison by now."

"Yes – her report came in. She confirmed it was ricin," McTeish said.

"That helps explain it—it's something that could be ingested without Dr Chen knowing, and acting some hours later." Nguyen paused, then after a moment spoke again. "And there's another thing. Are there CCTV cameras in the foyer of the Badeker? We know Dr Chen went to the cafe on the ground floor. Check whether he met anyone that day. Particularly Euston, Kosic or Lee. They could have slipped him the ricin, and because it would have taken a while to act, he would've gone back to work oblivious, and the ricin acted in the middle of the night. And we know Kosic was making a party drug in the lab. What was it? And Lee could have compounded ricin through his pharmacy. Ditto Euston, he could have got it from HA. I'm flying back this afternoon— a day early. And we need to get search warrants for Euston's house. And probably Kosic and Lee's. Anything else? I have to get going."

"All good," Brothers said.

"Keep me in the loop. I should be home Saturday morning Melbourne time."

"Thanks, Boss," McTeish said.

BACK AT HER DESK, McTeish watched the video taken outside Con and Sue's Coffee in the courtyard near the Badeker, fast forwarding through the day of Chen's death, stopping when customers came in, then fast forwarding to—she stopped. Terry Euston walked up to the cafe and entered; it was just before 10:30 am. Twenty or so seconds later Dr Chen walked up and entered. Euston and Chen? She made a note and switched to normal speed. They left the cafe together about twenty minutes later, but walked in different directions. She noted the times before fast forwarding again. There were no people of interest until about 2:45, when Dr Chen reappeared, this time with Simon Lee, and they entered together. Almost fifteen minutes later Lee left, alone, then a short time later Chen left. McTeish noted the times again, and resumed fast forwarding. Nothing else of interest came up before the cafe closed at 4:30pm.

What was Chen discussing with these two? And why hadn't either mentioned they'd talked with him on the day before he died? She went back and watched the two entries closely. There was no doubt about it.

69

"WELL, LET'S GET THIS UNDERWAY," Brothers said. They walked back to the interview room and he unlocked the door.

Euston was sitting at the table, drumming his fingers. He looked up and said, "About time."

McTeish and Brothers sat down opposite him. Brothers switched on the video recording equipment and stated the time and date. "Present are Detective Sergeant Graham Brothers, Detective Constable Carol McTeish and Mr Terry Euston." He sat up, regarding Euston for a moment, then nodded to McTeish.

"Tell me, Mr Euston—"

"Terry, if you don't mind," Euston interjected.

"What did you talk to Dr Chen about on the morning before he died?" she continued, ignoring him.

Euston shut his mouth, then opened it. "What are you talking about?"

"At the cafe near the Badeker?"

Euston sat silent, as if considering something. Then he smiled, "Oh, that."

"Yes, that. Well?"

"I had a coffee with him."

"I presume that's what you do when you're in Con and Sue's Coffee."

"You have me there, Carol. Yes indeed."

"Cut the crap, Euston," Brothers said. "You heard the question. What did you talk to him about?"

"Ah ha," Euston said, breaking out into a smile. "He invited me for a coffee. Is that against the law?"

"He what?" Carol burst out before she could stop herself. "He invited you?"

"For a coffee. Remember I told you earlier that I didn't really know what Dr Chen was doing?" He looked at both of them. "With his research, I mean?"

"So?"

"He invited me to tell me about it."

"And you didn't think to mention it to us earlier?" McTeish said.

"Sorry, Carol. Must have completely slipped my mind." He added, "By the way, speaking of coffee, any chance of a drink?"

McTeish and Brothers exchanged glances.

"If you're helpful you'll get a drink," Brothers said.

"And what did he tell you about the research?" McTeish said.

"Surely you know better than me?" Euston smiled complacently.

"Wouldn't your mate at Howarth-Acfield have told you?" Brothers said.

"My mate...?" Euston looked puzzled for a moment, then again smiled. "Ah, you must mean Fred Lovell."

"That's right, Frederick Lovell, the President of Howarth-Acfield," McTeish said.

He looked at them both, hesitated and smiled. "He told me nothing." He cocked his head, as if studying them.

"So he just wanted you to photograph the protesters? Is that it?" McTeish said.

"Exactly. Carol, you're the one—so quick on the uptake."

Brothers smacked his hand on the table. "If that's all he wanted you to do, why did he fly you to Baltimore three times. And why did you call him yesterday?"

"Sergeant Brothers," Euston said in a soft voice. "Didn't you a moment ago refer to Mr Lovell as my mate?"

Brothers sat eyeing Euston, stone-faced.

"And can't a mate call a mate? They wouldn't be mates if they didn't chat, would they? And last time I looked that wasn't against the law. At least not here in sunny Melbourne. Not even in rainy Melbourne."

McTeish sat back, cleared her throat. "One thing I don't understand, Terry—"

"Ah," breathed Euston.

"—is why you went to all that trouble kidnapping my mother, if all you are is an innocent photographer."

Euston's face set in a snarl. "I already told you it wasn't a kidnapping."

"Seemed like it at the time. Why go through all that?" She paused. "Oh, I remember, because you wanted us to leave you alone."

Euston wreathed his face in another smile, though as usual McTeish saw his eyes remained cold. "See—you understand! That's exactly why."

"I'll tell you what I think *exactly* happened," Brothers said, leaning forward. "Dr Chen may have invited you for a coffee. In fact I couldn't understand why you'd met up with him, but that is as good an explanation as any. And you took the opportunity to slip the poison into his coffee, which killed him later that night.

"He had tea, not coffee."

Brothers slammed his fist on the table again. "Tea, then." He took a deep breath. "Whatever he drank, that's how you poisoned him. Admit it."

"Sergeant, are you feeling all right?" Euston asked. "Why on earth would I do that?"

"Because that is what your mate, Fred Lovell, paid you to do."

"You're out of your mind." He glared at Brothers, then suddenly laughed.

"This is no laughing matter." Brothers returned the glare.

"It is a laughing matter, *mate*." Euston said. "If I, or anyone else— because it wasn't me—if I poisoned Dr Chen in the morning, and he died that night, what the hell did I use?"

McTeish stared at Euston. "You tell us," she said.

"I don't know too much about poisons, but are there any with a delayed effect? With most wouldn't you feel the symptoms straight away, or pretty soon after—and then you'd try to get help. Let's not get too Hollywood about this. The only one I can think that could work is thallium. But if I'd used that it would've had to have been a couple of weeks earlier. Thallium doesn't work the same day." Euston sat back, his arms relaxed on the table. "You with me, Carol? Sergeant?"

"Our forensics people will tell us what you used," Brothers said. "And maybe your mate at Howarth-Acfield supplied you with something." He leaned back.

"Supplied me …?" Euston said.

"They are a big pharma, after all," McTeish said. "They do manufacture drugs."

Euston for once made no immediate comment. Then he said, "You lot have to take the prize. So now my employer is supplying poisons. And which poison?" He made a raspberry sound. "You've got to be joking."

"As I said before," Brothers said, "this is no joking matter." He shook his head. "Interview suspended at—" he checked his watch and noted the time. He and McTeish left the room.

Outside in the corridor, Brothers signaled to McTeish and they walked down a bit. "Let's get Simon Lee in. Find out what he talked to Chen about. And why he didn't mention that to us."

"Got it—I'll call him and get him here. He runs a chemists in South Melbourne, doesn't he?"

"I put the details in the file," Brothers said.

"Seems he could also source a poison, him being a pharmacist," she said.

Brothers rolled his eyes. "Heaven help us." Then he grinned and said, "Let's keep Euston stewing in there."

McTeish thought about that. She tried to imagine Euston stewing. "A good idea, Sarge, but don't you reckon that might just give him time to invent more ridiculous explanations? Still, at least we can get on to Lee." She had another thought. "And I'll get a glass of water for Euston."

70

McTeish found Simon Lee's contact details in the murder book, as Brothers had suggested, and rang his mobile. It went to voicemail, and she left a brief message for him to call her. A few seconds later her phone rang.

"Simon Lee here, Constable—sorry I didn't answer your call. I get so many scammers, and I didn't recognise your number. If they're a cold caller, they never leave a message."

McTeish said, "We need to follow up on your interview with Detective Nguyen. Can you come to the station in South Melbourne?"

"What sort of follow up? Can't we do it on the phone?"

She sighed. "You understand we do need to do this in person?"

"Why's that?" Lee sounded querulous. "Last time, Sergeant Brothers came to my pharmacy. It's busy here, you know."

"Mr Lee—you know this is a murder investigation. We just need to record the interview. It won't take too long."

There was a pause. "Okay. Understood, I suppose. When do you want to see me?"

"Can we talk to you today?"

"Hmm," Lee said. "Let me just check—okay, I could come in early this afternoon. Would around 1:30 be okay?"

"Fine, thanks." She gave the address details. "I'll see you at one thirty."

Just before one thirty McTeish received a message that Simon Lee was downstairs. She alerted Brothers and went down and brought him up to interview room 5. Brothers greeted him and switched on the recording equipment, specifying who was present and the time.

"Thanks for coming in, Mr Lee," McTeish said.

Lee nodded. "Why all this?" He waved his hand at the recording equipment."

"As I said, we need to follow up on what you told Detective Nguyen. For example, did you see Dr Chen on the day before he died?"

Lee sat back. "Well …" he gave a sheepish smile. "I did see him in the afternoon. We had a coffee together."

"Whereabouts?" Brothers asked.

"At the cafe near the Badeker."

"Is that Con and Sue's Coffee?" McTeish asked.

"Yes, that's the one. Not bad for a place in a food court."

"You didn't feel it worth mentioning this to me before?" Brothers asked.

"Didn't I?" He paused. "Maybe not. Does it matter?"

"What did you meet him about?" McTeish asked.

"He rang me, asked to see me."

McTeish and Brothers exchanged glances.

"What about?" McTeish asked.

"He said he wasn't feeling the best, and wanted to know if I could bring him something."

"Bring him something?" Brothers said.

"Well, he was a bit embarrassed. He had diarrhoea and wanted something to keep it in check. I told him he should go home, or see a doctor, but he said he was at a crucial stage with his project and had to be there for a few more hours."

"What time was this?" he asked.

"Early afternoon. Half past two or thereabouts."

McTeish nodded to Brothers.

"And did you bring him something?"

"As well as the runs—not too bad, he said—he had aching joints. I thought he might have a mild case of the flu, so I brought him some

Kaopectate, and ibuprofen. I told him that should keep him going for the short term, but he should see a doctor if it got worse."

"And you didn't mention this—even though Dr Chen was poisoned?"

"He said it was all pretty mild. Frankly, I didn't think about it. How was I to know he'd been poisoned? In any case neither of the tablets I gave him need prescriptions. They're just stop gap. For most that's all people need. And if he was poisoned, how would they have made a difference."

"Not a difference to you, maybe. But probably to Dr Chen," McTeish said.

"Why, what was he poisoned with?"

"It doesn't matter what he was poisoned with. Could giving him those medications have masked the symptoms, whatever they were?" she asked.

"Jesus," Lee said, his face going pale. "That's the last thing I would have thought of. He just said he needed something to tide him over."

"If you hadn't given them to him, he may well have sought proper medical help."

"So," Lee put his head in his hands, then looked up, his face pained. "Are you saying I caused his death?"

"I'm not saying anything at this stage. What do you think? You're the chemist."

As if to himself, Lee muttered, "What was the poison? What symptoms could some tablets of ibuprofen and Kaopectate mask? What poison causes diarrhoea? Or the flu?" He looked at both of them, sweat on his brow. "Did I kill him?"

McTeish and Brothers said nothing.

"Oh my God." Lee moaned. "Oh, no."

"You didn't kill him, if that's all you gave him," Brothers said. "Maybe contributed to it?" He left the question hanging.

"Hang on a minute." Lee straightened himself up. "If someone gave him ricin, for example, there's no cure for it, so no matter what I gave him it would have made no difference. Except perhaps to delay things.

He could have continued what he was trying to do." He glared at them both. "So don't try to guilt trip me. I was just helping a friend." He pondered for a time. "Even if it was some other poison ... what else causes diarrhoea and aches?" His voice died down to a murmur, talking to himself. "Vomiting, perhaps, but he wasn't vomiting. Thallium? But he would have had to have that days earlier—the chances of an antidote would have been too late." He stared again at them. "No, I don't think what I did would have changed the ... outcome. Just eased it." He placed his hands on the table. "Can you tell me what he was poisoned with? Then I'll know for certain."

Brothers said, "I don't suppose it matters to let you know. It has been confirmed to be ricin."

"Then although I may have helped treat his symptoms, I didn't inadvertently kill Doug. Whew!" He sighed.

"Thanks for coming in," McTeish said, standing up. "You've been most helpful."

Lee sat there for a moment, then stood, and she led him out.

After she returned she said to Brothers, "What'll we do with Euston?"

"Yes, good point. Can we charge him? What with? It's a bit hard to say, given your mother has cleared him of abduction."

"So. Do we have to let him go?"

"Let's have another talk with him," Brothers said, and they moved to the room Euston was in.

"About time," Euston said. "I've decided I want my solicitor now. I won't say another word until I see him." He folded his arms across his chest.

"Do you want to call him?" McTeish asked. She handed him his phone.

"Yes." Euston grabbed it from her.

"That's another word," Brothers said.

Euston ignored him, and dialled a number.

Outside in the corridor McTeish asked, "How long can we keep Euston locked up?"

"Hmm." Brothers said. "What we've got is purely circumstantial—assuming the abduction wasn't an abduction." He paused. "Maybe there's an advantage in letting him roam. We can see what else if anything he gets up to."

"Shall we let him out, then?" she said.

Brothers took a couple of paces back, nodded his head. "Yes. I think we should do that." He suddenly smiled. "It will save us having to deal with his lawyer, too—whoever that is. And given his attitude to you, it'll be better if I take him out."

71

NGUYEN FLEW BACK TO MELBOURNE from Baltimore on Saturday morning, and took an uber home, where his wife Hahn and daughter Minh hugged him.

"Daddy, did you get me anything?" Minh said, looking up with her big eyes.

He hoisted her into his arms and smiled. "Let's get inside and we'll see."

"How did it go?" Hahn asked. "Did you get what you wanted?"

Nguyen rarely talked about his cases at home, but he'd outlined the purpose of the Baltimore trip. "I think we've had some success, and the people there were very helpful," he said as they walked inside, Nguyen dragging his large bag while cuddling Minh, and Hahn taking his carry-on. "How's it been for you?"

"We're okay." Hahn ruffled Minh's hair. "The usual. You're away a lot anyway."

"What?" Nguyen looked at her.

She grinned. "Don't worry. All's good. Just teasing."

There was some truth in what she said, though, he thought. Work often kept him away. It did go with the job. He unpacked and brought out two wrapped items. Minh grabbed hers and ripped the paper off to reveal a Renee Barbie doll. Her eyes glittered. "Thank you, Daddy!"

Hahn looked at him with a raised eyebrow.

"I thought Barbie was now sort of a feminist icon," he said. "This is for you. I hope you like it." He handed her a small package, which she opened.

"Thanks." She kissed him and carefully took out a pair of pale green earrings. She inspected them and read the label: "Trebol Amazonite Dangle Earrings. Hmm." She smiled and put them on. "Thanks again. They're great. How do they look on me?" She moved her head from side to side.

"Don't ask me. Look in the mirror." He wondered whether she really liked them, or whether he'd made a mistake again. He remembered she usually preferred to select jewellery herself. "They're from a craft shop in Baltimore. They're made by artisans."

"They're beautiful, Johnnie. I love them. Now—would you like some tea?"

HE SET UP A debrief with Brothers and McTeish on Sunday late morning. They met in his office and Nguyen stood by the whiteboard, marker in hand. He looked none the worse for wear, despite the travel.

"Let's look at the groups," he said. He drew four boxes. "One: Dr Chen, his partner and friends. Two: Dr Chen's work colleagues. Three: The Green protesters. Four: The HA people. Maybe they're part of Two, the work group."

He drew four more boxes. "And now, the possible suspects."

He wrote down Euston and Kosic. "One of the Greenies, one of Chen's colleagues."

He wrote Lucy and Lee in the first box. "Chen's partner, or maybe Lee."

"I think we can eliminate some of the Greenies," McTeish said. "They'd be a long shot, as none of them seem to have had any chance to poison Dr Chen."

Nguyen stared at her for a moment, then said. "I agree they are the least likely, but let's not be too hasty. We haven't really explored them, except for Euston." He folded his arms, head bowed. He looked up at them. "As an exercise, let's examine the possible scenarios. First, Euston. What do we know about him?"

"He's a smart arse," Brothers said. "He annoys the shit out of me."

"By the way," McTeish said. "Sergeant Ladbroke rang back. Apparently ASIO hasn't got anything on him; all he seems to have done is use a different name from his passport, which is Australian."

"Never mind," Nguyen said. "ASIO would be more concerned with things like terrorism and political threats. But he's certainly been active in our patch."

"Yes," McTeish said. "He was paid by HA," She raised one finger of her right hand. "And he visited Baltimore to see them, at least three times." She raised a second finger. "He abducted my mother—or pretended to." She raised a third. "He was seen with Dr Chen on the morning of the day he died." She raised a fourth.

"And," Nguyen said, "he had the opportunity. You can tick off another finger." He flashed a grin. "His link with HA means he could have got the poison from them. Another finger. What's that, six? The question is, why would HA want Chen dead? That's a pretty big call."

McTeish and Brothers looked at Nguyen, waiting for the next bit.

After a moment Nguyen said. "It could be they wanted to own all the research, and Chen was holding out. If the work got out and HA didn't own it, it could have a big financial hit on their fertiliser business. Without the upside of earning from more productive wheat."

Nguyen underlined Euston in the fourth box and turned to face them. "Next, Kosic."

McTeish reddened, then said, "He was caught by Dr Chen making psychedelics in his lab, and Chen said he'd report him. This was a day before he died. Kosic's career could be in danger. That's a motive."

"*Was* in danger," Nguyen said. "Not *could be*."

"How'd he get the poison?" Brothers said., then laughed "Maybe he made it when he was finished with the psychedelics. That's a couple of fingers, Carol—motive and opportunity."

Nguyen underlined Kosic in the box, then said, "Next?"

"Simon Lee," Brothers said. "His missus was screwing Chen. Motive: jealousy."

"And as a chemist he could source the poison," McTeish said.

Nguyen wrote Lee in second the box.

"And Lucy Bottega," Brothers said. "She seemed upset all right, but was that an act? She found out about his affair with Yasmin, so, the same motive as with Simon Lee. Jealousy."

"Motive and opportunity." Nguyen wrote Bottega in the first box.

"Lots of people have affairs. Doesn't mean they're murderers," McTeish said.

"True, true," Nguyen said. "But it doesn't mean they're not, either."

"But how would she have got the poison?" she asked.

"Good point—but that's not impossible." He stared at the whiteboard. "Maybe you were right, and for the moment we should forget about a disgruntled Greenie. Or not prioritise them. That's a bit too left field. If none of the others pan out we can explore them." He turned around to face McTeish and Brothers. "So: we have Euston, Kosic, Lee and Bottega. Any suggestions?"

They looked at the whiteboard, thinking.

Nguyen said, "Carol. How about you bring Kosic in. We need to find out more about what he was making in the lab."

"He said psychedelics," McTeish said. "And he certainly seemed pretty distressed about Dr Chen finding out."

"Could he have made something poisonous, by mistake? As Graham suggested?" Nguyen said. "When he's here, I'll join you."

"What about Lee and Bottega?" Brothers said.

"They both had the opportunity to poison Chen. I must say I did think Lee was genuine when he got upset, thinking he might have contributed to Chen's death, you know, by alleviating the symptoms. Could've been put on, of course. Same for Bottega."

"Maybe Lucy and Lee worked together," Brothers said. "Lee would have been just as pissed off about his wife with Chen as Lucy would have been."

"Does that happen very often?" McTeish said. "I mean, have there been other cases where the partners of an adulterer team up?"

"There can always be a first time for everything," Nguyen said, grinning. "Though it does seem a bit far-fetched ..."

"But we can't rule it out," Brothers completed the sentence, also grinning.

72

Early in the evening McTeish had just got home when her phone buzzed. It was an unknown number. She hesitated, then put it to her ear. "Hello? Detective Constable McTeish speaking."

"Ah, Carol." The stomach-curdling purr of Euston.

She waited a moment, composed herself. "Yes?"

"Now your colleague has released me from the interview room—and I must say, there's a case to examine the fittings in police interview rooms, wouldn't you say?" He paused, and she waited. "Are you still there?"

"What do you want to say?"

"Ah, Carol. Carol. It's not just what I want to say, it's what I will say."

She could imagine his supercilious smile. "Yes?" She gritted her teeth.

"Your mother and I would like you to come over."

"My mother? What are you doing with her?"

There came an odd sound through her phone. She realised he was laughing.

"Not the sort of question a daughter should ask, don't you think? Not if you want to know the answer!"

She waited. Why had she phrased it like that? As he made no further comment, she said, "Where are you?"

"The Pullman Hotel, in East Melbourne." He chuckled. "Interesting name, isn't it?"

"Why do you want me to come over?"

"There's a few things to straighten out, don't you think?"

Against her better judgment she said, "When?"

"No time like the present, as the actress, er," He stopped. "Can you come over now? Of course, you *can* come now, but *will* you?"

She sighed. "Okay." She checked her watch. "I'll be there at 7:00 pm." She hung up, then dialled Nguyen, and told him that she was going to see Euston and her mother at the East Melbourne Pullman.

"Would you like me to come with you?" Nguyen asked.

"I should be okay. If there's any funny business I'll call you again."

"With Euston, you can guarantee there'll be funny business. Don't forget, he's still very much in the frame for Chen's murder—in fact, I will come with you."

"But he's with my mother."

"All the more reason. Where are you?"

"I'm at home."

"Okay. Can you meet me in the hotel lobby in half an hour? And while we don't have all the evidence on Euston, let's hope we can get him before he does something to your mother."

"Does something? To my mum?" McTeish shuddered, her thoughts flailing.

"See you at the hotel." Nguyen finished the call, and she stared at her phone.

After a moment, she texted Euston that she would be at the hotel in 30 minutes. She shook her head, grabbed her bag and jumped in her car. She arrived at the Pullman, parked in the basement and entered the lobby. She checked her watch: Winner should be there in ten or so minutes.

"Constable McTeish!" She heard Euston's unmistakeable voice, and spun around. Euston was striding towards her from a lift. "A little early—but then that's how you get the worm, isn't it?" He clasped her right arm. "Come with me!"

"Let go! What are you talking about?" She walked back a step.

He followed. "If you want to see you mother in, shall we say, one piece, then come with me. Now!" He snapped the word out, and pulled her towards the lift.

As she was being dragged in, McTeish looked around for her boss. There was no sign of him. The doors of the lift closed, and the lift descended.

"Stop this. Don't be ridiculous." She paused for breath. "Where is my mother?"

"You'll see, soon enough. Just get into my car."

"No," she said.

"What was it Sinatra said about regrets? I can tell you that if you don't come with me, you'll have a few."

She grabbed his free arm, turned and kneed him between the legs. He bent over for a moment, gasping, then straightened up and slapped her across the cheek.

She reeled. The force of the blow nearly knocked her over.

"I won't forget that," he snarled, and dragged her by the arm out of the lift, down a row of cars. He clicked a remote and opened the front passenger side door of a dark grey sedan while still holding on to her. "Get in. Now!"

She looked around. No one. The grip on her biceps tightened. It was painful. She made a decision and sat down. He released her arm and slammed the door shut. She watched as he went to the rear and opened the boot. After a short time he opened the driver's door and sat down opposite her. Before she realised what he was doing he'd put handcuffs on her right wrist, and grabbed her left hand, putting the other cuff on.

"Mr Euston," she said.

"Terry!" he snapped.

"This is not a good idea. Whatever you may have done earlier, you're now definitely up for assault and kidnapping."

He ignored her, started the engine, reversed out of the parking bay and drove around towards the exit. As they did she saw Winner in his car drive past in the opposite direction. She shouted out, but the car was past them. Euston drove out into the street outside the hotel, waited a moment, then accelerated east.

"What are you trying to do?"

"Shut up," he said. "Or do I have to shut you up myself?"

She closed her mouth. Her phone rang.

"Ignore it!" Euston said.

Would it be Winner? she thought. He'd be in the hotel lobby by now, wondering if she had been held up.

Euston drove north, then east until they arrived at a tall apartment block, parking at the kerb. He turned to her. "This can be easy, or not easy. I should say, it *will* be easy or not easy. It's up to you. If you come quietly, without protest, it will be easy. If you try to make trouble, you know who will suffer?" He watched her eyes. "Yes, your mother. Which is it going to be?"

A light rain had started to fall. She nodded, and they walked through the drizzle to the lifts, and rode up to Level 24.

Euston stood close to her, a fleeting idea that she push a lift button and jump out she immediately dismissed as impractical. Would Winner realise she was not at the Pullman? She had to keep Euston talking, distract him somehow.

"What is this all about, Terry?" she said.

He grunted and otherwise ignored her.

"You like my mother? Why drag me into it?"

"Shut up," he said.

"Come on, can you explain it to me" Before he could say anything she added, "I know you *can*, but *will* you?"

He glanced at her, a slight smile tugging at his lips, which then firmed into an angry sneer. "I *can*, as you correctly state—but I won't." He shut his mouth, just as the lift pinged its arrival at level 24. The doors slid open and he pushed her forward. "To the right," he said.

He unlocked the door to apartment 2403, and pushed her in the back again so she stumbled forward. The lights were on but she could see no-one. There was an open kitchen to the right, a settee and two armchairs facing a large TV, and a closed door to the left. "Where's my mother?"

Euston said nothing.

"Come on, Terry. The lights are on, surely someone is at home?"

"All in good time, Carol. Sit." He pointed at an armchair.

"What about these?" She raised her handcuffed hands.

He looked at her for a moment. "That will depend,"

"Depend? On what."

"Shut up." He paced in front of her, glancing at the door that led, presumably, to a bedroom or bedrooms and bathroom.

So, was her mother in there? And if so, was she free or also tied up? She got to her feet, warily watching him. He regarded her, then went to the kitchen and poured a bourbon.

"You want one?" he asked.

A drink? The absolute gall! She shook her head and walked to the window, overlooking the city. There was a balcony, accessible via a sliding door. Useless unless she got the cuffs off. Maybe a drink might work. She returned to the chair and said, "A drink would be good. What do you have?"

"That's better! What would you like?"

"A glass of water." She saw his expression harden. "To start with," she added.

He seemed to relax, or at least he took a glass, filled it from the tap and brought it over to her.

She held up her hands, holding the glass with difficulty.

He looked steadily at her for a time, then took a swift glance around the apartment. "Can't hurt, I suppose," he said, and extracted a key from his pocket, unlocking the handcuffs.

"Thank you," she said.

"That's better." He stood back, surveying her.

"Can I look around?" she said, nodding her head towards the door. "Is the bathroom through there?"

"It can't hurt," he muttered again. "Go ahead."

She took a sip of water, put the glass down on a small table near the chair, and opened the door. There was a short corridor with three doors.

"First on the right," he said.

She opened it, entered and sat down on the toilet seat lid and looked around. It seemed a standard bathroom: a bath, shower and basin. There were no toothbrushes or toothpaste in evidence, no cosmetics, just a hand towel and two water glasses next to the basin. Did anyone actually live here? She flushed the toilet, waited some seconds, rinsed her hands in the basin, dried them then opened the door. He was not in the hall—still in the main area, she presumed. She quickly opened one of the two other doors, revealing an empty bedroom. No Claire. She opened the door of the other room—and saw her mother tied up in a chair, with a gag taped over her mouth.

She ran over, removed the tape and untied the rope binding her to the chair.

"Oh, darling," her mother said, and slumped in the chair.

McTeish felt her pulse. She decided to check the hallway. The door leading to Euston was locked. So he's locked us in, she thought. Good. She went back to the bathroom, and filled a glass with water, and took it to her mother. She was still lolling in the chair.

"Mum. Here, drink this."

Her mother opened her eyes and smiled feebly at her. She sipped, then said, "I've been so foolish." She sipped again.

"Don't be silly. Of course you haven't been foolish. You're the victim. Euston is the culprit, not you."

"But still," her mother trailed off. "I should've known better."

"Let's not worry about that—do you need the bathroom?" She clasped her mother's hands. They were cold.

"Yes, please."

She helped her to her feet and to the toilet, left the door open. There was still no sign of Euston. She heard music start up in the other area, a regular low bass thumping

"Where's Terry?" her mother whispered.

"In the living area. I don't know why but he's let me go here. He even took off the hand cuffs."

"Hand cuffs?" Her mother burst out sobbing. "He put hand cuffs on you?"

"Don't worry, Mum. We'll get you safe."

But how? She helped her mother back to the chair. She had a thought. "Hang on a sec." She darted out into the hallway and checked the door again. Still locked. "He's locked us into this section of the apartment."

"Is that good?"

"Better than having him in here."

"But why did he bring you here?"

"I've no idea. But first, how did he get you to come here?"

"You know Terry," she said, tossing her hair. That was more like her mother, she thought. "He said we'd have some fun. Then, when we got here, he tied me up." She burst into tears again. "What an idiot!"

"He's the idiot." She walked to the window and looked out. The balcony extended along the wall. "Mum. I've had an idea. Let me tie you up again."

"What?" He mother cried out. Her face was taught with anxiety.

"Shoosh. It'll just be loose. Just for appearances. I'll climb out the window and try to go next door."

He mother's face relaxed, and she nodded. "I suppose...."

McTeish retied the rope, loosely, and put the tape back over her mother's mouth. It still stuck. "Okay?"

She nodded.

McTeish opened the window, climbed out and slid the window shut behind her. The fine drizzle had if anything increased, and the surface made up of dark ceramic tiles was wet. At the end of the balcony there was a gap of a metre or so to the next one. She clenched her fists. Could she get across? The wall had uneven brickwork. Also wet. She put one hand out to wedge it between two bricks for stability, and climbed onto the railing. She looked down to the black shining street, a huge drop of about a hundred metres. Her stomach lurched. Looking down was a big mistake. She steadied herself on the railing, fixed her gaze on the opposite balcony. Come on, you can do it. Stop hesitating, she told herself. It's only a metre.

She jumped.

73

Nguyen parked and took the lift to the lobby of the Pullman. He checked his watch. It was 6:55 pm. There was the usual bustle of people, a couple dragging wheeled bags to check in, and no sign yet of McTeish or Euston. There was a circular staircase leading up to the hotel's conference centre, and he took a few steps up it, but there was no one on them. He walked back and looked around, and sat down on a leather chair that gave him a view of the lifts and the front doors.

A waiter came up and asked if he wanted anything, and he shook his head. Where was Carol? He checked his watch again. Five past seven. She'd said they'd meet in half an hour, at seven, and she was normally on time. He drummed his fingers on the arm rest, then called her. The phone rang for a time but there was no answer.

Five minutes later he jumped up and walked around the lobby. No sign of her. He rang again, and still she didn't answer. Could she have gone up to Euston's room? He went to the counter, showed his identification, and asked which room Mr Terry Euston was in. The receptionist, a slight young woman named Eva, according to her badge, keyed at her computer.

"I'm sorry sir. We have no guest of that name staying with us." She smiled.

"What about McCauley, Terry McCauley?"

Eva searched again and shook her head. "Sorry, sir. No Mr McCauley either. Anyone else?"

"No, thanks." He scowled in frustration. He called Brothers, who answered on the second ring.

"G'day, boss. What's up?"

"Have you heard from Carol?"

"No. Should I have?"

"I'm meant to be meeting her at the Pullman Hotel in East Melbourne, about quarter of an hour ago."

"The Pullman?"

"Yes. Euston called her and said he had her mother here. She was going to meet him at seven, but there's no sign of either of them, and he's not registered as a guest."

"Could he be using another name?"

"He'd have to have a credit card, or some other form of identification. I suppose it's possible, but I doubt it."

"Maybe she got delayed by traffic."

"Maybe—but Euston and Claire McTeish as well?"

"Good point."

There was a pause. "Something doesn't seem right," Nguyen said. "I'll try calling her again." He hung up and did so, but the call went to voicemail. "Carol. Call me as soon as you hear this," he said.

74

McTeish hit the partition, her abdomen landing on the rail, winding her, her body face downwards towards the tiles, her hands wet. Made it. She scrambled over and stood up, heart beating. She felt her stomach. All seemed okay, and she rubbed her hands dry. She moved to the sliding door. It was locked, and there was no light inside. Shit. She moved shakily to the end and stared at the next apartment along. There was yellowish light coming from behind its glass sliding door.

The leap this time seemed easier. She stood up on the railing again, hand on the bricks keeping her steady, the bricks for some reason not so wet, and jumped.

She landed in a similar fashion to last time, midriff on the rail, face towards the tiled floor of the balcony. Again she scrambled up, again her stomach was winded. Apart from that everything was fine. She glanced back. There was no movement on the balcony she'd come from.

She shook her head, and rapped at the sliding door. There was movement inside, and shortly the window slid open.

"Who are you?" A short woman in her eighties glared at her. "I may be old but I'm not afraid! What are you doing here?"

"I'm trying to escape," McTeish said. The woman stepped back, her mouth open. "I was locked in apartment 2403, and need to get out." She smiled; would the woman help her?

"Apartment 2403? Isn't that that nice Mr McCauley?"

"That's the one." She looked at the woman. Nice Mr McCauley indeed. "Can I come in, please? And use your phone? I'm a police officer. Carol McTeish."

The woman eyed her for a time, then shrugged and relaxed. "Yes, dear," she said. "You seem awfully young to be a policeman." She stood aside and let McTeish through. "I'm Fiona Callahan," she said, as she picked up her phone from a couch, touched her finger to it and handed it to her. "It's not locked."

"Thank you," McTeish said. "I'll explain in a minute." What was Winner's number? It was so easy when numbers were in your phone. She recalled the prefix digits, and Nguyen emphasising the need to learn by heart his and Brother's numbers, for just this sort of situation when you didn't have your phone. Then she recalled the rest of the number—she hoped. She dialled, and Nguyen answered immediately.

"Yes? Who is this?" His voice was brusque, impatient.

"It's me." She said. "Oh god." She breathed out heavily, gasping in relief.

"Carol? Where the hell are you?" he said. "I'm waiting in the lobby. I thought you said half an hour. And there's no sign of Euston. What held you up?"

"Euston took me, Boss. He hand-cuffed me. He hit me." She sobbed, after a moment biting her lip to stop.

"He what?" Nguyen said.

"He hit me, slapped me, hard." She took a breath, steadied herself. "I did kick him in the balls."

"Good on you, dear," Fiona Callahan said. "That's exactly where you should kick someone who does that to you."

Briefly she told Nguyen what had happened.

"Where are you? And who's that who spoke?"

"That's a very helpful lady. I'm in her apartment. I don't know where we are—Euston drove North then East, so maybe in Hawthorn. It's an apartment block. I was in 2403. But now I'm in—" she looked at Callahan.

"We're 2407," Callahan said, eyes wide.

"Apartment 2407." She nodded to Callahan, who gave a weak smile.

"I'll be there straight away," Nguyen said. "Is your mother okay?"

"She was when I left her." McTeish grimaced at the thought of her mother still tied up.

"Euston must be wondering what he's got himself into," Nguyen said.

"I doubt he ever wonders that—what's the address here?" she asked Ms Callahan, who stood watching her with her mouth open. She passed on the information to Nguyen.

There was a thump from outside on the balcony.

"What next?" the old woman said. She moved behind the kitchen island and grabbed a frying pan, which she kept below the bench top. "Another one?"

"Get down!" McTeish said, and the older woman ducked down behind the bench.

The sliding door opened and Euston stormed in.

"He's here, Boss," McTeish yelled, as Euston wrestled the phone from her hand.

"Mr McCauley!" Callahan called out. "What on earth are you doing?"

Euston looked up, while attempting to twist McTeish's arm holding the phone. "Why, Mrs Callahan. What does it look like I'm doing?" he snarled. He grabbed the phone while trying to force McTeish's arm upwards behind her back.

As he spoke McTeish sagged back into him, relieving the pressure on her arm for the moment, then crouched and jerked him over her to the floor. Callahan darted out from behind the kitchen island and smacked the frypan on his forehead. Euston slumped. She raised the frypan— cast iron, McTeish saw as she panted—and whacked him again. Euston appeared to lose consciousness.

"That'll teach the brute!" Callahan said, with a gleam in her eye. "I may be old but I'm not useless."

"Thank you," McTeish said, shaking her head in amazement. She focused. "Do you have any string, or tape? I need to tie him up."

Callahan pulled out a drawer in the bench and rummaged around. "Nothing here, I'm afraid." She shut the drawer. "Hang on a sec." She went through a doorway and soon emerged with two pairs of tights. "Will these do?" There was a gleam in her eye. "I haven't had this much fun since … I dunno. Since whenever."

McTeish took the tights and tied Euston's arms with one pair and his legs with the other. She stood up and saw the phone on the floor and retrieved it. Nguyen was still on the line.

"Did you hear any of that?" she asked.

"What happened? Can I speak to Euston?"

"I'm afraid Mr Euston is all tied up at present." She told him he was out cold, on the floor. "Thanks to Mrs Callahan."

"We'll be over quickly."

She finished the call, and handed the phone back to Mrs Callahan, who had slumped into a chair.

A thought suddenly occurred to her. "My mother. I'll have to check she's okay." The prospect of climbing back over the balconies did not appeal, and she searched Euston's pockets, who groaned as she did so. She found a set of keys.

"Mrs Callahan—" McTeish began.

"*Miss* Callahan," the old lady said, sitting up straight in her chair.

"Sorry. I need to check how my mother is. She's in 2403."

"Okay, dear," she said, smiling and sitting back.

McTeish found the key to apartment 2403 on the bunch she had taken, opened the door and rushed to the room where her mother sat slumped in the chair. For a moment she feared the worst, then Claire groaned softly. McTeish untied the ropes, and hugged her.

"Are you okay?" she asked.

"Oh …" her mother mumbled into McTeish's hair. "Thank you, darling." She pulled back and looked into McTeish's face. "Where were you?"

"Hush. It's all right now." Holding her mother brought a range of feelings to the surface. Relief that she was okay. Anger that she had got herself into this mess in the first place. And a swelling love that brought tears to her eyes. She was hugging her spiteful mother. She looked into her eyes. "Mum." She hesitated. "You *are* okay, aren't you?"

"Yes, dear." Her mother hugged her back, breathing heavily.

A few minutes later she heard a door open and shut, and Nguyen appeared. She looked up and he smiled. "You both all right?"

McTeish nodded. Claire hugged her tighter.

"Graham is with Miss Callahan. Amazing old bird, that," he said. "He's cuffed Euston. When you're up to it, bring your mother down. Or does she need an ambulance?"

Claire tried to stand up, and stumbled against McTeish. "I'm okay," she said in a soft voice. "Can I go home?"

"I'll take you, mum."

Nguyen nodded. "Take her home. Stay with her."

"What about Euston?"

"You can come in tomorrow. We'll take him back for another little chat. He's not going anywhere."

"Euston took my phone."

Nguyen reached into his pocket. "Here it is. It was on the coffee table."

"Thanks." She took it and thought for a moment. "Hang on a sec." She took photos of her mother in the chair, the doorway to the balcony, and went out and photographed the further balconies and the long drop between them. "Oh," she said. "My car. It's still at the Pullman."

"Graham can drive you. We came in separate cars. Sit with your mother while we get Euston."

"I want to thank Miss Callahan. You should have seen her!" McTeish mimed the whacking down of a frying pan.

"Make sure your mum is okay first." He left.

"Mum, will you be okay if I go next door. Then I'll take you home?"

"Carol. Could you stay a minute, please?" Her voice was subdued, listless.

"Come into the other room." She led her into the living area. "Sit down here, on the couch." She sat her mother down. "Are you warm enough?"

Claire nodded. "I'm okay." She shivered.

McTeish searched around and found a blanket in the bedroom. "It's the shock," she said, wrapping it around her mother's shoulders.

"Thanks, darling." She gazed at McTeish, her lower lip quivering.

McTeish hugged her again, and her mother collapsed and sobbed against her shoulder. A little later she stopped, sat erect.

"I'm okay now."

"Okay if I go? It'll only be a minute or two. Then I'll take you home."

Her mother smiled sheepishly and nodded.

In Miss Callahan's apartment, Euston stirred on the floor. He lay face down where Brothers had hand cuffed him. Nguyen and Brothers stood looking down at him. "Whatever else he may have done," Nguyen said, "he'll certainly go down for kidnapping."

"Twice," Brothers said. "Carol *and* her mum." He looked sideways at Nguyen. "What about Dr Chen?"

Nguyen rubbed his chin, glanced meaningfully towards Miss Callahan, who stood watching them from behind her kitchen bench.

"Right, right," Brothers said.

"Thank you, Miss Callahan," Nguyen said. "You helped us enormously. Probably saved our colleague, too."

"Oh, I don't know," Fiona Callahan said. "You just do what you've got to do. Would you like a cup of tea?"

Brothers eyed Nguyen, who shook his head. "Thank you, but no thanks," the latter said. "We'll get this guy out of your apartment."

Euston moaned and moved his arms. "What …?" he said. He turned his head. "What …? Hey! What's happening?" Then, as if a light had gone on, he moaned. "Oh. Shit."

"Don't tell me." Brothers sniffed. "He grinned at Nguyen. "All good, boss." He reached under Euston's shoulder, turned him over and sat him up. "What's happening is that you're going back with us for a long conversation."

Nguyen reached down and took a phone from Euston's pocket. "Ah ha," he said, grinning at Brothers.

McTeish knocked on the open door to Miss Callahan's apartment and looked in, saw Brothers and Nguyen getting Euston to his feet.

Euston saw her and his face drooped briefly, then a gleam came back into his eyes. "Detective Constable!" he said. "Fancy meeting you here! Do you come here often?"

Brothers led him past her, out into the corridor. Nguyen followed and said, "Get your mum home. We'll see you tomorrow."

McTeish went up to Miss Callahan, who came out from behind the bench. "Thank you so much, Fiona," she said. "You certainly were a great help today."

Fiona Callahan blushed. "As I said to the Inspector, it was nothing, really. Anything to help."

Without thinking, McTeish hugged her. "I wish everyone was as brave as you."

"Oh, tush." Miss Callahan smiled sweetly at her. "It was a bit of fun, wasn't it?"

76

BACK AT THE STATION Brothers led Euston to one of the interview rooms, uncuffed him and sat him down.

"We'll be back shortly." He left, locking the door, and joined Nguyen in his office. "He's in room 503," he said to him.

"Let's interview him while everything's fresh," Nguyen said. "Before he has the chance to concoct some new story. Let's focus on the abductions. Then we can get to Dr Chen. And let's get his phone analysed. There may be messages from Baltimore."

"Why would he have abducted them unless he was desperate?" Brothers said.

"Let's try to find out." He looked at his watch. It was quarter to eleven. "It's late, and he's not going anywhere. We'll get first impressions, then let him stew overnight." He glanced down and picked up Euston's phone, waving it a little, as if weighing it up. "He's a smart arse, isn't he," he muttered, and went to open the phone. The entry code screen came up. What, thought Nguyen, would a smart arse have for a code. A dumb smart arse. Something simple, something he thinks no one would ever use because it's too obvious. So, let's see … He keyed in 12345. Nothing. He rubbed his jaw, then keyed in 54321.

Bingo.

"You got it?" Brothers said, his eyes widening. "Are we allowed to do this?"

"We'll get the authorisation. A little task for you. Let's look at his Messages." Nguyen flicked it open, scrolled down. "Hello! He's been in touch with our Baltimore friends. And with Fred Lovell."

He scrolled down further, and handed it to Brothers. "We'll need a print-out of this."

The first thing Euston said was, "I want my lawyer. I won't speak until she's here."

"You want your lawyer? No problem. Who should we call?"

"Susan Ashton. She's with McDonald Grewing."

Brothers searched his phone and called her. The phone rang and went to voicemail. "No luck. Must be a bit late for her."

"I won't speak until she's here."

Brothers gazed at him, switched on the recording devices, gave the date and time, and said, "Terry Euston, you have been arrested on two charges of abduction, and of assault. There will be other charges, I'm sure. I must inform you that you do not have to say or do anything but anything you say or do may be given in evidence in court."

Euston stared with his jaw thrust out. "As I said, I'm not saying anything until Susan is here."

"That's your right," Nguyen said. "We can get a duty solicitor, if you like."

Euston shook his head. "Susan Ashton, or nothing," he said.

"Tell me, while we're waiting—"

"It'll be a long wait if the call went to voicemail," Euston said.

"Why abduct Detective Constable McTeish? And her mother?" Nguyen continued.

"Who says I abducted them?"

"They do."

"La di da di dah," Euston said. "That's all you'll get out of me."

"What about Dr Chen?" Brothers said. "Why did you kill him?"

"Dr Chen? I told you I had nothing to do with him."

"I can understand you saying that," Nguyen said. "Murder is a lot, lot worse than kidnapping."

"Well, fuck you, too." Euston clamped his mouth shut and sat back in his chair.

"Charming. We had a quick look at your phone messages. Seems you have been a good correspondent with Fred Lovell."

Euston's eyes flickered, but he said nothing.

"We'll get a print-out tomorrow morning," Nguyen said, watching Euston for any reaction.

"Good for you." Euston said.

There was a call on Brother's phone. "This is Susan Ashton. You rang?" Brothers checked his watch. A bit after 11 pm. "Yes, sorry for the hour, but it seems a client of yours wants to speak to you. A Terry Euston." He put the phone on loud speaker and laid it on the table.

"Ms Ashton?" Euston said. "I'm being pestered by the Victorian Police and I wonder if you can help me."

"What's he in for?" Ashton said.

"Kidnap and assault at the moment. Possibly murder," Brothers said.

They heard a muffled expletive, that might have started with an f sound.

"This is Detective Inspector John Nguyen, Ms Ashton. Can you come in? We're at the South Melbourne station."

Again there was a muffled exclamation, then, quite clear, Ashton said, "I'd like to speak to my client in private, please."

"Happy for you to do so. Come to Reception and they will buzz me and I'll come down and take you to him." He finished the call, and his lips quirked. To Euston he said, "We'll leave you for the moment," and shut off the recording equipment.

He and Brothers left the room. In the corridor, Nguyen said, "Fancy a coffee?"

Brothers shrugged, seemed about to say something, but then said, "I'll get them. Okay with the vending machine?"

"Not really, but this late it will have to do."

77

"How long do you think she'll take to get here?" Brothers asked, as they walked back to their offices, sipping their coffees.

"The lawyer? Half an hour or so." Nguyen rubbed his jaw, thought about Euston and muttered to himself, "The turd kidnapped a police! And her mother. He hit McTeish. It'd be different if we'd nabbed him for some sort of white-collar crime—" Nguyen broke off and glanced at Brothers. "Funny, isn't it, how white-collar crime always seems to be the grey area? Anyhow, it doesn't matter if the solicitor stops Euston talking. We've got enough on him to get him locked away for years."

There was a buzz on his desk phone. The lawyer had got there quicker than he had expected.

"Graham, can you bring her up? I'll meet you at the interview room.

Susan Ashton was a tall woman, in her late thirties or early forties, Nguyen estimated. She seemed weary—not surprising, he thought, given the time—but didn't display the arrogance he had expected. He introduced himself outside the interview room.

"Your client is inside. As I said, you can talk to him in private, first."

"Thank you, Inspector. What are you holding him for?"

"For the moment, as I said on the phone, two counts of kidnapping and of assault."

"Who do you say he kidnapped?" She spoke quietly.

"My colleague, Detective Constable Carol McTeish, and her mother."

Ashton's eyes widened. "And the assault?"

"On Constable McTeish. And on her mother."

"Mmm." She paused, about to enter the room, and turned back to Nguyen. "You mentioned murder? Did I hear right?"

"Yes. He's a person of interest in the death of Dr Chen Du, at the Badeker Institute."

Ashton's face was impassive. "Of interest, eh?"

"Of great interest."

"Then you'd better let me talk to Mr Euston."

Nguyen gestured with his right hand for her to enter.

FIFTEEN MINUTES LATER SHE knocked on the door and Brothers opened it.

"My client is willing to agree that he detained Constable McTeish, but he denies kidnapping her. Or her mother. He says they both accompanied him voluntarily. And he denies any assault, and certainly any involvement in Dr Chen's death. Furthermore, he will sign a statement to that effect, but will otherwise remain silent for the time being."

Nguyen smiled at her. "Thank you, Ms Ashton. About what I expected. If he won't speak for the time being, that's fine with us. We'll get an earlier night's sleep. But we'll be keeping Euston here."

"That's what I expected, too," she said.

78

THE NEXT MORNING McTEISH arrived at the station about 7:30 to find Nguyen already there. Brothers arrived a few minutes later.

"Are you okay after last night?" Nguyen asked her.

"Fine. Slept like a log, even though I was at Mum's place. She's pretty upset, though. I'll check on her later."

"Euston got his lawyer in last night. He won't speak for the time being, she said. But he she says he admits to 'detaining' you and your mother, but says you went voluntarily. And he denies any assault."

"Voluntarily? No assault?" McTeish went red in the face. "That lying arsehole!"

"Calm down, Carol. No jury will believe him. He's in deep shit."

"What about Dr Chen?" she asked.

"I reckon we can get him on that, too," Nguyen said. "There's plenty of circumstantial evidence. We know Howarth-Acfield paid him to be at the Institute. We know he met Dr Chen the day he died, and I think any reasonable silk can convince a jury that that's when he poisoned him. No matter how much he denies it—and which criminal arsehole admits they did the deed?—I reckon a jury will convict. Particularly when we get this open—" Nguyen held up Euston's phone—"and find the evidence trail. And we can cross off Kosic, the Lees and Chen's partner, Lucy Bottega."

McTeish nodded. "Certainly simplifies everything."

"I think so. We've got motive—financial on the part of Howarth-Acfield. And we've got opportunity—he was paid to be there at the Badeker, and he saw Chen at the cafe the day he died. I'll let the boss know."

"He didn't help himself kidnapping my mum and me," McTeish said.

"Seems his blood left his brain for another part of his anatomy," Brothers said, then shut his mouth.

"I suspect he knew he was done for the murder, and went for broke," Nguyen said.

"Too clever by half," McTeish grinned.

"And we'll have the satisfaction of putting that clever dick away. For a long time." Nguyen said.

79

Superintendent Forell looked up at Nguyen as he entered her office. "I trust you're not bearing bad news," she said, her face impassive.

"Last time I said we had good and bad news. This time it's good."

She cocked an eye. "Do tell."

"We're charging Euston with kidnapping and assault."

"Euston or Macauley?" she said. "I recall there was some confusion about who he is."

"Euston will do."

"And Dr Chen? The murder?"

"That, too."

Forell raised an eyebrow. "What aren't you telling me, John?"

"He denies it, in fact denies the kidnapping and assault too, but we have all the evidence we need to put him away for a long time."

"Evidence, hmm," Forell said, sitting up straighter and staring at Nguyen. "How good is the evidence? We don't want this one to fall apart."

"The kidnapping and the assault—we have witnesses."

"Who are they?

"Detective Constable Carol McTeish and her mother." Nguyen let out a breath he hadn't realised he'd been holding.

Forell's lips curved. "Mr Euston has been busy. What happened?"

Nguyen told her of the past 24 hours.

"And Dr Chen?"

"Circumstantial—the evidence, I mean. Euston was paid by the pharma, Howarth-Acfield. We've got confirmation on his phone. Text messages, emails. He was doing their bidding."

"His phone? How did you get that?"

"He had it on him when we arrested him for kidnapping McTeish and her mother."

"And how did you unlock it?"

Nguyen grinned and told her about the passcode.

"What's that saying? Bullshit baffles brains. Is that relevant? Good work, John. Excellent." She stretched her arms and looked at him again. "So that looks like a result. Good. Good." Her brows furrowed. "And Dr Chen? What about him?"

"Here's the thing, Sup. He met Chen the morning of the day he died. At the coffee place next to the Badeker Institute. That's when we reckon he poisoned him, in his coffee."

"You *reckon*? Why would he do that?"

"This is where it gets interesting. It's the reason Dr Chen had to go." Nguyen paused a moment, and Forell raised her eyebrows again. "You see, Howarth-Acfield, the pharma that was paying Euston, stood to lose a motza if Chen's work paid off."

"Hang on a sec." Forell frowned. "Didn't you tell me Howarth-Acfield invested in Chen's research?"

"They did. Or rather, they didn't."

"John, John. You're giving me a headache. They either did or they didn't. Which is it?"

"They invested in the Badeker, but Dr Chen refused to sign up. And apparently his work looked like bearing fruit."

Seeing Forell's mouth tighten, Nguyen said, "The Badeker has two teams working on wheat, with different approaches. The other team signed up and got the money. But Chen held out. He wanted his IP to be in the public domain. And get this—after Chen died Howarth-Acfield signed up his team."

"So they now own the IP?"

"Exactly. And that's why they can now bury the research."

"You're confusing me again. Why would Howarth-Acfield lose if Chen's research worked out? Wouldn't it be the other way around? Wouldn't they benefit?"

"You'd think so, wouldn't you?" Nguyen said, then, on seeing Forell tighten her lips, hastily added. "But their fertiliser business is much, much more important to them than the pharmaceutical side. Into the billions. Apparently they didn't get any of the gravy—"

"Gravy?"

"The Covid government money. They missed out on all the Covid vaccine contracts.

"What sort of gravy are we talking about?"

"A very big pot, into the billions. So their pharmaceutical business missed out on that—and they faced losing a huge chunk of their fertiliser business."

"How so?"

"Think about it."

Forell winced.

"Sorry. I'm sure the prosecutors will explain it nicely. Here's what we've worked out. Chen was increasing the protein in wheat. But not just that—he was also making it resistant to pests and making it much more effective in sucking nutrients from the earth. Hence farmers would have no need for their fertiliser. They stood to lose those billions. That's why they wanted Dr Chen dead. If he finished his research then they wouldn't even get revenue from the new wheat seed. Euston was their tool."

"So the farmers wouldn't need the pharma?" Forell stared at Nguyen, a glimmer of a smile on her face.

"What? Oh, yes." He forced a chuckle. "Good one, Sup."

Forell was silent for a time, then said, "What about Chen's wife. Didn't you tell me Chen was having an affair?"

"Yes. And no." Nguyen reddened a little as Forell narrowed her eyes. "Yes," he said. "We think he was having an affair. But no, she wasn't his wife. Just his partner."

Forell took a deep breath and sat back, regarding Nguyen, again without speaking. He felt as if she saw him as some sort of unpleasant insect. "And the lab guy, Kosic? The one with the party drugs in the lab?" she finally said.

"We don't think he did it, either."

Forell raised an eyebrow.

"He had the opportunity, sure. And I suppose the motive, if he thought Dr Chen was going to report his extra mural activities."

"Extra mural? I like that," Forell said, without a smile.

"It just doesn't add up. Although he was at the lab that evening, he left early, and there's no evidence he poisoned Chen."

"But he could have slipped him something during the day?"

"That's possible, I suppose. But, I doubt we could mount a case to convince a jury, when we've got Euston. I always thought that Kosic was the least likely."

"Hmm." Forell gazed up at the ceiling, then back at Nguyen. "And the husband of the woman he was having it off with?"

"Same." Nguyen kept his voice calm. "As I say, we're pretty sure it was Euston, doing HA's bidding."

"Pretty sure, eh?" Forell regarded him steadily.

"Particularly when you take in the kidnapping and assault. And the messages on his phone. We think we have enough for a prosecutor to convince a jury to convict. Opportunity, motive, both."

"And you say Euston poisoned Chen the morning he died?"

"Yes—sneaked ricin into his coffee. The ricin we presume he got from Howarth-Acfield. Then Chen felt symptoms a few hours later. Chest tightness, difficulty breathing, maybe the runs. He called his mate Simon Lee, the pharmacist, wanting him to give him something to tide him over so he could finish his work overnight. He must have thought he was getting the flu or something. And the ricin was able to kill him sometime around midnight. Lee was pretty upset when he realised that if he'd known Chen had been poisoned he might've saved him."

"Okay. What are you waiting for?" She picked up a sheet of paper on her desk and started reading it.

80

As HE LEFT NGUYEN thought about what he had just said, that Euston would be convicted. But what if he was telling the truth when he said he'd had nothing to do with Dr Chen's murder? What if they had dismissed the other possible culprits too easily? Did it matter, as long as they got a conviction? Euston was a jerk, and a kidnapper and he had assaulted McTeish. And he had been paid by HA, and HA had a big motive to take out Chen. But what if one of Chen's colleagues or friends or his partner had done it? Did that matter as long they got a conviction?

He called Brothers and McTeish into his office and outlined his concern. "Part of me thinks, there's a really solid circumstantial case against Euston to get the prosecutors salivating. Particularly from his phone." He paused and looked at the other two. McTeish was focussed on what he was saying, and Brothers was fiddling with a hangnail.

"Are you saying we should check the other possibilities again, boss?" McTeish asked.

Brothers clasped his hands together. "Why bother?" he asked.

"All roads seem to lead to Euston," Nguyen said. "And he did kidnap and assault you, Carol, and your mother—"

"I don't think he assaulted my mum, but he certainly kidnaped her. And me too, of course."

"Quite right, Carol." Nguyen rubbed his jaw. "But could we sleep comfortably if someone else did the actual murder, and we left a killer walking around, free?"

Brothers scratched his belly. "So you want us to check up on Ms Bottega and the others—just in case?"

Nguyen nodded. Brothers groaned. McTeish looked down at her lap.

"I see you're both delighted by the prospect." He chuckled at their expressions. "If it's not Euston, the ones I'd focus on are Bottega and Kosic." A thought occurred to him. "What about the leader of the other team, Felix Robertson?"

"What about him?" Brothers said. "You reckon he found Dr Chen too much competition and knocked him off?"

"No, well, you're probably right, Graham. Come to think of it, they did work at the same place for several years. Why would he suddenly want Chen dead? He's got his funding; Chen hasn't. Forget it. I shouldn't have brought it up."

"But with Kosic, didn't his colleague Dr Shildduck know he'd been messing about in the lab?" McTeish asked. "Surely that gets him off the suspects list? If his job was in danger, then he'd have had to get rid of her as well."

Nguyen rubbed his chin again. "Good point, Carol. So it's really just Bottega who's left as a possibility. So you and Graham talk to Bottega. I think there's no point casting our net any wider—even though I started to."

McTeish and Brothers stood up. "Okay, boss," Brothers said. "Carol, come with me."

"It may not amount to anything, but it'll put my mind at rest." Nguyen put his elbows together on the desk, interlacing his fingers with his chin resting on them. "Let's do this quickly. At the same time, we'll try to crack Euston. He's still the most likely. So set up interviews with Bottega for tomorrow, and we'll get to Euston now."

"You know, boss," McTeish said as she and Brothers stood up to leave. "A thought occurred, seeing Euston seems so fixated on me and my mum."

"What's that?"

"Well, he didn't really do any harm to us, physically, I mean. Apart from the thump he gave me. He certainly frightened me, and mum. But what if that was a double bluff?"

"How do you mean?" asked Brothers.

"What if he did all that to throw us off the scent that he is the real murderer. I mean, wouldn't a good lawyer say all that, about us not being hurt, to get him a light sentence?"

Nguyen pondered for a moment. "Hold that thought, Carol."

81

Nguyen and Brothers commenced the interview with Euston, with Susan Ashton present, at 10:00 am on the dot. Brothers set the recording equipment in play and read out the caution. The room was cool and there was a slight antiseptic smell from the cleaners.

"Mr Euston," Nguyen said. "First, there's the matter of you kidnapping Detective Constable McTeish and her mother, and assaulting them both."

"My client has admitted he detained them. He did not kidnap them," Ashton said.

Nguyen ignored her and spoke to Euston. "So tying up Mrs McTeish, handcuffing her daughter, and taking them both, against their will, to your apartment, isn't kidnaping? Come off it. You're going down for quite a stretch for that."

"Just having a bit of fun," Euston muttered. "No harm to either of them. In fact, come to think of it, I might have a case of assault against that old biddy who whacked me on the head."

Ashton nudged Euston on the shoulder, and he stopped talking.

"We'll see how the court treats that," Nguyen said.

"As I said last night, my client might be willing to plead guilty to certain charges, as a gesture of good will. But not to assault."

Nguyen sat back and regarded the two of them. "Well, let's get to the more serious matter. The poisoning of Dr Chen Du."

"I've told you I had nothing to do with that," Euston said.

"Hmm, funny you should say that. We have these print-outs of messages and emails from your phone." He put his hand on some papers in front of him.

Euston sat stolidly; Ashton sat up straight. "How did you get the print outs?" she asked.

"Quite easily," Brothers said. "Used Bluetooth, and it goes straight to the computer. Then we print them out."

Ashton sucked in her breath. "How did you get access to the phone? That's a breach of privacy."

"Mr Euston left his phone with us when we caught him attempting to recapture Detective Constable McTeish."

Ashton glanced at Euston. "You gave them your phone?"

"I was indisposed," he said. "As I said, my neighbour hit me over the head."

Nguyen pushed a sheet of paper across the table. "You'll see here text messages between you and Fred Lovell.

The package arrived. All good to go.

"That's from you to Lovell, a week before Dr Chen's death. That would be the ricin arriving, wouldn't it?"

Euston's lips tightened but he said nothing.

"And this, also from you to Lovell."

Set up a coffee with Dr C.

"So?" Euston said. "So I had a coffee?"

"You told us you didn't know him."

"That's why I had the coffee—to get to know him."

Nguyen pointed further down the sheet.

All good. Will let you know.

"Seems an odd thing to text, wouldn't you say?" Nguyen said.

"It must have been a pleasant day."

"That text was sent at 10:43 am on the day of Dr Chen's death. We have you on camera entering Con and Sue's Coffee at 10:29, where you met up with him. And you sent it after you put ricin in his coffee."

"Could mean anything," Euston said.

"Certainly could, Mr Euston. But we know what it means, don't we? And," Nguyen said, pushing another sheet across the table. "Look at this text:

Problem solved

"I had a problem … with my camera." Euston faltered and stopped talking.

"You sent that to Lovell the day after Dr Chen's death. That was the problem you solved."

Euston's face sagged, but he said nothing.

"And this."

Check your account.

"From Lovell to you," Nguyen said. "Did you check your account?"

Ashton sat tight-lipped, and Euston said nothing.

"We're getting copies of your banking transactions shortly. We'll see what landed in your account." Looking at Ashton, he said, "We're getting the authorisations."

Ashton grimaced.

"And we have further messages between the two of you, that demonstrate what Howarth-Acfield really hired you to do. It wasn't just to photograph protests by Greenies outside the Badeker, was it Mr Euston?"

"It was just meant to—" Euston started, then shut his mouth.

"Just meant to what?" Nguyen asked.

Euston remained silent. Then he muttered, "That stupid bitch. She didn't even give it a chance."

"Which stupid bitch, Terry?" Nguyen asked. "I hope you're not referring to my colleague—or do you mean her mother?"

"Where is she?" he snarled.

"Who? Constable McTeish or her mother?"

Ashton made a shushing motion with her right hand. "You don't have to answer that." She sat upright. "Is that all you've got?" she said. Her heart didn't seem to be in it.

Nguyen grinned. "It's enough, don't you think? Enough for us to go on with, anyway." He stared at Euston. "Come on, Terry."

Euston looked up, his face pallid despite hearing his first name.

"If you want to have any chance reducing your time inside, admit your guilt."

Euston gazed at the table top.

"Terry, Terry. Come on, man. You're not stupid. Think about it. If you continue to bullshit us and fight it you'll get a long, long sentence." Nguyen emphasised the word long, stretching it out.

Euston sat back but said nothing. Nguyen could see that he was thinking about it.

Ashton said, "Can I have a word with my client, alone?"

Nguyen nodded, and Brothers shut down the recording equipment. They left the room

Outside in the corridor Nguyen said to Brothers, "You won't need to talk to Lucy Bottega now."

Brothers nodded. "That's for sure. Do you reckon he'll come clean?"

"I'm sure Ms Ashton is doing her best to persuade him."

TWENTY MINUTES LATER ASHTON left the room, and negotiations started. Euston would agree to poisoning Dr Chen, and the assault charges would be dropped.

"What about the kidnapping?" Ashton asked.

"That will depend on Detective Constable McTeish and her mother. If they'll consider not pressing charges then those can be dropped, too. But I'll only ask them if the murder charge sticks."

"And pleading guilty will lead to a reduced sentence?"

"I'm sure you know the court system better than me. But don't you think twenty years sounds a lot better than forty? And with good behaviour? Who knows."

They shook hands.

82

Nguyen checked the time difference and phoned Major Janne Fleischer in Baltimore. After the preliminary greetings he said, "It looks like Terry Euston will plead guilty to the murder."

"That's fantastic, John. You got a result! I hope we were of some assistance."

"You certainly were—you found the motive. And speaking of which, you might like to take action against Fred Lovell. He paid Euston to do the job."

"Can you send over any evidence we can take a look at?"

"We've got a series of texts and emails between the two of them. They're incriminating here in Melbourne, and I hope you find them useful in Baltimore."

"Look forward to getting them. Lovell's a tricky bastard, and we'll need it to be pretty watertight."

"Euston had a top lawyer here, and she realised we had the goods. Give me a call once you get the stuff."

"Will do. If it holds up, we may need you to come and testify. Fancy coming to Baltimore again?"

"Why do you think I'm calling you?"

83

THE NEXT DAY MCTEISH called on her mother, and inspected her when she opened the door. "Are you all right, mum?"

"Of course, darling," Claire said. "Why wouldn't I be?"

McTeish shook her head. "You know. After what he did." She wasn't going to mention his name.

"Oh, you mean Terry? Come and sit down while I make a pot of tea."

"Yes. Do you understand now?"

"Just a bit of excitement, wasn't it?" Her eyes gleamed.

Excitement? "He kidnapped us, mum. He tied you up. Is that excitement?"

"Oh, you do get things out of proportion, don't you? I suppose you have to, being a policewoman. Anyhow, he did I suppose take things a little too far. But," she looked dreamily at her. "No harm done."

"No harm done? He killed Dr Chen Du. He's a murderer. He hit me. In the face." She grasped her mother by the shoulders. "Can't you see?"

"You're just ..." Her mother trailed off. Then her face set hard. "Well, he seemed nice enough to me. At least at first."

McTeish let her go. She realised that nothing had changed with her mother. Why did she always go for such men? She breathed out in a mixture of despair and annoyance. At least she seemed back to normal. Her phone rang. She glanced at it and saw it was Tamas Kosic.

"I've got to go, Mum." She answered the call while shutting the front door.

"I heard you've caught the killer of Dr Chen," he said.

"Hang on a sec." She moved out of the kitchen, away from her mother. "It's going to court. How did you find out?"

"It's in the news."

She'd forgotten that Euston's arrest and the charges against him had been announced.

"Does that mean I'm no longer a potential suspect—and I can ask you out now?"

"For god's sake …" she muttered. She felt her cheeks warm, and tried to suppress the feeling. "I suppose it does."

"Well—would you like to go out with me?"

"Tamas," she said. "Is that a good idea?"

"Why not?" he said. "I think it's a very good idea."

He seemed to have gained a confidence she hadn't seen before. "Okay," she said.

Acknowledgements

Many thanks to those who read drafts of this novel and provided encouragement: Rob Sessions, Paul Morgan, Tony Wildman, Janeen Webb, Noel Turnbull, my Thriller-tique colleagues Gareth Bodie, Sara Ennis, Kirsten Moore, Saralyn Richards and Eleanor Shelton, my Sandy Writers Group colleagues Richard Bell, Tania Cossich, Brenda Cullen, Breda Hertaeg, Leo Jahn, Prue Mercer and Kim Robyn Smith, and especially my partner Maggie Gerrand. And David Grigg for his excellent design and setting of the book. Without your support the book would have been the lesser. Any faults, however, are to be laid solely at my feet.

About Norstrilia Press

Norstrilia Press is a specialist publisher of eclectic books. Founded in 1975 with the publication of Philip K Dick: Electric Shepherd, edited by Bruce Gillespie, it continued into the late 1980s when it went into cold storage. It was revived in 2022.

NORSTRILIA PRESS books

I've Come To Talk With You Again Leo Jahn
Up Shit Creek In a Barbed Wire Canoe Muriel Cooper
The Book Blinders John Clute
Proud and Lonely Leigh Edmonds
Aliens & Savages: The Voice in Australia Janeen Webb and Andrew Enstice
Charm, Strangeness, Mass and Spin Stephen Dedman
The Millennium Job Rob Gerrand

The Plains Gerald Murnane
Landscape With Landscape Gerald Murnane
Philip K Dick: Electric Shepherd Bruce Gillespie (editor)
The Altered I Lee Harding (editor)
An Unusual Angle Greg Egan
The Dreaming Dragons Damien Broderick
Moon in the Ground Keith Antill
Dreamworks David King (editor)
Where Pussywillows Last in the Catyard Bloomed and Other Poems
    Roger Zelazny
In the Heart or in the Head: An Essay in Time Travel George Turner
Lavington Pugh Jay Bland
The View from the Edge: A Workshop of Science Fiction Stories
    George Turner (editor)
The Stellar Gauge: Essays on Science Fiction Writers
    Michael Tolley and Kirpal Singh (editors)

www.norstriliapress.com

www.ingramcontent.com/pod-product-compliance
Lightning Source LLC
Chambersburg PA
CBHW030609170726
48283CB00002B/533